An Bhóinn agus an Bhóchna
The Boyne and the Sea

Philip O'Leary
Eagarthóir/Aistritheoir

An Bhóinn agus an Bhóchna
The Boyne and the Sea

Liam P. Ó Riain
(Cara na nÚdar a scríobh)

An Bhóinn agus an Bhóchna
The Boyne and the Sea

Foilsithe in 2019 ag
ARLEN HOUSE
42 Grange Abbey Road
Baldoyle
Dublin 13
Ireland
Fón/Facs: 00 353 86 8360236
Ríomhphost: arlenhouse@gmail.com

Dáileoirí i Meiriceá Thuaidh
SYRACUSE UNIVERSITY PRESS
621 Skytop Road, Suite 110
Syracuse, NY 13244–5290
USA
Fón: 315–443–5534/Facs: 315–443–5545
Ríomhphost: supress@syr.edu

978–1–85132–205–3, bog/paperback

Clóchur ¦ Arlen House

Tá Arlen House buíoch de
Chlár na Leabhar Gaeilge
agus d'Fhoras na Gaeilge

CLÁR : CONTENTS

Brollach

Nuair a bunaíodh Conradh na Gaeilge sa bhliain 1893, bhí cruthú nualitríochta as Gaeilge ar cheann dá phríomhchuspóirí. Cuspóir dúshlánach, uaillmhianach a bhí ansin gan amhras ag an am nuair a chuimhnítear ar ghéarchéim na Gaeilge ag deireadh an naoú haois déag – labhairt na Gaeilge ag trá go tubaisteach in aghaidh na bliana, an Ghaeilge ceilte ar chóras na bunscolaíochta agus gan litearthacht sa Ghaeilge maíte ar dhream Gaeilge ar bith sa tír, beagnach. Bhain litearthacht le mionlach daoine nár de bhunadh na tuaithe iad den chuid is mó. Cad as a dtiocfadh an corpas nualitríochta seo, mar sin?

Bhíothas ag brath ar an mionlach beag sin a raibh léamh agus scríobh na Gaeilge acu le litríocht a sholáthar. Ach cén traidisiún litríochta a leanfadh siad sin fiú dá mbeadh féith na cruthaitheachta iontu? An litríocht is mó a raibh cur amach acu air litríocht an Bhéarla. Ba bheag an chabhair dóibh litríocht na Gaeltachta nár mhair di ach an fhilíocht agus an scéalaíocht agus bhain an t-earra sin le muintir na Gaeltachta ach go háirithe. De bharr na gcúiseanna sin ar fad, níorbh aon ghaisce na chéadiarrachtaí liteartha as Gaeilge.

Ar an chéad ghlúin de na scríbhneoirí Gaeilge sin bhí Liam Pádraig Ó Riain a rugadh i dTiobraid Árann sa bhliain 1867 agus, cosúil le go leor de Ghaeilgeoirí luatha na hAthbheochana, b'fhada agus ba thimpeallach a thuras i dtreo na Gaeilge. D'fhoghlaim sé an Ghaeilge as a stuaim féin i dTiobraid Árann nuair a bhí sé óg agus chuir spéis i gcúrsaí polaitíochta ansin fosta. Bhí sé ina thuairisceoir áitiúil ag an *Freeman's Journal* agus foilsíodh dánta Béarla leis ar nuachtáin agus irisí náisiúnaíocha an ama sin. Lean sé leis an iriseoireacht nuair a bhog sé go Londain agus bhí sé ag obair ar nuachtáin mhóra Shasana ar feadh na mblianta taobh amuigh de thréimhse a chaith sé i mbun gnó san India. Bhí baint mhór aige leis na cumainn liteartha Éireannacha agus le Conradh na Gaeilge nuair a bunaíodh iad thall i Londain.

Le Béarla a tógadh é, i mBéarla a fuair sé a chuid scolaíochta agus an Béarla a chleacht sé ina cheird mar iriseoir. Ní hiontas ar bith, mar sin, gur leabhair Bhéarla is luaithe a tháinig óna pheann ag deireadh an naoú haois déag, mar atá, úrscéalta agus leabhar ar athbheochan liteartha na hÉireann. Níor thosaigh sé ag scríobh na Gaeilge go dtí 1902. D'fhill sé ar Éirinn in 1905 agus rinne cónaí san Uaimh áit a raibh sé mar eagarthóir ar an *Irish Peasant*. Ina dhiaidh sin, chaith sé saol corrach idir Éire agus Sasana, ag plé le cúrsaí iriseoireachta agus ag scríobh as Béarla agus Gaeilge i seánraí éagsúla.

B'iriseoir agus ba scríbhneoir ildánach é nach raibh mórán cosúil leis ag saothrú na Gaeilge ina lá. Ba scríbhneoir *engagé* é a raibh a mhéar aige ar chuisle an násiúin ina am. Bhí baint aige, gan amhras, le Conradh na Gaeilge agus leis an idé-eolaíocht agus smaointeachas a bhain leis i rith a shaoil. Ach bhí sé tógtha go mór le cúiseanna eile a bhí chun tosaigh go mór ina lá: cúrsaí polaitíochta, sóisialachais, talmhaíochta agus comharchumannachais chomh maith le ceisteanna a bhain le comhionannachas ban, ceisteanna fealsúnachta, staire, litríochta, intleachta agus misteachais. Is deacair cuimhneamh ar aon scríbhneoir Gaeilge – nó Béarla dá n-abróinn é – a raibh oiread de *zeitgeist* a linne léirithe ina shaothar.

Tá rian saoil agus smaointeachais Uí Riain in uachtar go mór sa *roman à clef* seo *An Bhóinn agus an Bhóchna* a foilsíodh mar shraithscéal ar *An Claidheamh Soluis* idir 1915 agus 1916. Ní bhfuair an saothar seo an aird ná an t-aitheantas atá tuillte aige ar an ábhar, mar rud amháin, nár foilsíodh i bhfoirm leabhair riamh é. Tá an scéal sin leigheasta anois óir tá an téacs cóirithe i bhfoirm chaighdeánaithe agus aistriúchán Béarla curtha leis mar áis do phobal níos leithne léitheoireachta. Chomh maith leis sin tá réamhrá cuimsitheach curtha ag an eagarthóir leis an leabhar áit a rianaíonn sé saol Uí Riain chomh maith le cuntas mion a thabhairt ar chomhthéacs agus ábhar an úrscéil seo.

Tá an tOllamh O'Leary, a bhfuil lucht léinn na Gaeilge faoi chomaoin mhór aige cheana as a chuid taighde i rith a shaoil i ngort na léirmheastóireachta , le moladh go mór as an úrscéal dearmadta seo a chur inár láthair arís agus a mhíniú dúinn. Is mithid fosta, más mall, aitheantas cuí a thabhairt do Liam Pádraig Ó Riain as casadh nua-aimseartha, dúshlánach, intleachtach a bhaint as nua-litríocht na Gaeilge an uair ba ghann agus ba riachtanach sin.

– Nollaig Mac Congáil
Gaillimh

Focal ón Eagarthóir/Aistritheoir

Is mar shraithscéal in *An Claidheamh Soluis* (11/9/15–15/1/16) a foilsíodh *An Bhóinn agus an Bhóchna* den chéad uair. Mar ba ghnách ag an am sin ba sa gcló 'Gaelach' agus i litriú Fhoclóir an Duinnínigh a bhí an téacs. San eagrán nua seo den téacs, ní raibh le déanamh agam ach dornán botún cló a cheartú agus an téacs ina iomláine a chur sa gcló 'Rómhánach' agus sa litriú caighdeánach. Gaeilge na Mumhan a chleacht Liam P. Ó Riain den chuid is mó, ach mar a dúirt sé féin sa réamhrá dá leabhrán *Inghean Mhanannáin* (1917):

> there is a noticeable 'inter-provincialism' in my Irish with regard to both vocabulary and pronunciation. I make use of pronunciation and vocabulary from every province when I feel the need.

D'fhonn blas éigin dá chuid Muimhneachais agus den 'inter-provincialism' sin a bheith le sonrú sa téacs seo, d'fhág mé corrfhocal agus abairt nó dhó nach de réir an chaighdeáin iad sa téacs ach iad a bheith inaitheanta gan deacracht ag léitheoirí an lae inniu.

Sa réamhrá bainim úsáid as an leagan Gaelach d'ainm agus de shloinne an Rianaigh. Déanaim sin chun an tranglam a leanfadh dá n-úsáidfinn na leaganacha go léir ar bhain sé féin úsáid astu ag brath ar an gcomthéacs ina raibh sé ag scríobh a sheachaint. Sna nótaí, áfach, úsáidtear an leagan atá ar an leathanach teidil. Tugtar sleachta as na saothair Ghaeilge i mBéarla sa téacs, ach tá an bhun-Ghaeilge (chaighdeánaithe) le fáil sna nótaí. Eisceacht, áfach, is ea *An Bhóinn agus an Bhóchna*. De bhrí go bhfuil an t-úrscéal Gaeilge ina iomláine anseo, ní dóigh liom gur gá sleachta faoi leith i nGaeilge a chur ar fáil.

Maidir le *The Boyne and the Sea* ní miste cúpla focal a rá faoin aistriúchán féin. Nílim go hiomlán sásta leis na focail agus na téarmaí 'Gael,' 'Gaelic,' agus 'Gaelic culture' nó rud éigin den sórt mar aistriúcháin ar na focail 'Gael,' 'Gaelach,' agus 'Gaelachas.' Ach is léir go raibh an Rianach agus a chomhghleacaithe bródúil as gluaiseacht na hAthbheochana. Is 'Gaeil' a thugadar orthu féin mar chomhartha ar an difríocht shuntasach a mhothaigh siad a bheith idir iad féin agus a gcomh-Éireannaigh a bhí patfhuar faoi chúis na hAthbheochana. Is d'fhonn béim a chur ar an difríocht sin a d'fhág mé ainmneacha agus sloinnte na gcarachtar sa mbun-Ghaeilge. Os a choinne sin, bhain mé feidhm as leaganacha Béarla de na logainmneacha toisc gurb iad san is mó a mbeadh aithne orthu ag an ngnáthléitheoir.

Is míshásúil agus is achrannach é an focal 'cine' mar aistriúchán ar 'race.' Bhí tuiscint níos simplí – agus níos aineolaí – den téarma conspóideach sin an-choitianta nuair a bhí Ó Riain ag scríobh. Ba é sin ré na 'Irish Race Congresses' le gan ach sampla amháin a lua. B'fhearr liom féin aistriúchán a mbeadh níos lú staire ag baint leis, ach is é 'race' an téarma a mbaineadh an Rianach agus a chairde leas as agus iad ag plé na ceiste i mBéarla agus, mar sin, is é a úsáidim anseo. Agus, lena cheart a thabhairt dó, ní raibh an Rianach féin compordach leis an bhfocal ná leis an míthuiscint gurbh fhéidir a bhaint as an téarma – agus as an gcoincheap – pointe a ndéanaim tagairt dó sa réamhrá.

Cé go n-aistrítear 'spéirbhean' go minic mar 'sky woman,' bainim féin feidhm as an bhfocal 'goddess,' mar go bhfeictear dom go bhfuil blas na scannán sárlaochra ó Hollywood ar 'sky woman.' Ó am go ham tugann an Rianach 'buachaillí' agus 'cailíní' ar charachtair a dtabharfaí 'fir óga' and 'mná óga' orthu i gcaint an lae inniu. Bainim leas as focail an údair anseo mar gurbh é sin nós na haimsire sin.

Anois ba mhaith liom buíochas ó chroí a ghabháil le Brian Ó Conchubhair, Joyce Flynn, Alan Hayes, agus go háirithe le Nollaig Mac Congáil, a bhí sásta ceisteanna a fhreagairt agus comhairle thuisceanach a chur orm. Orm féin atá na lochtanna.

Introduction

I: Liam P. Ó Riain, Life and Works

> My own existence is a futility in the complex of futilities. Only in my hidden life have I poise or peace or joy. My career as known to friends and fellow-workers seems a sorry patch-garb that I shrink from ever wearing again, or as a secret of which I am sorely ashamed.

Thus in 1920 Liam P. Ó Riain (William Patrick Ryan or O'Ryan) passed judgment on 'my crawling of years, my feeble life-building, the parody of myself I have exposed in the universe.'[1] Whatever may be said about this 'hidden life' – a topic about which, as we will see, he had a good deal to say – he was far too hard on himself with regard to his career in the world he shared with his friends and fellow-workers.

Born in 1867 in Castleiney near Templemore in County Tipperary, Ó Riain attended the local national school and started studying Irish, working his way through books published by the Society for the Preservation of the Irish Language. He also began his long career in journalism as a local correspondent for the *Freeman's Journal,* before moving in 1886 to London, where he worked for a variety of English papers including *The Catholic Times*, the *Morning Leader* and the *Daily Chronicle*. He returned to Ireland in 1905 to edit the *Irish Peasant* until he was forced to resign as the result of episcopal opposition to his heterodox views on a wide range of issues. He then went on to found and edit his own paper, *The Peasant*, which was soon re-named *The Irish Nation* and lasted until 1910. He provided a lightly fictionalised account of his adventures as a progressive and iconoclastic editor taking on the mighty monolith of traditional Irish Catholicism in his 1910 novel *The Cross and the Plough*.[2] From 1911 he would live almost entirely in London, where he was assistant editor of the pro-labour *Daily Herald* and continued to play an important role in Irish language and literary circles. He died after an accidental fall in 1942.

Among the Irish organisations of which he was a member in London were the Southwark (later the Irish) Literary Society and the London Branch of the Gaelic League (Conradh na Gaeilge), whose journals *Guth na nGaedheal*, *Inis Fáil* and *An tÉireannach* he edited. Actually, Ó Riain was an inveterate joiner of Irish societies during this time of national revival. Before leaving his native Tipperary he had already served as secretary of the local Gaelic society and the local branch of the Land League and he would go on to be an original member of the Socialist Party of Ireland, to involve himself with the Gaelic League in Dublin and Meath, and to regularly attend both the formal meetings of a mystical society founded by 'AE' (George Russell) and the more informal discussions at AE's weekly at-homes.[3]

Ó Riain's interest in literature began early in life so that while still in Castleiney he was already publishing poems in papers like *The Nation*. He would go on to have a prolific career as an author in several genres in both Irish and English. His novels were *The Heart of Tipperary: A Romance of the Land League* (1893), *Starlight through the Roof*

(1895), *The Cross and the Plough* (1910), *Daisy Darley, or the Fairy Gold of Fleet Street* (1912), *Caoimhghin (Caoimhín) Ó Cearnaigh: Sgéal Úrnua* (A novel, lit. 'An original story') (1913), and *An Bhóinn agus an Bhóchna* (The Boyne and the Sea) serialised in *An Claidheamh Soluis* in 1915–6. For the stage he wrote *Grádh agus Gréithidhe agus Drámanna Eile* (Love and crockery and other plays) / *Plays for the People* (1904), which in addition to the title play included *An Mí-Ádh Mór* (The great misfortune) and *The Wake of the People*; *An tOide as Tír na nÓg* (The teacher from *Tír na nÓg*) (1910); *Cuaird na Bainríoghna* (The Queen's visit) (1910); *The Jug of Sorrow*, performed at the Abbey Theatre in October 1914; *From Atlantis to Thames* (1926); *King Arthur in Avalon* (1934); *The Song of the Salmon God* (n.d.); and *Feilm an Tobair Bheannuighthe* (The Farm of the Holy Well) (1936). Collections of poetry were *Inghean Mhanannáin: Laoi a Bhaineas le n-Ár Linn Féin* (The Daughter of Manannán: A poem dealing with our own time) (1917); *Féile na nÓglach maille le Laoithe Eile na Linne seo* (The feast of the heroes along with other poems of this time); and *Poets in Paradise* (1931). His *Seanchas Filidheachta* (1940) was an exam-time crash course in Irish language poetry from Aogán Ó Rathaille to Agnes O'Farrelly,[4] and he also tried his hand at writing for children with *Sídheoga ag Obair* (Fairies at work) (1904), a collection of stories.[5]

In all probability it is, however, on his non-fiction that his reputation now rests, and while some of his books have aged less well than others, most continue to be useful sources for the cultural, intellectual and literary history of a tumultuous period in Irish life. Readers can still benefit from books like *The Irish Literary Revival: Its History, Problems and Possibilities* (1894); *The Labour Revolt and Larkinism* (1912); *The Pope's Green Island* (1913); *The Celt and the Cosmos* (1914); *The Irish Labour Movement From the 'Twenties to Our Own Day* (1919); *Eden and Evolution: A Record of Evenings in Avalon* (1926); and *Gaedhealachas i gCéin* (Gaelic Culture Abroad), an informed survey of the contributions of non-Irish scholars to the study of the Gaelic literary tradition (1933), as well as the Gaelic League pamphlet, *Lessons from Modern Language Movements* (1902, new ed. 1926). Perhaps less memorable are *Literary London: Its Lights and Comedies* (1898) and *The Romance of the Motor Mission: With General Booth on the White Car Crusade* (1906) – although members of the Salvation Army may disagree about the latter. And of course he was a prolific and wide-ranging writer of editorials, articles and essays, among them pieces like 'Tús Staire na hÉireann: Sean-Sgéalta agus Sean-Déithe na nGaedheal' (The beginning of Irish history: The ancient stories and the ancient gods of the Gaels);[6] 'Cúis na bhFear Oibre' (The workers' cause) (*ACS*, 13/9/13); 'Éireannaigh agus Greugaigh/Finnscéaluidheacht an Dá Threabh' (Irish and Greeks/The legends of the two peoples) (*Misneach*, 1/5/20); 'Na Draoithe: A Réimeas agus a dTeagasg' (The druids/Their era and their teaching) (*Misneach*, 22/5/20); 'Rúindiamhra na Sean: Draíochas agus Críostuíocht' (The mysteries of the ancients: Druidism and Christianity) (*Misneach*, 5/6/20); 'Aspalacht agus Éigse/*Épopée* Phádraig Naofa' (Apostleship and poetry: The *épopée* of St Patrick) (*Misneach*, 19/6/20); 'Príomh-Éigeas na hÉireann: Johannes Scotus Eriugena' (The premier scholar of Ireland) (*FL*, 15/3–17/5/24); and 'Gaels and Obsessions,' his contribution to a lively debate in *The Leader* concerning the role of the native speaker of Irish in the development of a modern literature in the language (*Leader*, 19/4/41). In addition, as 'Sliabh Bladhma' he wrote a regular column in English in the bilingual journal *An Gaedheal* in the 1930s.[7]

This record of achievement was certainly no sign of 'futility in the complex of futilities.' Still, one could argue that while his engagement with central issues in the cultural and intellectual life of Ireland over four decades was both prolific and provocative, he seems ultimately to have made few converts to his ideas.[8] Again and again, he returned to the same questions, pondering them from different angles, arriving at different provisional answers, but never convincing most of his readers of the truth of doctrines and theories he so profoundly believed gave meaning to his own life and that of his emerging nation.

Ó Riain believed that the Irish, indeed all Celts, had been deeply spiritual people from as far back as their history could be traced – and farther. Indeed that history, whether factual or legendary, was a 'romance' of 'the wonderland, the lightsome civilisation and the mystic mind, of the vanished ages of Gaeldom.'[9] And that civilisation had always had an august destiny, one as magnificent as that of classical Greece or the India of the *Mahabharata*. As he wrote in *Gaedhealachas i gCéin*:

> The mysteries of ancient Ireland have a special place in the spiritual history of the west. They prepared the way for the revelations of Christianity and new directions in the divine and human Pilgrimmage.[10]

For Ó Riain, the tragedy was that the overwhelming majority of the Irish people were 'petulant and worldly' (*casaoideach saolta*) as the result of 'a lack of true insight: They do not like to develop the mystic life of ideas' (*easpa fiorléargais: Rúnbheatha na smaointe ní gnaoi leo saothrú*).[11] Such people were, as the goddess Grian says in *Inghean Mhanannáin*, 'sham Gaels, senseless and ineffectual./Alas many of them are not really people' (*samhalta Gael, gan chéill gan éifeacht/Ní daoine go fíor iad, faraor, a lán aca*). Consequently, 'this country is a desert altogether' (*Amuigh is 'stigh tá an tír 'na fásach*), or as Fergus O'Hanlon, the protagonist of *The Cross and the Plough* puts it, 'Ireland's worst disaster was that her mind had shrunk, that as a whole she had lost the heroic consciousness, that her inner life had grown weedy, pessimistic and vexatious.'[12]

Nevertheless a stubborn optimism characterises Ó Riain's work over the years. Thus in *The Pope's Green Island* he declares: 'We can see, as the ideal of Ireland grows from mind to mind, it tends to assume the character of a sacred land.' Despite all of the frustrations and disappointments he experienced, he was certain that such a sacred land was steadily evolving:

> The soul-fact, the heavenly truth, is the inner Kingdom of Eirinn, / The psychic and mental selves that in stress and dream she has fitted / For the farther and grander faring in the wider cosmic saga.[13]

Grian, who as a divine being should know, shares this view in *Inghean Mhanannáin*:

> The universe is evolving – a tree of mystical beauty / That will be developing and flowering forever. / Countries and stars are its branches and flowers, and a spirit in everything is evolving with them.

Since Colm Ó Domhnaill, the human protagonist of the poem, has grasped this truth, he is able to experience 'Ireland as it is' (*Fódla mar tá sí*).[14]

Here Ó Riain is, of course, invoking a central tenet of mystical thought around the globe: the idea that what appears to us as real – the visible, tangible, corporeal world we seem to inhabit – is only an illusion, the true reality being invisible, immaterial, spiritual. This belief runs throughout his work. For example, he writes in *The Celt and the Cosmos* that:

> there is a self that ever inspires and ever eludes the self which works in time and place. It is here, it is now, it is everywhere, it is timeless, it bides in me, in all the reaches of the visible and invisible. Every unit of the race and of all races,[15] has even such a master-self. The more we realise it the more we enlarge our sense and power of progression ... Our normal selves are dim reflections of our inner selves. Our inner selves are manifestations of the One and Ultimate Reality.[16]

In *The Cross and the Plough*, Fergus O'Hanlon tells his beloved Elsie O'Kennedy that:

> there's only a slight, all but spiritualised bodily vesture like gauze between your spirit and the infinite. So you are your own fairyland. Your mind can always revel [sic] and see wonder.[17]

Fergus believes that:

> one had to crucify the lower nature continually. As one did so a Master Self, unknown to normal consciousness, and indifferent to self-hood in the ordinary sense, became dimly but ever more and more realizable. The soul becomes more radiantly alive and active, in more conscious relation with the Divinity ruling the higher reaches of life ...[18]

Ó Riain was convinced that, like individuals, nations – the planet itself – possessed what for want of a better word we might call a soul, and that that soul was immortal, cycling through the illusions that are time and space in superficially-different incarnations. Indeed such a belief in re-incarnation underlies much of Ó Riain's thinking about both personal self-realisation and cultural and national revival, what he called 'the nationality of the spirit.'[19] Moreover, he insisted that there was nothing in this belief alien to the Celtic or Gaelic mind. Thus in *The Celt and the Cosmos* he refers to 'the old Celtic doctrine ... once widespread ... of re-incarnation.'[20] In *The Pope's Green Island*, he writes of 're-incarnation or re-embodiment':

> For various people who have come under the spell of the Gaelic idea it has a great attraction. The thought that their real selves worked through bygone personalities and bodies in a far-off Gaelic civilisation, and that their present enthusiasm means the stir and response of something stored from the past in higher and permanent reaches of their being, proves attractive.[21]

Nothing gives more striking proof of the continuity of one's sense of place than the uncanny conviction of having previously lived in a specific spot, usually one with powerful mythic resonances. One of the most resonant of those spots was the Boyne Valley, which Ó Riain knew well from his time in Navan editing *The Peasant*. In *The Celt and the Cosmos* he refers specifically to places near the Boyne he feels he had known in previous ages: 'And a Self obscured long days, felt the gleam and call of the godhead … and I knew I was part thereof, and my everyday self was a shadow.'[22] In *Inghean Mhanannáin* no less a being than the mythic Aonghus Óg appears to Colm Ó Domhnaill and his beloved Méabh Ní Mhaoláin and shows them 'many states of being' (*an iomad neamhstáid*) so that they realise 'how Tara and the territory of Clíona/Are linked with the paradise of the Boyne and the Mystical Sea of the west' (*mar ceangaltar Teamhair 's críoch Chlíona/Le parthas na Bóinne 's Rún-Bhóchna an iarthair*).[23] It is, then, no surprise that writing as 'Sliabh Bladhma' in *An Gaedheal* in 1934, Ó Riain called for 'a noble re-building of Teamhair in our mental world,' declaring that 'it is a fascinating task, and the spiritual profit is great' (*Gaedheal*, 1/9/34).

In Ó Riain's true Ireland of the spirit, the heroes of the ancient Irish past – Cú Chulainn, Fionn mac Cumhaill and others – can live again in their full reality, for 'there was a great difference between the primary Cú Chulainn – the spiritual Cú Chulainn – and the Cú Chulainn of the *Táin*.'[24] Indeed in his 1925 poem 'Cuchulainn' he calls Ulster's great champion 'the light's mystic Source' and continues: 'You routed all the fell foes of the race:/Pride, hatred, lust, despair./You cleared man's course/For thought and growth and grace.'[25] He also elevated Fionn to divine status:

> It is clear that much of this saga has nothing at all to do with the ordinary world … They [Fionn and his men] are from regions more profound than Scandinavia or the ordinary Ireland.[26]

The Nirvana of Ó Riain's mystical cosmology was the native Irish *Tír na nÓg* or Land of the Young that in *The Celt and the Cosmos* he calls 'the wonderland beyond the World of Waters' that 'symbolises a soul-state, experience of a part of the Kingdom of Heaven within.'[27] He develops this idea in more detail later in the same book:

> The Earth-World, the World of Waters, and *Tír na nÓg* or the Land of Immortal Youth ... They correspond esoterically to the physical, psychic and mental planes of certain mystical literature.[28]

In *Tír na nÓg*, the illusions of ordinary life vanish and all questions and conflicts are resolved, as Colm Ó Domhnaill learns when he goes there in *Inghean Mhanannáin*: 'He understood the wonder, the great mysteries, the many joys/Of the mystical, real, eternal world.'[29] As we will see below, this is the realm to which Créide, the female protagonist of *The Boyne and the Sea*, aspires.

Yet Colm opts to return home to Ireland, for in keeping with the Buddhist influences on Ó Riain's thinking, he believed that the most enlightened of the spirits who reached *Tír na nÓg* willingly gave up all of its wonders and returned to our world to help those still mired in illusion. That is, they became Boddhisatvas. For example, the children in *An tOide as Tír na nÓg* decide to forego life on a higher plane of existence in order to remain on earth and serve Ireland, a decision their Otherworld teacher finds laudable.[30] But the most important of Ó Riain's Boddhisatvas was his friend AE (George Russell), who was a major influence on his thinking with regard to matters both mystical and pragmatic, and who as Feargus Ó Ruanaí is apotheosised by Créide Ní Chonghaile in *The Boyne and the Sea*:

> Feargus is a wonderful person. He takes as much interest in potatoes as he does in visionary knowledge, in tillage as in the cosmos, in bees as in Brahma. When I am listening to him I feel that the human race is noble and that Ireland is a rich and spiritual country. I feel that I am near *Tír na nÓg*.[31]

Later Feargus himself explains his mission as Boddhisatva:

> I would love to be like Ruairí, far away on a delightful island in the sea of wonder – in a way I sometimes am – but I still have a great deal to do here in Dublin. I have great things to

> accomplish with the co-operative movement, great things no one else is willing to do at present.[32]

That Ó Riain understood how difficult that sacrifice must be is clear in *Inghean Mhanannáin* where even Cú Chulainn and Fionn attempt to escape it. Fionn makes his case forcefully:

> But alas! The creatures that are in our place today!/To be re-incarnated amongst them! I'd be afraid of it. /My state would be contemptible: it is not spiritual growth/That would be in store for me, but growth in baseness.[33]

Grian does, however, convince them to accept the challenge.

Ó Riain was well aware of the magnitude of that challenge. There was 'great work facing everyone' (*ollsaothar roimh cách*) in Ireland. But he also knew that that work was being done, above all by the various new organisations committed to national revival – mystical societies, the co-operative movement, the women's movement, and, above all, by organised labour and language activists.[34]

Ó Riain shared AE's conviction that, in the words of the AE figure Feargus Ó Ruanaí, 'the co-operative movement is the hope of Ireland – the hope of the world.'[35] For example, in *The Pope's Green Island* he called the Irish Agricultural Co-operative Society (founded in 1894) 'one of the most important forces in the country … one of the great constructive movements in modern Ireland.'[36] And needless to say he felt that that importance and greatness extended far beyond the purely agricultural and social aspects of the movement, writing of AE's co-operative work that 'he leads the man on the land to the knowledge of earth-powers and earth-goddesses he can appreciate' and that at times:

> he seems to set the farmers engaged in the planting of potatoes on as high a plane as the creative spirits of mystic literature beginning the fashioning of a cosmos after a Night of Brahma …[37]

Ó Riain's support for the women's movement was also consistent throughout his life. He was, for example, proud that a short while after the founding of the Gaelic League 'woman [sic] of various classes and degrees had come out smiling from the concentration camp in which the clergy would keep her [sic]' and that though

> far from satisfactory as it is in a hundred places and ways, the position of Irish women is at any rate improving, inasmuch as several have seized all the possibilities of education to the full and are spreading progressive and generous social ideas amongst their sisters, and their brothers for that matter.[38]

In *The Cross and the Plough*, Fergus O'Hanlon clearly feels that at least some of those brothers had indeed espoused such 'progressive and generous social ideas,' declaring of what he calls 'Young Ireland':

> Our young men, to be sure, are human and chivalrous and reverent towards woman-kind; but the great desire of their hearts in these days is to prepare for a human and self-reliant and creative nation. Woman to them is the comrade-thinker and the comrade-builder, not a toy or a slave, or even a golden creature of romance.[39]

In his novels in Irish Ó Riain explored what such an understanding would mean for the lives of those striving to build a new Ireland.[40]

Risteárd Ó Glaisne saw Ó Riain as 'a Socialist of some kind' (*Sóisialach de shaghas éigin*).[41] While Ó Riain was always too independent to follow any party line, there can be no doubt of his lifetime commitment to the socialist economic and social agenda. As noted above, he was an original member of the Socialist Party of Ireland and he always stood with the working class, as is clear from his front page piece in *An Claidheamh Soluis* during the great Dublin lockout of 1913 where he wrote:

> We must understand that we cannot have a true nation until poverty and ignorance are banished. Every person will have to

> have [sufficient] wealth (both material and intellectual) (*ACS*, 13/9/13).[42]

Several characters in his novels also make clear in very practical terms their solidarity with the workers. For example, in *The Cross and the Plough* Fergus O'Hagan's sister Maeve decides to devote her life to work in the Dublin slums, as do Dan Deegan, whom Fergus calls 'the great, racy Slum Doctor';[43] the theosophist Miss Lefanu, 'that revolutionary American woman';[44] and Elsie O'Kennedy, who tells Fergus that

> I have craved some such labour for years ... But Dublin's odious slum-land and the lovely, empty, wasted Boyne Valley separated by so short a space! – isn't it an awful irony?[45]

In *Caoimhghin Ó Cearnaigh*, Úna Ní Chuilleannáin joins her friend Canon Ó Maoilbheanna to work in his slum parish, for '*tá dúil mhór agam in obair den tsaghas sin, agus tá sí ag teastáil go géar sa gcathair.*'[46] And in *The Boyne and the Sea*, Ruairí's friend Cathal Ó Cinnéide says that a part of him hopes 'there would be armed warfare and a war for the exploited workers in Ireland.' For Cathal, 'there will be no Gaelic culture in Ireland until we put an end to serfdom and poverty.'[47] And, of course, those in the urban slums were not capitalism's only victims. The progressive priest Father Dónall Ó Dálaigh is disgusted by some of the 'Gaels' he sees at the Meath *Feis*, including 'farmers who were not willing to cultivate the soil or treat the labourers fairly,' for

> it was neither fitting nor sensible for people like that to have the nation's land. If that land were in the care of the nation, as it should be, it would be easy to get rid of serfdom and poverty.[48]

Ó Riain was a pioneer in and a lifelong supporter of the Gaelic League. In *The Pope's Green Island*, he wrote of the League that

> In an ever-deepening degree it has re-discovered Ireland for them [i. e. 'many thousands of Irishmen and Irishwomen, whose lives might otherwise be wasted'], or, to express it in another way, it has enabled them to discover something hitherto undreamt of in themselves.[49]

It was, of course, its commitment to revive Irish as a spoken and literary language that made the League so significant, as Feargus Ó Ruanaí explains in *The Boyne and the Sea*:

> No more important work is being done in all of Ireland than the teaching of Irish. It is even more important than the co-operative movement. We don't understand how important it is, but it will be understood some other time – in a thousand years perhaps.[50]

For Ó Ruanaí – and doubtless for Ó Riain as well – 'we have a great need of it [Irish], a mystical need as well as a worldly need.'[51]

We also get some idea of the mystic force of the language and the League from the communal spirit it creates among activists, most notably at League events like local *feiseanna* and the annual national *Oireachtas*.[52] Indeed the Meath *Feis* in *An Bhóinn agus an Bhóchna* gives those present a glimpse of the reality behind the superficial stagnation of contemporary Ireland:

> It had been said that the Province[53] was a desert, that the majority of the people were interested in nothing but cattle and money. And behold! They had created a lively *feis* worthy of ancient times.[54]

Caoimhghin Ó Cearnaigh develops this idea:

> What is the Irish language movement? A revolt by the 'true people' against the 'ordinary' people. Divinity, mysticism, true love, true poetry, true music, charity, empathy – all of these are the life and work of the 'true person'.[55]

For those in the movement, the *Oireachtas* was the central event of the Gaelic year:

> They thought it a pity that the *Oireachtas* was not always there just as Tara and the joy of Tara existed from one end of the year to the other long ago.

But as the progressive priest Muiris Mac Cathmhaoil responds to such regrets: 'They are greatly mistaken. The *Oireachtas* is always there. The *Oireachtas* is in ourselves.'[56]

Nevertheless, Ó Riain did have some reservations about the League, most notably with regard to its often bourgeois attitude to the labour movement. In his history *The Irish Labour Movement*, he wrote that while it had had a considerable influence on 'elements' in the labour movement, 'the League on the whole did not attempt nearly as much for the social and intellectual fortunes of the Labour world as it might and ought to have done.' Moreover, he felt this failure was due to the League's 'lack of courage or vision,' the result of which was that the language movement 'failed to see that to save and strengthen Irish in the *Gaeltacht* a thorough-going economic and social scheme was essential.'[57] Engaging in a bit of counter-factual history, Ó Riain pondered what might have happened if greater financial security in his youth had given James Connolly the opportunity to work with the League:

> Connolly as a Gaelic League pioneer would have made history for the League and for Labour ... For many Gaelic Leaguers had need, and still have need, of more Gaelic culture, particularly of the social species.[58]

Ó Riain found this failure of the League to make common cause with labour especially unfortunate since both Gaels and workers as well as those in other progressive movements often faced the same powerful and implacable adversary. That opponent was, of course, the institutional and hierarchical Catholic church to whose priests and above all to whose bishops the majority of Irish people at that time gave their almost unquestioning allegiance.[59] Somewhat surprisingly, despite his own bitter personal experience of the power of the hierarchy and priests subservient to it – experience that, of course, provides much of the plot of *The Cross and the Plough* – Ó Riain did not see the issue exclusively in terms of power and prerogative.[60] He believed the Church's opposition to movements he supported was rooted in something far deeper:

> While bishops and other ecclesiastics deliver alarmed and woeful pronouncements that are really a criticism of human nature, this eager young Ireland believes more and more in a certain divinity inherent in human nature.

And once again he refused to cede the cultural high ground to opponents eager to dismiss his ideas as threateningly alien:

> And here of course is really a clash of two old religious, indeed two Christian, theories. Here is the immemorial contrast of the exoteric and the esoteric, the ephemeral and the mystical view.

Thus while clerics looked at 'the passing, personal man, the superficial life' and developed 'the theory of the miserable sinner, the human worm with no godliness in him,' Irish progressives had 'a sense of the higher self, the divine ego, in whom is the Kingdom of Heaven.' For Ó Riain

> nothing is more notable in Ireland than the contrast between the implicit faith of lay workers and some of the rising priests and the explicit pessimism of the generality of the ecclesiastics.[61]

This opposition created the paradoxical situation that 'non-believers, we are given to understand, are the trouble in other lands,' while 'we are banned in Ireland, or some would like to ban us, for believing too much.'[62]

In addition to asserting that his brand of mysticism was entirely consistent with historical Christian tradition, Ó Riain once again claimed that his beliefs were also in tune with ancient Gaelic beliefs. Thus in *The Pope's Green Island* he wrote that 'doubtless in their deepest and purist essence essential Christianity and Gaelicism are at one.'[63] This case is made forthrightly by Father Muiris Mac Cathmhaoil in *Caoimhghin Ó Cearnaigh*:

> The spirit of today's Gaels is truly like the spirit of the Gaels who lived in the time of Cú Chulainn and in the time of the Fianna. The spirit of Christ is in these Gaels now, and the spirit of Christ was in those Gaels then ...[64]

Of course he also saw similarities between his own faith and beliefs and those of the Church, similarities that would have scandalised more than a few Irish lay people, most of the priests, and probably all of the bishops. Thus when in *The Boyne and the Sea* Father Micheál Ó Gadhra declares that Ruairí is 'in danger of forgetting the qualities and the heritage of the Celts and taking too much interest in the books and the visionary beliefs of the East' and that 'Christ and Krishna and the Celts are in conflict with each other,' Ó Riain's *alter ego* responds: 'You are greatly mistaken, Father Micheál ... I will not admit that there is any dissimilarity between the visionary beliefs of the East and the true philosophy of the West.'[65] Ó Riain must then have felt both sympathy and vindication when he wrote in *The Celt and the Cosmos*:

> Yet how the Irish Catholic countryman has tragically tried for ages to reconcile himself at one and the same time to fairyland, *Tír na nÓg*, and the Vatican, how he has accepted both Finn and the Devil ... is one of the romances of theology and life.[66]

There was, however, nothing romantic about Ó Riain's struggle to inspire new thinking in his countrymen, especially the Irish-speaking ones. Risteárd Ó Glaisne says of Ó Riain:

> But he was opposed to so many systems and institutions that were long established in the life of Ireland and the world, and his mind was so open to new ideas of various kinds that he left many people suspicious and troubled.[67]

Readers of Irish may have been comfortably familiar with Cú Chulainn, Fionn, Tara and *Tír na nÓg* (if not with his version of them), but many of them must have been baffled by his discussions of mysticism, re-incarnation and Immanentism, as well as by his references to Plato, Plotinus, Dante, Goethe, Hegel, Emerson, Whitman, Flaubert and Mistral – not to mention Krishna and 'Congfútsa' (Confucius)![68] But other and more powerful people moved quickly from bafflement to relentless opposition. Ó Riain believed that Ireland needed a new kind of missionary (*soiscéalaí*) preaching a new gospel to an emergent nation, 'the gospel of man's divinity and the ideal of a nationality of the spirit ...'[69] Moreover he felt that he himself had been called to be one of those missionaries, knowing full well that

> in mud and mire and misery to-day we are laying, though we know it not, the foundations of the House of Life. And the meanest of wage-slaves shall be master-builders.[70]

In fact he knew quite well what foundations he was laying and, despite all the formidable obstacles he faced, we find a consistent optimism in his Irish writings. For example, in *The Pope's Green Island* he states:

> When people are re-discovering themselves, are mentally alive, there is always magic, whatever the opposing powers may be. To work and look inward is better than to look towards the stars ... That way lie riches and a renewal of wonder, a joy which can neither be expressed nor argued about, – and a strength, individual and collective, which is likely to prove unaccountable and embarrassing to opponents who are always looking outward and afar.[71]

Or to put it more simply, as Ruairí Ó Duibhir does in *The Boyne and the Sea*, 'Rouse up your courage ... The Kingdom of Heaven is in us and the soul always wins.'[72]

It goes without saying that Ó Riain did not expect that victory to be either quick or easy, but that was no reason to lose hope:

> Even here I realise that there are many interpenetrating worlds. I shall be fully conscious of them all in due season. I can afford to be patient; I have manifold cause to be joyous.[73]

II: *The Boyne and the Sea* in Context

A superficial reading of Ó Riain's creative work dealing with Ireland could lead one to think that he had in fact only written variants of a single book. There are certainly many obvious similarities among these novels and plays as well as his long poem *Inghean Mhanannáin*.[74] Thus the question of love, marriage and gender roles in the lives of Irish progressives and Gaelic activists is central in *The Cross and the Plough, Caoimhghin Ó Cearnaigh, The Boyne and the Sea* and *Inghean Mhanannáin*. In the first the focus is on Fergus O'Hagan and Elsie O'Kennedy; in the second on the eponymous protagonist and Úna Ní Chuilleannáin; in the third on Ruairí Ó Duibhir and Créide Ní Chonghaile; and in the fourth on Colm Ó Domhnaill and Méabh Ní Mhaoláin.[75] In all of the above works in addition to the play *Feilm an Tobair Bheannuighthe*, the male protagonist is torn between the apparently uncomplicated communal life of the native place he has left (and sometimes returned to) and the intellectual excitement and opportunities for personal development and service to the national revival he finds in the urban environment. Predictably enough from what we have seen of Ó Riain's own mystical interests, among the major themes in all of these works, as well as in the early play *An tOide as Tír na nÓg*, is the opposition, real or illusory, between our corporeal world and a superior spiritual realm; between an apparently 'real' Ireland and a Greater Ireland waiting to be (re)discovered; between the Gaelic and the universal; between the warped Christianity of the institutional, hierarchical and exclusive Irish Catholic Church and the true Christianity that is but one expression of an all-inclusive faith in life's divinity and diversity; between an understandable and all too facile pessimism and a brave optimism.

Moreover, *Caoimhghin Ó Cearnaigh* and *The Boyne and the Sea* are both *romans à clef,* with the male protagonists obviously based on Ó Riain himself.[76] But we also meet, among others, Piaras Béaslaí, Arthur Griffith, Cathal Mac Gairbhigh, and Tadhg Ó Donnchadha ('Torna') as 'Pilib na gCleas,' 'Art Aonair,' 'Gruagach an Ghrinn,' and 'Taidhgín an Éigse' respectively in *Caoimhghin Ó Cearnaigh*; and 'John Eglington' (J.K. Magee), Douglas Hyde, Seán P. Mac Éinrigh, Micheál Mhag Ruaidhrí, Agnes O'Farrelly (Úna Ní Fhaircheallaigh) Patrick Pearse, and George Russell ('AE') as 'Eagleton,' 'An Dochtúir Ó Dúda,' 'An Dochtúir Mac Shligigh,' 'Micheál Mag Tuireadh,' 'Áine Ní Fharaile,' 'Pádraic Mac Éanna,' and 'Feargus Ó Ruanaí' respectively in *The Boyne and the Sea*. The female protagonists of the novels – Elsie in *The Cross and the Plough,* Úna in *Caoimhghin Ó Cearnaigh* and Créide in *The Boyne and the Sea* – seem more like composite figures based on such female activists as Máire de Buitléar, Máire Ní Chillín and, perhaps the most important, Eibhlín Nic Niocaill, a lively university graduate (B.A.) who drowned near the Great Blasket Island in 1909.[77] In like manner, Ó Riain seems to have used several models for his progressive priests, among them Fathers Michael Moloney, Michael O'Hickey and Walter McDonald.

Yet despite the many parallels that run throughout Ó Riain's works, there are also significant differences in the way characters and themes are presented and developed. For example, with regard to marriage and gender roles, we find that *The Cross and the Plough* ends ambiguously with both Fergus and Elsie committed to serving Ireland but Fergus still wondering if he is 'a sort of after-thought, the inevitable postscript' in her future plans.[78] In *Caoimhghin Ó Cearnaigh,* Caoimhghin is far more interested in marriage than is Úna, who at one point tells him a little parable about a young couple of 'noble nature' (*ardnádúr*) living in 'a pure happy state' (*staid ghlan shonasach*) and having 'great work to do' (*obair mhór le déanamh*). However as a result of 'a low, worldly, uncharitable nature' (*nádúr íseal shaolta mhícharthanach*) that neither of them can escape, they forget their better selves and think only of 'love … pleasure … idleness' (*grá … pléisiúr … díomhaointeas*) and fail to realise their proper destiny, leaving them 'unhappy, weary, vice-ridden, tormented' (*mí-shonasach tuirseach duáilceach cráite*), their lives ruined.[79] With time Caoimhghin comes to share Úna's viewpoint, deciding that while love might be 'delightful' (*aoibhinn*) and 'useful' (*acrach*) for most people, there were some like himself with 'great uncommon work to do' (*obair mhór neamhchoiteann le déanamh*) for whom it was 'necessary … to guard against love' (*riachtanach … an grá a sheachaint*).[80] Úna offers a solution: 'We will always be loving towards each other … I will be working among the poor; you will be working diligently for Ireland and for your own people.'[81] However ideologically sound, this plan has no chance of working and, by novel's end, we find them married and comfortably ensconced in Sandymount. Needless to say, as Úna makes clear, their higher natures and commitments survive the shock of wedlock:

> To be as we are now, so joyful in ourselves, with so much happiness around us as there is here by Dublin Bay and so much work to be done for the poor and for our country – wouldn't we be happy forever?[82]

The long poem *Inghean Mhanannáin* also ends conventionally for the lovers, but only because the otherworldly intervention of Manannán's daughter Grian is able to overcome the rather priggish Colm Ó Domhnaill's dismissal of Méabh's love for him as 'too worldly' (*róshaolta*).'[83] Grian tells Colm: 'Without love in his heart, fresh, genuine, and tender,/And he forever loyal to it, it is futile for anyone/In the world to be thinking that he is truly alive/Ever, no matter how powerful or learned he may be.'[84] The main problem with the love-gender theme in this poem is that Colm is not particularly likeable and Méabh is pretty much a cipher, her only role to keep Colm busy and to inspire a paean to human love from Grian.

The female protagonist of *The Boyne and the Sea* is anything but a cipher. While there are certainly similarities between Créide Ní Chonghaile and other Ó Riain heroines – beauty, intellect, wit, commitment to progressive causes, for example – she is the most complex and interesting of them. As is usual with Ó Riain, the course of true love does not run smooth for Créide and Ruairí. But whereas like Úna in *Caoimhghin Ó Cearnaigh* she worries that love and marriage might not be compatible with the full expression of her (and Caoimhghin's) spiritual potential or with their service to higher causes, Créide's reservations are more specifically feminist. Thus, although she later admits to having fallen in love with Ruairí at first sight and does let him kiss her on a moonlit night by the sea, she quickly replies to a long letter from him to disabuse him of any misconception that she holds conventional views of romance:

> The discussion of love was genuinely poetic. But what does it have to do with me? Did you make a mistake? Were you writing a novel and did you put a bunch of pages from it into your letter? If that isn't it, what else could it be?

When he sends her a letter similar to the first she responds:

> You seem to have put the whole novel in this time! … I see that it deals mostly with love and, as is fitting in a love story, there is talk of marriage.

At this point she shifts to Aristophanic mode:

> But if I were the girl I would let the 'hero' know a few things in particular. Things like this: 'You say I am a goddess and that it is what is wonderful in me that is inspiring you to great deeds. You need to prove that. Don't say another word about marriage until you have done something great for your

> country and your people in the form of a book or a heroic action. I will believe you then.

Indeed she tells him she wants to start a club for young women committed to that very principle, adding that she faulted the goddesses of Greece, Ireland and other ancient societies for attaching 'too much interest in lovers, in themselves and in the very idea of love, and too little in their countries, the human race and their own duty.[85] Eventually she does decide to marry and settle down with Ruairí, but then again has second thoughts and sets out to fulfill a higher destiny.

The home Ruairí and Créide briefly planned for themselves was to have been in his native place, on the 'patch of ground' where his parents eke out a living. Ruairí left the farm for the intellectual ferment of Dublin, but he still feels a deep attachment to it, wondering:

> Was he faithful to his heritage? Was it worth it to ask questions about the universe? ... Wouldn't it be better for him to be working on the farm still and not be bothering with city life at all?[86]

Yet he knows full well that a return to the 'patch of land' will mean a surrender of his ambition for himself and his country.

Caoimhghin Ó Cearnaigh, teaching in the local national school in his native Cluain Tobair, imagines Dublin as a place 'as wonderful as was Tara in the time of Cormac mac Airt or Emain Macha when Cú Chulainn set out for it' (*chomh hiontach agus a bhí Teamhair in aimsir Chormaic Mhic Airt, nó Eamhain Mhacha ar dhul do Chúchulainn Óg ar a triall*).[87] After a bit of homesickness in his early days in the big city, he seems to forget both Cluain Tobair and his parents. At any rate, for all practical purposes he loses touch with his mother and father to the extent that it is only after the fact that he learns poverty has forced them to emigrate to America to join their other sons and daughters.

Despite her anti-intellectualism it is hard to fault his mother for her disappointment with her author son:

> A book is an insignificant thing to a mother's heart compared with a son. Och. I was always afraid of those books. And now my dear son has left me forever because of them.[88]

To be fair, he does rush to Cluain Tobair – too late of course – when he learns they are in such dire straits and he does tax his own limited resources bringing them home to the farm, but it is still difficult to forgive his self-absorbed lack of interest in them when they were in such need of his help, financial and emotional. His friend Father Muiris Mac Cathmhaoil tells him he and Úna should go to Cluain Tobair where they can have 'a happy life on the little farm' (*saol sonasach ar an bhfeirm bheag*), but Caoimhghin says that while tempted to do so he intends to remain in Dublin and follow his vocation as a writer with 'things in my mind I should make known' (*nithe im' intinn gur cóir dom a gcraobhscaoileadh*).[89]

In *Inghean Mhanannáin,* Colm Ó Domhnaill is warned against the exotic ideas of faraway places by his mother:

> O stay home, on the land of the people; /The ordinary pious peaceful life is best for you; /Avoid knowledge from beyond the border of the countryside; /Do not abandon your heritage for foreign learning.[90]

Nevertheless he does leave - even reaching the Otherworld - only to finally decide as an improbable Boddhisatva to go home, where he has already begun to teach his neighbours the latest agricultural developments, built new houses, started a co-op and organised a *feis,* thereby creating a vibrant new Gleann Corraigh on a sound traditional foundation.[91]

Ó Riain's mystical beliefs are, predictably enough, central in all of his Irish writings. For example, in *The Cross and the Plough* Fergus O'Hagan asserts:

> Our spiritual selves, though much bound up with bodies, and consequently chained to the present, do not belong to it alone; I see no reason why they, eternal in essence as they are, cannot occasionally realise in some measure what is coming in time and space long before it arrives.[92]

Caoimhghin Ó Cearnaigh tells himself that

> There is nothing worth talking about except the spiritual state. Heaven itself is a spiritual state. If we ourselves were in a joyful spiritual state here and it was constant – and if we did not yield to insignificant corporeal things – we would be in Heaven.[93]

Once again, however, it is in *The Boyne and the Sea* that we find the most ambitious exploration of mystical themes in Ó Riain's Irish novels and plays, one that simply transcends the dichotomies noted above. Créide tells Ruairí that at a meeting of the Society of the Star of Knowledge Feargus Ó Ruanaí had declared of activists in the various revival movements that

> their ordinary minds do not understand the job that the Soul of the Universe (the high servant of God) has conceived for them, but their souls understand it, and it is their souls that inspire them to work unbeknownst to their ordinary minds.[94]

Writing to Ruairí from the Gaelic college, Créide herself states that 'there is another state of being and other work in store for us. You will realise that soon, my beloved.'[95] That realisation comes with a shock to Ruairí when he discovers that Créide has vanished without a trace from the college, never to be found despite intensive searches by people at the school as well as by Ruairí himself. Soon, however, he comes to understand that she has moved on to a higher spiritual state and that his mission is to quite literally tend his own garden on a remote island off the west coast while also cultivating greater enlightenment. As Feargus Ó Ruanaí says:

> But there exists a mystical, mental, and spiritual co-operation, and Ruairí and Créide, especially Créide, help with mystical

> co-operation, for she is in the most wonderful state of being. They are working in the great Ireland – a country holier and more profound than we perceive here in the ordinary Ireland.[96]

This comment underscores the link between the individual spirit and that of the nation as a whole that was a central tenet of Ó Riain's spiritual nationalism in both his explicitly mystical writings and in his creative work dealing with Ireland. For example, in *The Cross and the Plough*, O'Hagan tells Elsie that

> the great Ireland is in ourselves, and it is full of beauty, divine activity and boundless hope. The outer Ireland, agitated or stagnant, is something incidental to keep our souls in training.[97]

At the end of *Inghean Mhanannáin*, Grian expresses her satisfaction with Colm's spiritual progress, declaring: 'At last Ireland as it is is clear to you.'[98] In *Caoimhghin Ó Cearnaigh*, Caoimhghin explains to his friend Seán Ó Murchú that some philosophers believe that there is 'a special higher life in everyone unbeknownst to him' (*ardbheatha faoi leith i ngach duine gan fhios dó féin*), and continues that he thinks there might well be 'a special higher mind or a higher life in the case of every country as well – a hidden and profound noble life that emerges in certain periods of time' (*ardintinn nó ardbheatha faoi leith i gcás náisiúin chomh maith céanna – ardbheatha cheilte dhoimhin, a thigeas chun cinn in aoiseanna áirithe*).[99] By novel's end Caoimhghin is convinced of the reality of 'the invisible great *Gaeltacht*' (*mór-Ghaeltacht dhofheicthe*).[100]

What links the individual spirit with this true and greater *Gaeltacht* over the ages is, of course, re-incarnation, and in his creative work dealing with Ireland Ó Riain does not shy away from what was certainly in the minds of his compatriots one of his most heterodox and troubling theories. Thus Fergus O'Hagan believes that 'Death, after all, was but an incident of change, an essential turning in our time-and-space stage, the end of a chapter and a starting point.'[101] Caoimhghin Ó Cearnaigh is initially uncomfortable with the idea of cycles of rebirth, but he soon becomes a believer:

> The souls that were here in Tara long ago, they are somewhere and in some state in the universe. Perhaps some of them have come back again and are working in other bodies in places throughout Ireland.

As a result, 'there is no such thing as death, just a change of form and a change of state. Tara is not lost, just changed.'[102]

We find a similar acceptance of re-incarnation in *The Boyne and the Sea*, as when Ruairí tells his friend Cathal Ó Cinnéide:

> I think that there is in everyone a soul that comes into the world with a particular job to do, and that when it has done that it goes on to another state of being to do another job. If it doesn't finish the work, or doesn't do it right, I think that it must come back to finish it – in another body.[103]

More important, however, is the fact that Créide lives out this belief and at the end of the novel achieves just such a transition to a higher spiritual plane.

Any characters modelled so obviously on Ó Riain himself would have to engage in the same struggle between pessimism and optimism that marked his own passionate engagement with controversial issues in Irish life. Certainly he made no attempt to hide the discouragement those characters faced in their challenge to the conventional, conservative and Church-dominated Ireland of their time. All three of his alter-egos experience what in *Caoimhghin Ó Cearnaigh* is called 'sorrow and terrible loneliness without knowing why' (*dólás agus uaigneas uafásach … gan fios cén fáth*) when they feel that they and the whole human race are exiles (*deoraithe*), 'banished from their soul's inheritance because of some dreadful crime, and not knowing the way to get back' (*díbeartha mar gheall ar choir mhillteach éigin ó dhúchas a n-anamanna, agus gan eolas acu ar bhealach a bhfillte*), and that 'in some ways the people of Dublin and the people of Ireland are like the dead' (*ar shlite tá muintir Átha Cliath agus muintir na hÉireann cosúil leis na mairbh*).[104] This state of mind is exemplified in *The Boyne and the Sea* by Créide's father Fionntán, the sub-editor of a Dublin newspaper:

> He liked the great stories of ancient Ireland – or their mystical meaning I should say – and as for present-day Ireland, he didn't think it was worth a mention: its life had been withering for a long time, and not even a druid or a sage could revive it.[105]

This kind of depression must have been tempting for many taking on reactionary forces in the cause of national revival, but neither Ó Riain nor any of his protagonists ultimately surrender to it. Liam P. Ó Riain may not have been a very good novelist, but he was a very interesting one who lived at a time in Irish history that demanded both determination and faith, and he had both. The hallmark of all of Ó Riain's writings and of his creative work in particular, is a consistent, hard-earned optimism that enabled him to preach, in the words of Ruairí Ó Duibhir, that 'the Kingdom of Heaven is in us and the soul always wins.'[106] This is also, of course, the philosophy that enables Ruairí to survive and thrive after Créide's transition. It finds memorable expression at the end of *The Boyne and the Sea* when the AE figure Feargus Ó Ruanaí recites the epigraph from 'The City,' a poem by the actual AE quoting lines from the *Phaenomena* of the 3rd century BC Greek poet Aratus: 'The cities are full of Zeus, the harbours are full of Zeus, the myriad ways of people are full of Zeus.'[107]

We began with the self-doubts of Liam P. Ó Riain. We will now conclude with the belief that inspired all of his work for the Irish Revival: 'For men and races re-building is more glorious than proud remembering. The non-creators are the lost.'[108]

Notes

1 W.P. Ryan, *The Celt and Cosmos* (London, David Nutt, 1914), p. 38.

2 R.F. Foster writes: 'Ryan's cheerful secularism in educational matters, the subversive and quizzical editorial tone, his ridiculing of clerical opposition to mixed Gaelic League classes precipitated the paper's suppression, in its first incarnation, at the hands of Cardinal Logue.' See Foster, *Vivid Faces: The Revolutionary Generation in Ireland 1890–1923* (New York, W. W. Norton, 2015), p. 168.

3 Biographical information has been drawn from Diarmuid Breathnach and Máire Ní Mhurchú, *Beathaisnéis a hAon* (Biography one) (Baile Átha Cliath, An Clóchomhar, 1986), pp 96–8; and Risteárd Ó Glaisne, *Ceannródaithe: Scríbhneoirí na Nua Ré: Tuairisc Iriseora* (Pioneers: Modern writers: A journalist's account) (Baile Átha Cliath, Foilseacháin Náisiúnta Tta, 1974), pp 34–53.

4 It offered brief summaries of and comments on what Ó Riain felt were the major works of these poets.

5 There is a considerable body of unpublished material by Ó Riain in the W.P. Ryan papers in the University College Dublin archives.

6 This was a series that ran in *ACS* beginning 24/10/03.

7 I must thank Brendan McGowan, Education and Outreach Officer at Galway City Museum, whose superb detective work has recently established that Ó Riain was 'Sliabh Bladhma', a fact I wish I had known when I was writing *Gaelic Prose in the Irish Free State*.

8 Perhaps his most significant influence was on his son, the historian Desmond Ryan.

9 Ryan, *Celt and Cosmos*, p. 56.

10 Liam P. Ó Riain, *Gaedhealachas i gCéin* (Baile Átha Cliath, Oifig Díolta Foillseacháin Rialtais, 1933), p. 35. Tá áit faoi leith ag Rúndiamhra na sean-Éireann i stair spioradálta an iarthair. D'ullmhaíodar an tslí chun taispeánta na Críostaíochta agus cúrsaí nua san Oilithreacht dhiaga dhaonna.

11 Liam P. Ó Riain, *Inghean Mhanannáin: Laoi a Bhaineas le n-Ár Linn Féin* (Dún Dealgan, Uilliam Tempest, 1917), p. 13.

12 William Patrick O'Ryan, *The Cross and the Plough: A Story of New Ireland* (Dublin, Irish Nation Office, 1910), p. 344. See also Ryan, *Celt and Cosmos,* p. 7 and Ó Riain, *An tOide as Tír na nÓg: Dráma Cheithre Ghníomh* (Baile Átha Cliath, Connradh na Gaeilge, 1910), p. 15.

13 Ryan, *Celt and Cosmos,* p. 60. Writing as 'Sliabh Bladhma' in *An Gaedheal* in 1935, he stated: 'In regard to Gaelicism ... my own main and final reason for not trying to sum it up is that I look upon it as something which is ever growing ... It is not something completed and definite' (*Gaedheal,* 16/2/35). See also 'Cara na nÚdar (Ó Riain), 'Filidheacht agus Fíordhacht,' *ACS,* 12/9/14; and Ryan, *Pope's Green Island,* pp 324–5.

14 Ó Riain, *Inghean Mhanannáin,* p. 28. Tá an chruinne dá fás – crann na háille diamhartha/Bheas i mborradh 's i mbláth go bráthach na síoraí./Tá na tíortha 's réalta 'na gcraobha 's 'na mblátha dhe,/Agus spiorad istigh i ngach ní ag fás leo.

15 The term 'race' was used far more carelessly then than it is now and Ó Riain was very much a man of his time in this regard. It should, however, be noted to his credit that he was conscious of the misuses to which the concept could be put. For example, in *The Celt and the Cosmos* he warned against considering 'one race greater or more strange than another' and continued: 'It is only an entity with a different conscious and sub-conscious experience. We have lived and wrought in many races, we may be re-born in many more' (p. 24). Similarly, in *The Pope's Green Island* he writes: 'And to the terms "Gael" and "Gaelic" we are not necessarily to attach a particular racial significance. I mean by the Gael a unit or type of the age-old civilization that expressed itself through Irish, ancient, middle, or modern' (p. 25). Thus for him 'race' was primarily a linguistic not a genetic category.

16 Ryan, *Celt and Cosmos,* pp 30–1. See also pp 10, 49, 58; and O'Ryan, *The Cross and the Plough,* p. 10.

17 O'Ryan, *The Cross and the Plough,* p. 102. See also pp 67, 145–6.

18 O'Ryan, *The Cross and the Plough,* pp 358–9.

19 Ryan, *The Cross and the Plough,* p. 53.

20 Ryan, *The Cross and the Plough,* p. 14.

21 Ryan, *Pope's Green Island,* p. 201.

22 Ryan, *Celt and Cosmos,* p. 58.

23 Ó Riain, *Inghean Mhanannáin,* p. 23.

24 Ó Riain, *Gaedhealachas i gCéin,* p. 34. He added that Celtic scholars, however learned, rarely realised this fact. Bhí an-

difríocht … idir an Príomh-Chú Chulainn – an Cú Chulainn spioradálta – agus Cú Chulainn na Tána.

25 W.P. Ryan, 'Cuchulainn,' *Dublin Magazine*, March 1925, pp 509–10.

26 Ó Riain, *Gaedhealachas i gCéin*, p. 62. Is léir nach bhfuil baint ar bith ag an-chuid den saga leis an domhan gnách … As dúiche ní ba dhoimhne ná Lochlann nó an gnáth-Éire dóibh. On the other hand, in *The Boyne and the Sea* Ruairí tells his friend Cathal that 'we don't need the Fianna or other heroes of ancient times. I am glad that the Fianna are not to be seen or found in today's Ireland. They were always fighting and hunting. In some ways they were fine in their own day, but there is a more profound and intellectual spirit in us' (p. 13).

27 Ryan, *Celt and Cosmos*, p. 14. See also Ryan, *Pope's Green Island*, p. 235.

28 Ryan, *Celt and Cosmos*, p. 59. See also Ó Riain, *Inghean Mhanannáin*, p. 5. In *Gaedhealachas i gCéin* he gives a slightly different definition of the three planes: 'the ordinary mind, clear spiritual perception, beginning of enlightenment' (an ghnáthmheabhair, léiraireachtáil anama (fios anamdha), tús intsoilsithe) (pp 85–6).

29 Ó Riain, *Inghean Mhanannáin*, p. 11. Do thuig sé iontas, oll-rúin, ilaoibhneas/An domhain diamhartha, fhíorga, shíoraí.

30 The teacher is also, of course, a Boddhisatva figure. In Ó Riain's 1910 play *Cuaird na Bainríoghna*, it is also the pupils who teach their elders the value of the Irish language and its culture.

31 Ó Riain, *The Boyne and the Sea*, p. 39. See also pp 44, 68; and Ryan, *Pope's Green Island*, pp 199, 235 and 257. In the earlier version of a section of the novel entitled 'An Múinteoir Taisdil, Bhergilius, agus an Sagairtín' (The travelling teacher, Virgil and the young priest), this character is called Seoirse [George] Ó Ruanaí. There is, however, no difference in his characterisation. In the earlier version Ruairí states that Seoirse reminds him of Virgil when he discusses farming and of Plato when the subject is philosophy and mysticism (*ACS*, 2/11/12).

32 Ó Riain, *The Boyne and the Sea*, pp 84–5. Writing as 'Sliabh Bladhma' in 1938, Ryan did express some reservations about AE's ideas concerning *Gaelachas* or Gaelicism: 'Mr. George Russell, to the Gaelic view, is a puzzle. Some of his utterances on *Gaelachas* have been thoughtful and penetrative, some grudging and almost petulant …' (*Gaedheal*, August 1938, p. 1).

33 Ó Riain, *Inghean Mhanannáin*, p. 25. Ach monuar! Na créatúirí

inniu 'tá 'nár n-ionad!/Ath-ioncholnú 'na measc! Ba heaglach mé roimhe./Ba shuarach mo staid: ní fás spriodálta/A bheadh i ndán dom ach fás i dtáire.

34 See Ó Riain, *Boyne and the Sea*, p. 61, and *Celt and Cosmos*, p. 18.

35 Ó Riain, *Boyne and the Sea*, p. 85.

36 Ryan, *Pope's Green Island*, p. 254.

37 Ryan, *Pope's Green Island*, p. 253.

38 Ryan, *Pope's Green Island*, pp 87–8.

39 Ryan, *The Cross and the Plough*, p. 32.

40 The references to a 'chivalrous' and 'reverent' attitude towards women might set off warning bells. But Ó Riain was still a man well ahead of most of his contemporaries on this issue. It is, for example, worth noting that in all three of his Irish novels men tell women there are things too physically hard for them to do only to have those women accomplish even more challenging tasks.

41 Ó Glaisne, p. 52.

42 Ní foláir dúinn tuiscint nach féidir fíor-náisiún a bheith againn nó go mbeidh daibhreas agus aineolas díbeartha. Caithfidh maoin go leor (idir saolta agus intleachtach) a bheith ag gach uile dhuine.

43 Ryan, *The Cross and the Plough*, p. 353.

44 Ryan, *The Cross and the Plough*, p. 226. See also p. 354.

45 Ryan, *The Cross and the Plough*, p. 375.

46 Ó Riain, *Boyne and the Sea*, p. 67. See also p. 68.

47 Ó Riain, *Boyne and the Sea*, pp 57, 75.

48 Ó Riain, *Boyne and the Sea*, p. 65. This was a courageous position to take, for as Ó Riain wrote in *The Pope's Green Island*, virtually all of the Catholic clergy were opposed to 'anything that seems to savour of Socialism.' And in the same book he also discussed the powerlessness of progressive priests in the face of this all but universal condemnation of 'socialism' (pp 278–9).

49 Ryan, *Pope's Green Island*, p. 52. In a 1903 piece in *An Claidheamh Soluis*, Ó Riain called the London Branch of the League an organisation marked by '*l'idéalisme* agus *le romanticisme*' (*ACS*, 17/10/03). For a discussion of his work with the London Branch see Donncha Ó Súilleabháin, *Conradh na Gaeilge i Londain 1894–1917* (Baile Átha Cliath, Conradh na Gaeilge, 1989).

50 Ó Riain, *Boyne and the Sea*, p. 44.

51 Ó Riain, *Boyne and the Sea*, p. 45.

52 This was also true of the League *céilí*, a social evening with dancing. See Ó Riain, *Boyne and the Sea*, p. 13.

53 Ó Riain here uses 'province' instead of the expected 'county' to underscore the importance of Meath as one of the five ancient provinces of Ireland (the literal meaning of Ir. *cúige,* 'province,' is 'fifth').

54 Ó Riain, *Boyne and the Sea,* p. 64.

55 Ó Riain, *Caoimhín Ó Cearnaigh: Scéal Úrnua* (Baile Átha Cliath, 2014 [1913]), p. 93. Cad atá i ngluaiseacht na Gaeilge? Éirí amach na bhfíordhaoine in aghaidh na ngnáthdhaoine. Diagaireacht, diamhaireacht, fíorghrá, fíorfhilíocht, fíorcheol, carthannacht, comh-mhothú – 'siad san go léir beatha agus obair an 'fhíordhuine.'

56 Ó Riain, *Caoimhín Ó Cearnaigh,* p. 73. Ba thrua leo gan an tOireachtas a bheith ann i gcónaí díreach mar a bhí cathair na Teamhrach agus aoibhneas na Teamhrach ann ó thus deireadh na bliana anallód … Tá dearmad mór déanta acu. Tá an tOireachtas ann i gcónaí. Is ionainn féin atá an tOireachtas.

57 W. P. Ryan, *The Irish Labor Movement From the 'Twenties to Our Own Day* (New York, B.W. Huebsch, 1920), pp 9–11.

58 Ryan, *Irish Labor Movement,* p. 174.

59 One thinks here of the League's refusal in 1905–6 to back down when a parish priest in Portarlington, Co. Laois condemned the local League branch for holding co-educational classes in Irish, and of the organisation's leadership role in securing the acceptance of Irish as a mandatory subject for matriculation in the new National University of Ireland in 1910.

60 See, for example, Ryan, *Cross and Plough,* pp 82–3, 116–33, 181–7; and Ryan, 'Introductory' in *The Pope's Green Island,* pp 1–16, 20.

61 Ryan, *Pope's Green Island,* pp 26–7. See also p. 218.

62 Ryan, *Pope's Green Island,* p. 27. See also pp 2–4.

63 Ryan, *Pope's Green Island,* p. 74.

64 Ó Riain, *Caoimhín Ó Cearnaigh,* p. 50. Tá spiorad Ghaeil an lae inniu fíorchosúil le spiorad na nGael a bhí ina mbeatha in aimsir Chúchulainn agus in aimsir na bhFiann. Tá spiorad Chríost iontu seo anois; agus bhí spiorad Chíost iontu súd ansin …

65 Ó Riain, *Boyne and the Sea,* p. 37. Speaking to his friend Conall Mór in 'Brugh na Bóinne agus an Domhan Thoir' (Newgrange and the East), an early version of a section of *An Bhóinn agus an Bhóchna,* Ruairí says: 'There is a mystical meaning to the stories of *Tír na nÓg* and many others, and that mystical meaning is very similar to the philosophical essence of the East and to the

fundamental mystical teaching of Egypt etc.' (Tá ciall rúndiamhair le scéalta Thír na nÓg agus lena lán eile, agus tá an chiall rúndiamhrach sin fíorchosúil le brí fhealsúnachta an Domhain Thoir agus le bunteagasc rúnda na hÉigipte ⁊rl.). He adds that without an understanding of the 'sages' (saoithe) and 'spirituality' (spioradáltacht) of the ancients, the Irish would never be able to understand the story of Newgrange or the meaning of its symbols (scéal Bhrú na Bóinne ná ciall a chomharthaí) (*ACS*, 23/11/12).

66 Ryan, *Celt and Cosmos*, p. 17.

67 Ó Glaisne, p. 52. Ach bhí sé in aghaidh an oiread sin córas agus institiúidí a bhí seanbhunaithe i saol na hÉireann agus i saol an domhain, agus bhí a aigne chomh hoscailte do smaointe úra de chineálacha éagsúla, gur chuir sé amhras agus imní ar go leor daoine.

68 In 'Brugh na Bóinne agus an Domhan Thoir,' he also mentions 'Spinótsa' (*ACS*, 23/11/12).

69 Ryan, *Celt and Cosmos*, p. 55.

70 Ryan, *Celt and Cosmos*, p. 40. See also pp 15–6.

71 Ryan, *Pope's Green Island*, p. 323.

72 Ó Riain, *Boyne and the Sea*, p. 39.

73 Ryan, *Celt and Cosmos*, p. 49. See also *Pope's Green Island*, pp 358–9.

74 It is interesting that in both *Caoimhghin Ó Cearnaigh* and *The Cross and the Plough*, Ryan suggests that there may be a sequel in future, writing in the latter for example: 'Another day, and in a further story, we hope to follow the later fortunes of our friends in the deepening social and spiritual drama of their new Ireland' (p. 378). However instead of writing sequels he in some ways went back to the beginning in the two books in Irish that followed *The Cross and the Plough*.

75 Writing of *Caoimhín Ó Cearnaigh*, Alan Titley suggests that the conventionality of the novel's treatment of love may have been one of the reasons it has never gotten its due as a pioneering work dealing in Irish with challenging contemporary themes in an urban setting. See Titley, 'Réamhrá' (Foreword) in *Caoimhín Ó Cearnaigh*, p. 11. It is interesting that there is no mention of romantic love in either of the earlier versions of sections from *An Bhóinn agus an Bhóchna* published in *ACS* in 1912. Ó Riain's love plots can seem rather trite and even saccharine at times, but as I hope this introduction makes clear, he uses such storylines in his Irish novels to explore issues of political,

philosophical and mystical significance in the Ireland of his time.

76 Like Ó Riain, Caoimhghin Ó Cearnaigh and Ruairí Ó Duibhir are from a rural, more or less *Breac-Ghaeltacht* background, where they attend the local national school before leaving for Dublin and a career in journalism. All three are torn between an allegiance to their home places and a fascination with the intellectual life of the capital. They become activists, authors and misunderstood mystics, and fall in love with lovely, strong-minded and idealistic young women. Fergus O'Hanlon of *The Cross and the Plough* follows the pattern in everything except the rural, *Breac-Ghaeltacht* background. In his preface to the new edition of *Caoimhín Ó Cearnaigh,* Alan Titley writes: 'Mar adeir siad ar eagla na dlí go seachantach, níor ghá gurb ionann iad smaointe an údair agus smaointe a chuid carachtar, ach ar shlí éigin ní féidir gan a shamhlú nach bhfuil ach droichead gairid eatarthu' (p. 7). Among the unpublished material in the W.P. Ryan papers at UCD is 'Rúna Fáil,' the manuscript of another *roman à clef* in Irish.

77 See Micheál Ó Dubhshláine, *Óigbhean Uasal ó Phríomhchathair Éireann* (Baile Átha Cliath, Conradh na Gaeilge, 1992).

78 Ryan, *Cross and Plough,* p. 377.

79 Ó Riain, *Caoimhín Ó Cearnaigh,* pp 68–9. See also pp 74–5.

80 Ó Riain, *Caoimhín Ó Cearnaigh,* p. 87.

81 Ó Riain, *Caoimhín Ó Cearnaigh,* p. 88. Beimíd go grámhar dá chéile i gcónaí … Beadsa ag obair i measc na mbocht, beidh tusa ag obair go bríomhar ar son na hÉireann agus ar son do mhuintire féin …

82 Ó Riain, *Caoimhín Ó Cearnaigh,* p. 126. A bheith mar atáimid anois, chomh háthasach ionainn féin, an oiread sin aoibhneasa inár dtimpeall agus atá anso cois Chuan Átha Cliath, agus an oiread sin oibre le déanamh ar son na mbocht agus ar son ár dtíre – nach mbeimís sásta go deo …?

83 Ó Riain, *Inghean Mhanannáin,* p. 6.

84 Ó Riain, *Inghean Mhanannáin,* p. 20. Gan grá i n-a chroí, úr, íon a's ré-ghlan,/A's é dílis go bráth de, tá sé fánach ag aon neach/Sa tsaol bheith ag ceapadh gur 'na bheatha dáiríre/A bhíonn sé aon uair dá chumhacht a's saíocht é.

85 Ó Riain, *Boyne and the Sea,* pp 59–60.

86 Ó Riain, *Boyne and the Sea,* p. 42.

87 Ó Riain, *Caoimhín Ó Cearnaigh,* p. 18.

88 Ó Riain, *Caoimhín Ó Cearnaigh,* pp 85–6. Is suarach leabhar do

chroí máthar i gcóimheas le mac. Och, is orm a bhí eagla i gcónaí faoi na leabhra céanna. Agus anois tá mo mhac dil imithe uaim go deo mar gheall orthu.

89 Ó Riain, *Caoimhín Ó Cearnaigh*, pp 118–9.

90 Ó Riain, *Inghean Mhanannáin*, p. 9. Ó fan sa mbaile, ar thalamh na ndaoine;/Is fearr duit an gnáth-shaol cráifeach síthiúil;/Seachain an t-eolas thar teorainn na tuaithe,/Fá fhoghlaim i gcéin ná tréig an dúchas.

91 In *The Cross and the Plough* even the urban O'Hagan longs for the simple life at times. See pp 27 and 278–9.

92 Ryan, *The Cross and the Plough*, p. 67.

93 Ó Riain, *Caoimhín Ó Cearnaigh*, p. 26. Níl aon rud gur fiú trácht air ach cuma spioradálta. Is cuma spioradálta Neamh féin. Dá mba rud é go mbeadh cuma áthasach spioradálta orainn anseo, agus é a bheith seasmhach – gan sinne a bheith ag géilleadh do rudaí suaracha corpartha – bheadh Neamh againn.

94 Ó Riain, *Boyne and the Sea*, p. 61.

95 Ó Riain, *Boyne and the Sea*, p. 89. Of course her father Fiontán is also a mystic. See pp 23–9.

96 Ó Riain, *Boyne and the Sea*, p. 85.

97 Ryan, *The Cross and the Plough*, p. 373.

98 Ó Riain, *Inghean Mhanannáin*, p. 28. Is follas fá dheo dhuit Fódla ar tá sí.

99 Ó Riain, *Caoimhín Ó Cearnaigh*, p. 25.

100 Ó Riain, *Caoimhín Ó Cearnaigh*, p. 116.

101 Ryan, *Cross and Plough*, p. 281.

102 Ó Riain, *Caoimhín Ó Cearnaigh*, p. 94. Na hanamanna a bhí anso i dTeamhair fadó, tá siad in áit éigin nó ar staid éigin sa gcruinne. B'fhéidir go bhfuil cuid acu tagaithe ar ais arís agus go bhfuilid ag obair faoi cholainneacha eile in áiteacha ar fud Éireann … Níl bás dáiríre ann ach athrú cló agus athrú staide. Níl Teamhair caillte ach athraithe.

103 Ó Riain, *Boyne and the Sea*, p. 12.

104 Ó Riain, *Caoimhín Ó Cearnaigh*, pp 25–6. See also Ryan, *Cross and Plough*, p. 46.

105 Ó Riain, *Boyne and the Sea*, p. 23.

106 Ó Riain, *Boyne and the Sea*, p. 39.

107 AE, 'The City,' in *Collected Poems* (London, Macmillan and Co., 1935), p. 30.

108 Ryan, *Celt and Cosmos*, p. 57.

AN BHÓINN AGUS AN BHÓCHNA

I

Tráthnóna gréine sa samhradh 19– chuaigh ógbhean bhídeach ghleoite isteach in áras Chonradh na Gaeilge i mBaile Átha Cliath agus d'fhiafraigh de chléireach an raibh Diarmaid Mac an tSuaircis ann. Má bhí, ba mhaith léi labhairt leis ar feadh cúpla nóiméidín: Créide Ní Chonghaile ab ainm di, a dúirt sí de ghuth sámh ceolmhar.

Tháinig ionadh ar an gcléireach. Ba mhinic a chuala sé trácht ar Chréide, agus bhí sé amuigh uirthi go raibh sí an-léannta. Agus an ógbhean a bhí os a chomhair ní raibh rian an léinn uirthi, dar leis. Shíl sé go mbeadh bean léannta go mórálach agus beagán gruama. Agus maidir le Créide bhí sí simplí modhúil, agus cosúlacht leanbaíochta uirthi. Bhí sí seang, caol, clóghartha, agus gan ach timpeall le cúig troighthe d'airde inti. Bhí a gnúis fhionn dheas go soilbhir agus go smaointeach san am céanna, agus bhí a súile go síúil. Chuimhnigh an cléireach ar a lán filíochta faoi spéirmhná, ach ní tháinig leis cuimhneamh ar bhlúire di a bheadh oiriúnach mar thuairisc ar Chréide, ar a súile go háirithe. Samhlaíodh dó go raibh na filí róshaolta.

Phreab sé, agus chuaigh sé ar lorg Dhiarmada.

Bhí Diarmaid an-ghnóthach, ach tháinig sé go doras a

sheomra láithreach, agus chuir sé céad fáilte roimh Chréide. D'iarr sé uirthi teacht isteach agus cosúlacht bhróid air. Ba dhóigh le duine gur bhanfhlaith Gaelach í féin, agus gur taoiseach fial flaithiúil, ar a raibh sí ag tabhairt cuairte, Diarmaid.

Is é a bhí uaithi eolas cruinn (uimhreacha, ⁊l.) faoi fheiseanna, faoi mhúinteoirí taistil, faoi Choláistí Gaelacha, ⁊l. Cara san Oileán Úr a d'iarr uirthi an t-eolas a fháil di. Bhí sé ag teastáil i gcomhair aiste faoi Irisleabhar Aimiriceánach.

Thug Diarmaid an t-eolas di go prab, go cruinn, go fáilteach. Ba dhóigh leat gurbh é sin an t-aon rud a raibh sé ag fanúint leis le fada. Shílfeá nach raibh uaidh ach eolas iomlán ar imeachtaí na nGael a chur chun an Oileáin Úir.

Bhí Créide ar tí imeacht nuair a osclaíodh an doras, agus cé a bhuailfeadh isteach chucu ach an flaith iarthair, an file tuaithe, an scéalaí fial ón iargúil, an Dochtúir Mánas Ó Dúda? Las a shúile nuair a dhearc sé ar Chréide.

'Mhuise, tá áthas an domhain orm tú a fheiscint,' ar seisean. 'Is fada nár chasamar ar a chéile. Agus táir i do Bh. E. anois! An B. E. is óige in Éirinn, agus is áille déarfainn, ach ar eagla go mbeifeá ag rá go bhfuilim ag éirí plámásach.'

'Mar a bhíonn tú i gcónaí,' ar Créide.

'Ó! ó! ó!' arsa an Dochtúir. 'Mise ag éirí plámásach! Mise! Atá cráite, crapaithe le neart buartha agus laech agus cléireach ag bagairt orm agus cúram na mbithiúnach go léir mar an Diarmaid seo orm! Táir ag magadh fúm, a bhláth bhán na finne. Ach cá rabhais le fada in aon chor?'

'Bhíos ar lorg Éireann agus is deacair í a fháil,' ar Créide, agus rinne sí miongháire. 'Is ea, is an-deacair í a fháil. Anois agus arís, a Dhochtúir, ceapaim go mbíonn tú ag déanamh an-díobháil.'

'Ó mo ghaoth aduaidh,' arsa an Dochtúir.

'Is ea,' ar sise. 'Gríosaíonn tú sinne a bheith Gaelach, agus spéis a bheith againn sa nGaelachas amuigh is amach. Tá go maith, arsa sinne, agus léimid na seanscéalta móra go dtí go mbíonn ár meanma ag cur thar maoil le laochas agus le draíocht agus ceapann sinn gurb áit laochta fhileata í Éire –'

'Agus in ainm an Chonartha nach mar sin –'

'Ina ionad san is tír bhocht, chráite, mhí-ámharach í, mar is léir dúinn gan mhoill. Níl Éire na laoch, Éire Chú Chulainn, Éire na Féinne le fáil ar chor ar bith. Dá bhrí sin bímid buartha brónach. Bímid míshásta faoi gach uile ní. Tusa, agus daoine mar thusa, is ciontach leis sin.'

'Tá gliocas ins an méid sin,' arsa an Dochtúir. 'Ach a bhláth bhán na finne, táir róchrua orm ar fad. Gan amhras tá difríocht mhór idir saol do mheanman agus an gnáthshaol, óir is sáraoibhinn síúil an mheanma chéanna. Ach ní domsa ná do scéalta Gaeilge a bhuíochas sin ach do Dhia agus an Dúchas.'

'Nach raibh an ceart agam?' ar Créide le Diarmaid. 'Plámásaí críochnaithe is ea an Dochtúir.'

Rinne Diarmaid gáire. Ba ghnách leis a bheith ag gáire nuair nach mbíodh sé ag obair ar chroí a dhíchill.

'Cén chaoi a bhfuil mo sheanchara, agus dilchara na nGael, t'athair cróga, croílaochta?' arsa an Dochtúir le Créide.

'Leis an fhírinne ghlan a rá leat is beag eolas atá agam ina thaobh,' arsa an ógbhean go ciúin, mianúil. Is rúnmhar an fear é, agus is cosúil go mbíonn rud éigin ag cur buartha air de ghnáth. Tigeann sé abhaile ó oifig an pháipéir – *An Blobarán* mar a thug sé air fadó – go deireanach san oíche, agus ansin fanann sé sa leabharlann bheag ar feadh i bhfad. Ní fheadar cad a bhíos á dhéanamh aige. Bíonn sé tuirseach tostach lá arna mhárach. Ba dhóigh leat nach bhfuil baint aige leis an domhan ar aon chuma.'

'Is iontach an rud é,' arsa an Dochtúir. 'Dhéanadh sé an-obair ar son litríocht na Gaeilge blianta ó shin nuair ba ghann na hoibrithe sa saol Fódlach ar fad. Thráchtadh sé go bríomhar san *Irisleabhar* ar scéalaíocht agus ar shaíocht na sean. Is ait an rud é, agus is mór an trua é, nach mbíonn sé inár measc ins na laethanta so, agus croí óg ins na Gaeil.'

Ina dhiaidh sin dúirt Créide gurbh éigean di imeacht, ach an chéad nóiméad eile osclaíodh an doras agus d'fhéach fear óg isteach. Phreab sé.

'Gabh mo leithscéal,' ar seisean. 'Shíleas go raibh Diarmaid ina aonar.'

'Tar isteach, a Ruairí,' ar Diarmaid. 'Ná bíodh ceist ort. Níl ach cairde anseo romhat.'

Tháinig an fear óg isteach. Duine caol dathúil cúthail smaointeach ab ea é. Ach má bhí sé cúthail smaointeach féin ba léir go raibh sé fuinniúil neamhspleách, cé go raibh a shúile beagán brionglóideach. Cheapfá go raibh óglaíocht, laochas, agus brí filíochta measctha le chéile ann.

'Tá seanaithne agat ar an Dochtúir,' arsa Diarmaid leis, 'agus is dócha go bhfuil aithne agat ar Iníon Ní Chonghaile freisin. "Créide" den *Claidheamh* a scríobh na haistí fileata úd gur mholais chomh mór san agus sinne ag caint an lá faoi dheireadh.'

'Tá an-aithne agam ar "Chréide," arsan fear óg, 'ach ní fhaca mé Iníon Ní Chonghaile riamh roimhe seo.'

'Is aisteach é sin,' dúirt Diarmaid. 'Chualas tusa ag moladh na n-alt fileata a scríobh sise, agus chualas ise ag moladh na n-alt fealsúnachta a chum tusa. Tá sibh mór ag a chéile sa ndomhan intleachtach, mar a déarfá, ach gan aithne ar bith agaibh ar a chéile sa ndomhan gnách go dtí anois.'

D'fhéach sé ó Ruairí go Créide agus ó Chréide go Ruairí.

'Créide Ní Chonghaile, spéirbhean B.E. – Ruairí Ó Duibhir, múinteoir taistil, file na Teamhrach, agus fealsamh,' ar seisean go galánta.

Ghabh gáire gach éinne. Ba mhaith le Ruairí an gáire. Níor fhéad sé focal a rá le Créide. Tháinig cúthaileacht agus ionadh agus áthas air. Shíl sé gurbh amhlaidh – ar mhodh éigin nár thuig sé – go raibh seanaithne aige ar Chréide. Tháinig 'pictiúir' de sheanfheiseanna agus de chruinnithe ársa os comhair a shúl. Bhí seisean agus sise ina measc. Bhí ceol aoibhinn á sheinm agus guthanna neamhchoitianta le cloisint ina dtimpeall. Samhlaíodh dó go raibh a ghnáthchuimhne á leathnú ar shlí iontach.

Chuir an Dochtúir a lámh dheas ar ghualainn Ruairí agus d'fhéach sé ar Chréide.

'Anois mar tá aithne agaibh ar a chéile,' ar seisean, 'iarraim ort, a bhláth bhán na finne, gan mórán suime a chur i gcaint an Ruairí seo go brách.'

Rinne Créide miongháire.

'Ní cúis gháire é,' arsa an Dochtúir. 'Cúpla bliain ó shin bhí sé chomh simplí nádúrtha le sagairtín, ach amháin gur chreid sé ins na sióga, rud nach raibh amuigh ar shagart riamh. Ach chuaigh sé go cúige na Mí mar mhúinteoir taistil agus tháinig draíocht thar meán air i ngleann na Bóinne. Ba dhóigh leat go mbíonn an Daghda agus Aonghus Óg mar chomharsana aige. Ní chreideann sé go bhfuil an domhan sofheicthe dáiríribh, nithiúil. Is taibhse fealsúnach é. Agus cuid dá bharúla saolta is uafásach iad. Nótaí Gaelacha a scríobhann sé i gcomhair páipéir áitiúla sa Mhí cuirid scanradh orm. Agus óir a bhíos múinteoirí taistil eile agus Gaeilgeoirí eile ag déanamh aithris air tá trioblóid ag tuar. Beidh fadhb mhór nua le réiteach agam. Beidh *dies crisimus* eile againn in Éirinn na nGael.'

'Is geal liom an méid sin a chloisint,' ar Créide. 'Is aoibhinn liom go bhfuil daoine ann – nó duine amháin féin – a chreideas nach bhfuil an domhan mar a shamhlaíonn sé a bheith. Léas i leabhra go minic go "n-athchruthaíonn an Gael an domhan" go dtí go mbíonn sé ina chónaí i gcruinne faoi leith, cruinne spioradálta, cruinne síúil; ach tá eagla orm nach bhfuil ins an méid sin ach plámás. Má chreideann Mac Uí Dhuibhir nach bhfuil an domhan dáiríribh, nithiúil, is é an chéad fhíor-Ghael a tháinig im threo riamh é.'

D'fhéach sí ar Ruairí agus rinne sí miongháire arís.

'Ó! ó! ó!' arsa an Dochtúir. 'An chéad fhíor-Ghael an ea! Dála do scéil ní fíor-Ghael mé féin ná ár nDiarmaid calma croíúil ach chomh beag. "Ó, is é a bhreoigh is a chráigh mé!" Ba mhaith liom anois gan an domhan a bheith dáiríribh, óir ansin ní bheadh do dhrochthuairim dáiríribh ach an oiread.'

Bhí caint mhagúil ar siúl eatarthu ar feadh tamaill, an Dochtúir agus Diarmaid á rá go raibh an 'cruinne' agus an tsíoraíocht maith go leor d'fhealsúna ach gurbh éigean do dhaoine simplí macánta a bheith sásta lena dtír féin agus le hobair an lae inniu.

'Tá sibh deisbhéalach mar is gnách libh,' ar Ruairí, 'ach is é mo thuairim go bhfuil na Gaeil ag éirí róshaolta, agus go gcuirid an iomarca suime sa "náisiún" agus san "domhan," agus i ngach uile rud coiteann. Táim ag ceapadh le fada go bhfuil an "domhan" agus "an t-am" agus an "colainn" agus an "gnáthshaol" mar dhéithe bréige, agus ina dtíoránaigh is mó dá bhfuil le fáil. Tá a lán le rá againn faoi athbheo agus faoi shaoirseacht. Ionainn féin a bheadh an t-athbheo agus an tsaoirseacht dáiríribh dá mbeadh tuiscint againn agus misneach orainn. Ní heol do Ghaeil an lae inniu an bóthar go Tír na nÓg.'

'Agus cá bhfuil an bóthar san?' ar Créide go sámh. 'B'aoibhinn liom a bheith dá chur diom. Is deas iad na bóithre cois Chuan Átha Cliath agus na bóithre chun an tsléibhe ach ní shásaíonn siad mo chroí. An bóthar go Tír na nÓg! Cá bhfuil sé? Cá bhfuil sé? Nó an rún é?'

Rinne Ruairí miongháire. B'aoibhinn an rud, dar leis, bóthar go Tír na nÓg do thaispeáint di. Ach is é a dúirt sé os ard:

'Tá eagla orm go bhfuilir ag déanamh grinn. Is fada an scéal é – scéal an bhóthair chéanna – ar aon chuma.'

'Is trua liom é sin,' a dúirt Créide. 'Más amhlaidh atá an scéal ní foláir dom bheith sásta leis an mbóthar go Cill Iníon Léinín. Agus is mithid dom siúl anois.'

D'fhág sí slán acu agus d'imigh sí.

Tháinig síoruaigneas ar Ruairí. Ar feadh cúpla nóiméad bhí sé ar tí bualadh amach ina diaidh. Is beag nach ndearna sé dearmad ar an Dochtúir agus ar Dhiarmaid. Ansin chuimhnigh sé ar an áit ina raibh sé. Is amadán mór mé, ar seisean leis féin.

Rinne sé an gnó a bhí aige le déanamh le Diarmaid, agus chuaigh amach. Bhí a fhios aige go mbeadh Créide imithe, ach ina dhiaidh sin is uile bhí brón agus uaigneas air faoi nach raibh sí le feiscint. Mar sin féin bhí aoibhneas á mheascadh leis an mbrón agus leis an uaigneas.

Shíleadh sé go minic ins na laethanta roimhe sin go raibh mórán 'daoine' ann féin: ceann a raibh dúil in aonaracht aige, ceann eile ba mhian leis obair mhór shaolta a chur chun críche, ceann eile arís a bhí an-liteartha, agus mar sin de. Bhíodh sé fileata uair. Fealsúnach uair eile. D'airigh sé um an am so go raibh 'duine' eile ann, duine a raibh ceangal rúnda idir é féin agus Créide. Cén aontacht a bhí idir na 'daoine' seo go léir? Cén míniú a bhí ar bheatha an chine dhaonna ar aon chor? Bhí sé cosúil le farraige. Tháinig athrú uirthi gach uair agus ní raibh teora lena doimhneacht ná lena hiontas. Chuimhnigh sé ar líne file Fhrancaigh:

L'océan éternal où bouillonne la vie.

Sea, ach ba thrua é nach mbeadh tuilleadh eolais ar bhrí na 'bóchna' le fáil ag duine le linn na 'beatha.'

Ar dhul trí Shráid Uí Chonaill dó, d'fhéach sé ó thaobh go taobh le súil go mbeadh Créide le feiscint. Faraor ní raibh.

Is an-aisteach é, a dúirt sé leis féin. Níor chreideas i ndraíocht na mban riamh roimhe seo, agus is beag scéal grá in aon teanga a thaitnigh go mór liom. I bhfad uaim an grá céanna! Is saolta contúirteach an rud é de ghnáth. Níl sé oiriúnach do Chréide. Níl baint aici sin leis an ndomhan gnách. Is sióg, is spiorad í. B'aoibhinn liom fáil amach an tuairim atá aici faoi dhaoine agus faoin domhan, faoi chroí agus faoin gcruinne.

II

In aice le Droichead Uí Chonaill casadh múinteoir taistil eile ar Ruairí: Cathal Ó Cinnéide a bhí ag obair le tamall i Loch Garman. Bhí seanleabhra agus leabhra nua faoina ascaill aige, mar ba ghnách leis. Thagadh sé go Baile Átha Cliath gach Satharn beagnach, scrúdaíodh sé na siopaí leabhar de gach uile shaghas ar a shástacht, agus cheannaíodh sé a raibh taitneamhach leis – seanchinn go háirithe – má bhíodh an t-airgead aige.

'Bíodh tae againn, a fhealsamh na Teamhrach,' ar seisean, tar éis cúpla nóiméad. 'Táim chomh tuirseach le fear a bheadh ag éisteacht le miontuairiscí an Choiste Gnó.'

B'fhearr le Ruairí a bheith ag siúl ina aonar agus ag smaoineamh ar Chréide. Ach bhí an-chairdeas idir é féin agus Cathal, agus níorbh fhéidir a dhiúltú.

Chuadar go tigh ósta a bhí in aice leo. Fear óg aerach ab ea Cathal, ach dá aeraí é bhí sé dána go leor, go mór mór i dtaobh nithe intleachtacha. B'aoibhinn leis díospóireacht: faoi stair, anameolas, litríocht, agus ealaín. 'Namhaid na gnáth-thuairime' a thug sé air féin. Ní raibh sé chomh hard ná chomh caol le Ruairí, ach bhí sé dathúil, cumasach, glan; idir a ghrua churata, a rúisc bheoga, agus a cheann dubh dualach dea-chumtha. Bhí rian laoich dhea-chroíoch air.

'Tá beirt fhear ionam, a Ruairí,' ar seisean, agus iad ag ól an tae. 'Bíd ag troid le chéile gach lá. Teastaíonn claíomh ó cheann acu, agus an Barr Bua. Is mian leis féin an Fhiann a chur ar bun arís agus droch-Éireannaigh agus naimhde na hÉireann a threascairt agus a imchianadh. Chuirfeadh sé an ruaig ar fhormhór na bhfeirmeoirí agus na siopadóirí. D'fhágfadh sé sa tír corroide mar Phádraic Mac Éanna le fíoroideachas a chur ar bun i gcomhair chlann na mbocht go háirithe; agus bheadh an tAthair Dónall Ó Dálaigh, an tAthair Micheál Ó Gadhra, agus sagairt den saghas sin – níl mórán acu ann – in uachtar. Bheadh cogadh claímhte agus cogadh ar son na sclábhaithe in Éirinn. Ach an fear eile atá ionam, tá an tseandúil i litríocht neamhchoiteann aige –'

'B'fhéidir go bhfuil ceangal idir an bheirt acu,' ar Ruairí. 'Is saghas laochais í fíorlitríocht –'

'B'fhéidir é, ach táim ag éirí mífhoighdeach leis an bhfear liteartha. Tá troid níos oiriúnaí d'Éirinn an lae inniu ná an litríocht is doimhne. Dá mbeadh Fionn inár measc thabharfadh sé a sheacht mallacht ar litríocht agus scéalaíocht agus smaointí go dtí go mbeadh na naimhde buailte againn. Tá mo dhúil sna leabhra ag tabhairt náire dom. Mar sin féin tá cúpla seoid agam anso.'

Thóg sé *La Tentation de Saint Antoine* a scríobh Flaubert agus thaispeáin sé an leabhar do Ruairí.

'Ní maith liom Flaubert,' ar Ruairí. 'Bhí *le stile* go hálainn aige, ach sin a raibh.'

'Bhí an tuairim chéanna agam féin sula bhfuaireas an leabhar so,' ar Cathal. 'Bhíos á léamh ar feadh an tráthnóna, ins na sráideanna féin. Is feasach dom anois go raibh dhá Fhlaubert ann, agus an Flaubert a chum *La Tentation* ba fhile agus ba fhealsamh é. As leabhar mar é seo tuigeann duine áilleacht agus draíocht teanga. Go deimhin, éiríonn an teanga féin ina file, ina spiorad. Agus an t-aidhm atá mar bhunús an leabhair! Baineann *La Tentation* leis na *penchants naturels* go léir; baineann sé le háilleacht, le heolas, le cumhacht, le sárghrá. Scéal cruinneach, nó dán cruinneach, is ea é. Nach mithid dúinne, na Gaeil, nó ár bhformhór pé scéal é, ár slán a fhágáil ag prós na bprátaí agus ag filíocht na mbóithríní, agus iarracht a dhéanamh ar fhíorsmaoineamh, agus ar dhea-scríbhinn?'

Rinne Ruairí gáire.

'Is aoibhinn liom prós na bprátaí agus filíocht na mbóithríní féin, más nádurtha feiliúnach iad,' ar seisean. 'Dea-choda na cruinne prátaí, agus téann bóithríní go Tír na nIontas ina slí féin. Ach táim ar aon intinn leat faoi ardsmaointí agus mhóriarracht meanman. Déanaim féin mo dhícheall! Tosnaím ar *épopée* nua gach seachtain. Cuireann *La Tentation* i gcuimhne dom go ndearna mé iarracht uair amháin le dán rúndiamhrach a dhéanamh as scéal Chaoimhín Naofa –'

'Níorbh fhiú é,' dúirt Cathal. 'Dúnmharú Chaitlín! – B'uafásach an rud é.'

'Is samhlú a bhí sa scéal is dócha. An "naofacht" in aghaidh na bantrachta –'

Rinne Cathal gáire dóite.

'Ba cheart dúinn go léir naofacht na mban a thuiscint,' ar seisean, 'ach níor thuig bunáite na nÉireannach é ó aimsir na Féinne. Tá Éire lán de bharúla bréagacha leis na céadta bliain, agus is í an bharúil is measa díobh an bharúil bhréan i dtaobh na mban breá fíorga gleoite. Fan go scríobhfad mo leabhar fá "Fíor-Naofacht na Bantrachta." Beidh ionadh ar na filí mar gheall ar mo mhéid filíochta, agus ar na fealsúna mar gheall ar mo bhrí fealsúnachta, ach móidím go mbeidh a thuilleadh ionaidh ar na sagairt faoi mhéid mo dhiagaireachta agus rúndiamhrachta.'

'Táir óg fós, a Chathail,' ar Ruairí, 'agus táir laochúil, fileata, agus cuireann tú an-spéis ina bhfuil ráite ag na filí faoi na mná –'

Las a ghrua beagán. Chuimhnigh sé ar Chréide Ní Chonghaile. Maidir le scríbhinn, mheas sé nach mbeadh moill air féin.

'Taoi deisbhéalach, a fhealsaimh,' d'fhreagair Cathal. 'Ach cuimhnigh air seo. Cé go bhfuilim go mór ar thaobh na bantrachta ní hionann sin is a rá go bhfuilim ar thaobh mná nó cailín faoi leith. Nílim, ach an oiread agus atáim ar thaobh sióige faoi leith. Ba bhaolach míchéillí a leithéid – im chás-sa. Ní féidir le nádúr duine bheith slán muna mbíonn cairdeas croí, agus gean féin, aige don bhantracht. Bíonn sin chomh riachtanach aige, chomh tairbheach dó, agus a bhíos ealaín agus litríocht agus fealsúnacht. Ach b'aisteach an rud é duine a bheith tugtha d'aon phictiúr amháin nó d'aon leabhar amháin. Sa tslí chéanna –'

'Magadh fileata, a Chathail! Tá morán difríochta idir mná agus leabhra! Is féidir iad go léir a sheachaint nó grá a thabhairt do cheann acu: ach an "modh" ar a bhfuilir ag caint, is taibhreamh greannmhar é.'

'Bímid róthugtha do rialacha agus do bharúla, a Ruairí. Is ceart do dhuine triall ar a shlí féin. "Beatha duine a thoil" deir an seanfhocal, ach déantar dearmad air de ghnáth. Ní maith liomsa pósadh; níl slí bheatha dáiríribh agam sa gcéad áit, agus is gnaoi liom saoirseacht. Ach bíonn an bhantracht chomh haoibhinn liom agus a bhíos litríocht. Tá gean réidh deas intleachtach agam anois do sheacht gcailíní faoi leith. Ní gá dom a rá nach eol do cheann acu an scéal. Is mór an sásamh croí dom an grá céanna. Bíonn sé mar cheol sí nó mar radharc na farraige maidin samhraidh le héirí gréine.'

'Thar ar chualas riamh!' ar Ruairí. 'Ach dar Aonghus is deas an scéal é. Níl a shárú le fáil in ilscéalaíocht na meánaoiseanna féin. Buaitear ar *les troubadours* agus *Die Meistersinger* amuigh is amach. Go n-éirí an t-ádh leat agus leis na Seacht gCailíní! Ach ná bí róshásta, róbhrionglóideach, róleisciúil. Is cóir dúinn go léir Éire agus an t-aos óg a bhrostú. Seasann a lán orainn, na múinteoirí taistil. Ní thuigimid ár ndualgas ná leath ár gcumhachta ach chomh beag –'

'Cén ghaiscíocht eile, cén rud eile beag nó mór is féidir linn a dhéanamh?'

'A lán eile, a Chathail. Níl amhras ar bith orm mar gheall air sin. Is é a bhíos i ngach duine, dar liomsa, anam a thigeas ar an saol le gnó sonrach a dhéanamh, agus nuair a bhíos an gnó sin déanta aige téann sé ar staid eile le gnó eile a dhéanamh. Muna gcríochnaíonn sé an obair, nó muna ndéanann sé i gceart í, is dóigh liom gurb éigean dó teacht ar ais lena críochnú – faoi cholainn eile. Nílim sárdheimhneach fós faoin bhfíorobair atá romham, ach measaim go mbaineann sí leis an múinteoireacht taistil agus le rúndiamhra na sean-Éireann a athbheochan – thuigeas é ó thriallas ar an Mí. Téann an dá rud le chéile. Ord nua speisialta is ea na múinteoirí taistil. Más rúd é go mbeimid eolasach, neamhspleách, dúthrachtach beimid in ann smaointí a scaipeadh agus neart meanman a mhúscailt ar shlí iontach. Agus ansin –'

'Ina dhiaidh sin is uile ní léir dom gur féidir le múinteoirí taistil gaiscíocht a dhéanamh,' dúirt Cathal. 'Is mór an difríocht, faraor, atá idir sinne agus an Fhiann, nó idir sinne agus –'

'Fágaimis siúd mar atá sé. Ní theastaíonn uainn an Fhiann ná laochra eile na seanaimsire. Is geal liom nach mbíonn an Fhiann le feiscint ná le fáil in Éirinn inniu. Is fearr liom i scéalta ná sa saol iad. Ag troid agus ag sealgaireacht is ea a bhídís de ghnáth. Ba bhreá ar shlite ina laethanta féin iad, ach tá spiorad níos doimhne agus níos intleachtaí ionainne. Ar an ábhar sin ní foláir dúinn dul ar aghaidh agus saol breá fial speisialta aidhmeach a chur chun críche. Is mór an dearmad a bheith ag féachaint siar mar a bhímid. Sealbhaíonn sinn a raibh ann anallód – tá an t-iomlán againn nó ionainn ar shlí rúnda – agus is é ár ndualgas dul ar aghaidh agus síorchruthú a dhéanamh.

Is é an fáth go mbímid mí-ámharach dobrónach: gan *La Vie Créatrice* a bheith ionainn de ghnáth.'

'Is fíor fileata an chomhairle chéanna sin, a fhealsaimh mo chroí,' ar Cathal go haerach. 'Ach is mithid dúinn triall. Is mór an rud a bheith ag cur is ag cúiteamh faoin gcinniúint agus faoin gcruinne, ach – beidh céilí na hArd-Chraoibhe ar siúl gan mhoill. Dúirt Liam agus Art agus Críostóir liom go sáródh sí ar an bhféile ab fhearr a bhí acu riamh. Beidh an Dochtúir Ó Dúda agus a lán taoiseach eile ann, agus rud níos aoibhne ná san, beidh ceann de na Seacht gCailíní ann: A Mórgacht, Créide Ní Chonghaile, síbhean, B.E.'

D'éirigh sé go hobann. Phreab Ruairí. D'éirigh sé mar an gcéanna.

Lean Cathal ag caint go haerach, agus chuadar amach. Is beag focal a thuig Ruairí i gceart ar dtús. Tháinig uaigneas agus buairt air. Créide! Cathal! Dá mba rud é go mbeadh grá eatarthu! –

Rug Cathal greim ar a ghualainn.

'Dúisigh, a fhealsaimh!' ar Cathal go croíúil. 'Nílir i bhfásach na Mí anois, ach i Sráid Uí Chonaill. Cén cheist chrua atá ag cur buartha ort! Cad atá ar an gcruinne?'

Rinne Ruairí miongháire. Dúirt sé leis féin gurbh aisteach an rud é dearmad a dhéanamh ar an gcruinne mar gheall ar chailín.

III

Ar rochtain an halla mhóir do Ruairí agus Chathal bhí an céilí ar siúl go bríomhar beo; is é sin, bhí a lán daoine ag caint anseo agus ansiúd, agus gach éinne acu go soilbhir sonasach, de réir dealraimh. Saghas feise ab ea é, agus daoine nár chuir mórán suime i rince – mar Ruairí féin – b'aoibhinn leo a bheith láithreach. Bhí daoine ag déanamh grinn anseo, agus daoine ag cur síos ar phointí gramadaí ansiúd, daoine ag trácht ar litríocht i gcúinne áirithe, agus daoine ag díospóireacht faoi oideachas i gcúinne eile. Ba dhóigh leat ó na cainteoirí nach raibh teora le beatha intleacht na hÉireann, go raibh sí lán de bhrí agus d'fhuinneamh, go raibh sí lách agus neamhspleách san am céanna. Bhí oidí, lucht cléireachais go leor, freastalaithe siopa, ceardaithe, agus a lán eile nach iad, ann. De réir cosúlachta, ní raibh aon difríocht shaolta eatarthu. Níor airigh éinne ach croíúlacht agus duiniúlacht.

Le linn an chéilí sin – mar ba ghnách faoi chruinnithe den saghas céanna – b'fhuras do Ruairí a cheapadh nár briseadh riamh ar réim na nGael ná ar an nGaelachas. Ba dhóigh le duine, a dúirt sé leis féin, go raibh cine breá rúnda sa tír go síoraí, agus go dtéadh baill as an gcine sin chuig na tionólta Gaelacha. Ní deacair a mheas go raibh ceangal idir Teamhair na sean agus Baile Átha Cliath an lae inniu, nó go deimhin, gurbh iad muintir na seanaimsire a bhí i láthair: chomh beo agus a bhíodar riamh.

Sular airigh sé é d'éirigh aoibhneas in aigne Ruairí; bhí a cholainn féin go héadrom. Samhlaíodh dó go raibh ceol agus filíocht á n-éirí go ciúin réidh iontach ina mheanmain; ach ní raibh nótaí leis an gceol agus ní raibh focla leis an bhfilíocht; bhíodar mar bhunábhar ceoil agus bunábhar filíochta. Cá mbíonn fíorthús filíochta? Cén staid rúnda as a n-éiríonnn sí? 'Raibh sé ní ba ghiorra di ansin? D'airigh sé go raibh.

Is amhlaidh atá an scéal, ar seisean leis féin tar éis tamaill. Ní bhímid inár ndúiseacht dáiríribh, ní bhímid inár bhfíorbheatha, de ghnáth. Bíonn ár n-anamanna i gceilt orainn. Téann sinn trí fhásach. Sea, ach tigeann sinn anois agus arís chun feiseanna mar í seo, agus ar shlí éigin iontach is léir dúinn cumhachta doimhne agus taoidí rúnda na cruinne. Is rúndiamhair í, agus ní féidir í a mhíniú. Tá daoine anseo ag caint ar ghraiméar, agus daoine eile ag caint ar an ngrá, daoine eile arís ag trácht ar oideachas, ar náisiúntacht, ar leabhra, ar ealaín, ar an saol faoin tuath, agus mar sin de. Níl éinne acu ag caint ar an mbeatha ná ar an mbrí is iontaí sa gcruinniú agus iontu féin. Ach airíonn gach éinne iad, gríosaíonn siad gach croí, beag nó mór, agus athraíonn siad gach meanma. De réir cosúlachta is beag rud a thiteas amach le linn tionólta den saghas seo: ach ina ionad san is amhlaidh a bhíos eachtraí áille againn: eachtraí meanman – eachtraí spioradálta.'

Labhair sé lena lán daoine. Labhair sé leis an Dochtúir Ó Dúda faoi scéalaíocht tuaithe, le Pádraic Mac Éanna faoi oideachas anallód agus inniu, leis an Dochtúir Mac Shligigh faoi ghraiméar, le Taidhgín Éigse faoi sheanfhilíocht, le Diarmaid Mac an tSuaircis faoi shlacht scríbhinne, le hEoghan Ó Niallagáin faoi chreideamh na gCeilteach, agus le daoine eile faoi cheol agus faoi chomhoibriú. Bhí an seanchas go bríomhar gach uair, ach d'airigh sé go raibh rud ní ba bhríomhaire i ngach duine acu nár chuir sé i gcéill, agus go raibh an scéal céanna aige féin ó thús go deireadh. Bhí 'daoine' ag caint agus spiorada iontu ag faire agus ag éisteacht.

Tháinig Cathal Ó Cinnéide chuige sa deireadh.

'Táim tuirseach le neart rince agus le teann gáire,' ar Cathal. 'Is uafásach an rud é céilí. Baineann sé an chiall agus an chuimhne as duine. Saghas meisce a bhíos i gcéilíocht na haimsire seo. Tá gach duine dá bhfuil anso as a ghnáthmheabhair. Is toghachuid de *l'universelle illusion* céilithe. Bíonn draíocht i gcruinnithe. Bhí an ceart ag Naomh Antoine, Naomh Caoimhghin, agus na haonaráin naofa go léir. Réitíonn saíocht agus uaigneas, naofacht agus fásacha le chéile.'

'Tá a mhalairt de thuairim agam féin anois,' dúirt Ruairí. 'Fuaireas amach anocht go dtigeann filíocht agus diagacht na ndaoine chun cinn le linn na gcruinnithe croíúla. Is léir dom go raibh fáth rúnda le feiseanna na nGréagach agus le feiseanna na nGael fadó. Is léir dom, leis, go mbíonn brí éigin nach dtuigeann ár n-intleacht i bhfeiseanna agus céilithe an lae inniu. Bíonn na Gaeil níos tuisceanaí ná is dóigh leo. I bhfochair a chéile dóibh, ag déanamh grinn, agus ag rince féin, bíd á n-ullmhú féin i gcomhair saol álainn éigin; bíd ar bhóthar rúndiamhrach gan fhios dóibh –'

'Is aoibhinn é a chloisint,' ar Cathal go haerach, 'óir tá an-dúil agam i rince agus i ngreann anocht, agus is breá an rud go bhfuil brí rúnda iontu. Ardoíche is ea í seo. Cheapas nach mbeadh ach duine de na Seacht gCailíní anso, ach tháinig triúr acu – sea, triúr! Anois féin tá duine acu ag fanacht liom, óir tá an rince fada ar tí tosnú.'

D'imigh sé leis go haerach.

Tamaillín ina dhiaidh sin chonaic Ruairí go raibh sé ag rince ar a dhícheall le Créide. Bhí sise ag féachaint go deas, agus rinne sí an rince go beo, ealaíonta. Níor dhearc Ruairí uirthi ná ar an rince ach ar feadh cúpla nóiméad. Tháinig uaigneas agus saghas fiabhrais air. Ghluais sé chun an dorais. Dúirt sé leis féin go n-imeodh sé, ach nuair a shroich sé an doras níor mhaith leis imeacht. D'fhan sé in aice an dorais, agus é go smaointeach, buartha.

Chuala sé beirt fhear ag caint. An Dochtúir Ó Dúda agus an Dochtúir Mac Shligigh iad féin. Bhíodar ag dul abhaile, agus bhíodar ag díospóireacht faoi chruacheist ghramadaí. Bhí an Dochtúir Mac Shligigh á rá de ghuth ard go ndeachaigh gach éinne amú i dtaobh na ceiste ach amháin é féin agus Windisch agus an Laoideach. Bhí an Dochtúir Ó Dúda deimhnithe gur thuig gach seanbhean i gConnacht an ceart. Ghlaoigh sé ar Mhicheál Mag Tuireadh, an garraíodóir groí, a bhí in aice leo. Mhínígh sé an cheist dó. D'éirigh tine i súile Mhichíl. Thosnaigh sé ar óráid, a ghnúis ar lasadh, a ghéaga ag luascadh. Bhailigh daoine ar gach taobh de. Níor chuir cuid díobh suim ar bith sa gceist, ach chuireadar mórán suime i Micheál, agus rinneadar gáir mhór mholta is mhaíte.

Chualathas trácht ar Mhicheál go minic. Bhí a lán dá chuid scéalta i gcuimnhe Ruairí. Tháinig ionadh air mar gheall ar láidreacht agus líofacht a óráide – faoi cheist bheag ghramadaí! Mheas sé nach raibh tír eile faoin ngréin ina mbeadh a leithéid le fáil ó gharraíodóir. D'éirigh a chroí. Ba bhreá an tír Éire gan aon agó!

Bhí deireadh leis an gcéilí. Bhí daoine ag teacht amach ón halla, iad ag caint agus ag gáire; ba dhóigh leat orthu go raibh céad céilí ar siúl san am céanna.

'Bhí eagla orm go rabhais imithe,' ar Cathal Ó Cinnéide le Ruairí, ag teacht i ngar dó go hobann. 'Tá beirt spéirbhan anso agus ba mhian leo a bheith ag caint leat. Chualadar go bhfuil fuath agat do mhná, agus dá bhrí sin beidh tóir ar do mhullach. Focal i do chluas,' ar seisean os íseal, 'tá an bheirt acu ar na Seacht gCailíní.'

Créide agus cara di, Eilís Ní Anracháin, a bhí ann.

'Bhíos ag caint le Mac Uí Dhuibhir um thráthnóna,' ar Créide go croíúil. 'Cheapas gur Ghael nádúrtha é, ach níor chuir sé suim ar bith ionam le linn an chéilí.'

'Ó mo náire thú,' ar Cathal le Ruairí. 'Beidh droch-cháil ar na múinteoirí taistil go léir mar gheall ort. Scríobhfad chuig an gCoiste Gnó dod ghearán. Ach níl am agam le haighneas a chur ort anois: caithfimid dul chun Colún Nelson. Is dúr dearóil é an gnáthshaol, agus ní fhanfadh an riancharr deireanach le spéirmhná gleoite féin.'

Chuaigh Cathal agus Eilís ar aghaidh. Shiúil Ruairí agus Créide ina ndiaidh.

Bhí ardaoibhneas ar Ruairí. Ach theip air focal a rá ar dtús. Ansin d'fhiafraigh sé de Chréide ar thaitnigh an céilí léi.

'Thaitnigh sé go mór liom ar shlite,' ar sise. 'Ach céilí faoi leith ab ea é, dar liom. Ní bhíonn sonas orm de ghnáth le linn cruinnithe. Go deimhin bíonn uaigneas orm. Ach fuaireas amach anocht nó samhlaíodh dom, pé scéal é, go mbíonn brí mhór rúnda le tionólta na nGael.'

'Is iontach é sin,' ar seisean. 'Cheapas féin gur mar sin a bhíos an scéal. Bhí an smaoineamh céanna im aigne ar feadh na hoíche.'

'Ach más fíor é,' ar sise, 'ní hionadh go mbeadh sé in aigne beirte. Is é an t-ionadh nach dtuigeann a lán é.'

Mar sin féin shíl Ruairí gurbh iontach an rud é an smaoineamh céanna a bheith ag an mbeirt acu ar feadh na hoíche.

'Anois agus arís le linn an chéilí bhí ardáthas agus saghas scanraidh measctha le céile im aigne,' ar Créide. 'Shíleas go rabhas im chónaí in Éirinn go minic ins na haoiseanna atá caite. Chreideas go rabhas in Eamhain Mhacha, agus ina dhiaidh sin i dTeamhair, agus in iomad áit eile. Ansin a shíleas nach raibh ach aon aois amháin ann – aon mhóraois dhiamhartha amháin – ó thosach an domhain; gur sinne, daoine an lae inniu, na daoine céanna a mhair in aimsir Chú Chulainn, in aimsir na Féinne, agus mar sin de. Shíleas nach mbíonn i ngach gnáthshaol, nó i ngach gnáthaois, ach taoide den fharraige chéanna, mar a déarfá. Conas mar a mhíníonn tú é sin?'

'Téann sé go daingean orm é a mhíniú,' ar seisean. 'Is furas a cheapadh nach bhfuil an rud ar a nglaoitear "am" dáiríribh, nach bhfuil sé ach comórtasach, *relatif*. B'fhéidir go mbímid sa tsíoraíocht i gcónaí gan fhios dúinn féin – nó dár ngnáthintleacht – agus nach mbíonn ins an "am" agus sa ngnáthmheanma agus sa ngnáthshaol ach crapadh agus ceapadh.'

'Is ea,' ar sise. 'Cuireann sin i gcuimhne dom – óch, táimid lámh leis an gColún anois. Is breá liom a cheapadh go bhfuil an Colún gránna céanna – agus Baile Átha Cliath féin – go haimseartha, neamhbhuan: nach bhfuil baint acu leis "an domhan síoraí".'

Stadadar.

'Caithfidh mé slán a fhágáil agat anois,' ar Créide. 'Ba mhaith liom fanúint leis an mhórcheist úd a réiteach. Ach tá an riancharr deireanach ar tí imeacht, agus níl an tiománaí ag cur suime sa gcruinne; tá an fear bocht ag smaoineamh ar an mbóthar go Deilginis. Ó, sea, cuimhním anois: bhíomar ag caint i dtaobh bóthair eile – an bóthar go Tír na nÓg – um thráthnóna.' Labhair sí go réidh, sámh, aerach. 'Cén uair a thaispeánfaidh tú an bóthar iontach céanna dom?'

Shín sí uaithi amach a lámh dheas. Thóg Ruairí ina lámh dheas féin í.

'Is í an tsíbhean, an Niamh Chinn Óir a thaispeánas an bóthar i gcónaí,' ar seisean. 'Is aici agus a leithéid a bhíos an togha-eolas. Ní taise duitse. Táir i gceartlár Thír na nÓg cheana féin.'

'Briseann an plámás trí theagasc fealsúin. Mo náire thú!' ar sise.

'Beidh a lán de Ghaeil na cathrach ag dul ar thuras chun

an tsléibhe tráthnóna arna mhárach,' ar seisean. 'Ar shlí beidh an bóthar an-chosúil le bóthar go Tír na nÓg.'

'Más ea, rachad ann,' ar sise, 'agus –'

'Casfaimid ar a chéile,' ar seisean go haoibhneach.

Bhuail an tiománaí ar chlog. Scaradar óna chéile, iad ag gáire.

I gceann cúpla nóiméad eile, bhí Créide agus a cara sa riancharr, agus é ag gluaiseacht ar aghaidh.

'Ardoíche ab ea an oíche seo,' ar Cathal le Ruairí, agus iad ag siúl chun a dtí ósta. Mar sin féin ní raibh Eilís sásta léi. Bhí an-díospóireacht eadrainn. Chuir sí milleán ar na múinteoirí taistil agus ar na Gaeil óga go léir. Dúirt sí nach mbímid láidir léidmheach mar a bhíodh na Gaeil i ngach uile aois eile beagnach. Sinn Féiní críochnaithe is ea í. Tá athrú mór ag teacht ar na spéirmhná. Bhíos ag cuimhneamh ar Eoghan Rua Ó Súilleabháin agus ar fhilí móra eile le linn na díospóireachta. Dá mbeidís ina mbeatha anois bheadh a mhalairt de bhrionglóidí agus d'aislingí acu. Bheadh scéala nua ag na "símhná".'

Réitigh Ruairí leis sin agus thosnaigh sé ag caint go mear meanmnach ar Eoghan Rua agus a leithéid agus a gcuid aislingí. Bhí ionadh ar Chathal faoina raibh le rá aige ina dtaobh. Labhair sé mar sin de bhrí nach mbeadh air trácht i dtaobh Chréide. Ach is uirthi a bhí sé ag smaoineamh ó thús deireadh.

'Admhaím go n-éirím místhásta mar gheall ar na "haislingí" agus na "símhná",' ar Cathal. 'Ní bhaineann siad leis an domhan ná an duineatacht. Bíonn an iomarca ceangaltais idir na Gaeil agus an ghealach. B'fhearr liom rann amháin ó fhíorfhilí an ghrá, mar Chatullus, nó Burns, nó na daoine a chum amhráin ghrá Chonnacht, ná na haislingí go léir. "Mairimidne dáiríribh, mo Lesbia, mairimid agus gráimid go beo. Déanamid gáire dhóite faoi ilseanmóirí na seandaoine gruama ... tabhair dom míle póg" ... agus mar sin de. Bhí Catullus mar Ghael ar shlite.'

'Níor thuig sé síúlacht agus spioradáltacht an ghrá,' ar Ruairí.

D'éirigh Cathal beagán smaointeach.

'Dúras leat go bhfuil beirt fhear ionam,' ar seisean faoi dheireadh. Fear liteartha agus fear claímh. Tar éis na cainte le hEilís tá fear an chlaímh in uachtar. Ní féidir le fear óg a shaol a riaradh ina shlí féin. Nuair a cheapann sé go bhfuil gach rud socraithe aige tigeann cailín agus athraíonn sí an t-iomlán in ainneoin a dhíchill. Is tíorántach an obair í, ach bíonn aoibhneas ag baint léi.'

Rinne Ruairí gealgháire, ach má rinne féin bhí a fhios aige go maith go raibh an ceart ag Cathal.

IV

An tráth a bhí Créide ar an gcéilí bhí a hathair, Fiontán Ó Conghaile, ina shuí ina leabharlann bheag ina dtigín lámh le Deilginis faoi Chill Iníon Léinín. Bhí sé ann ó mhaidin. De bhrí gurbh é an Satharn a bhí ann níorbh éigean dó bacadh le hoifig an pháipéir, agus chaith sé an lá díreach mar a chaitheadh sé gach Satharn le fiche bliain – agus gach aon uair eile a bhíodh saor aige – ag léamh agus ag scrúdú leabhar agus ag scríobh síos a smaointí nuair ba thoil leis é. Bhain na leabhra le rúndiamhracht an tseansaoil, le draíocht na gCeilteach, le físíocht agus le saoithiúlacht. Ar shlí bhíodh dhá shaol aige ins na blianta sin: saol fo-eagarthóra san oifig – ba shaol míthairbheach é cé go raibh sé croíúil go leor dar leis – agus saol i measc na leabhar diamhartha. Ní chuireadh sé suim ar bith in aon ealaín a bhain le rudaí corpartha nithiúla, ná i bpolaitíocht, ná i ngnáthlitríocht fhreacnairceach. Ba ghnaoi leis mórscéalta na sean-Éireann – nó a mbrí rúnda ba cheart dom a rá – ach maidir le hÉirinn an lae inniu níorbh fhiú trácht uirthi dar leis: bhí a beatha ag feo le fada agus theipfeadh sé glan ar dhraoi nó saoi í a ghríosú. Ar theacht abhaile ón oifig dó gach oíche – nó go moch sa mhaidin –

théadh sé chun na leabharlainne agus d'fhanadh sé ann ar feadh i bhfad in ionad a bheith ina leaba. Aistí a scríobhadh sé faoi ainm cleite bhídís le fáil ó am go ham in irisleabhra fealsúnacha nach raibh mórán eolais orthu in Éirinn; ach ní raibh an chuid ba mhó dá scríbhinní i gcló fós. Agus níorbh eol d'éinne ach é féin agus corrdhuine thar lear go raibh a leithéid ann ar aon chuma. Bhí barúla faoi leith aige i dtaobh an tsaoil agus litríochta agus léinn; d'éiríodar ní ba láidre ó bhliain go bliain. Bheadh ionadh agus scanradh ar a lán daoine mar gheall orthu, dar leis. Iad siúd a bhí scríofa aige sa nGaeilge bhí sé cinnte glan nach gcuirfeadh éinne amach iad; agus dá gcuirfí amach iad ba bheag duine a bheadh ullamh rompu. Rud eile: ní raibh dúil aige i gclú ná i gcáil. B'aoibhinn leis smaointeoireacht agus scríbhneoireacht agus ciúnas.

Ní raibh a shaol gan bhuairt, agus buairt an-mhór leis. Nuair bhí sé ina fhear óg, d'éis teacht go Baile Átha Cliath dó, phós sé bean óg as a cheantar féin. Tar éis tamaill ba léir dó go ndearna sé dearmad mór. Níor réitigh an lánúin le chéile, agus bhí Fiontán go míshuaimhneach cráite ar feadh i bhfad. Thit sé amach ansin gur thug sé grá – cé gur grá glan, fileata é – do chailín gleoite, intleachtach, dea-chroíoch, agus gur thug an cailín – Eibhlín Ní Dhónaill ab ainm di – grá den saghas céanna dósan. Ach tháinig scanradh ar Eibhlín faoi dheireadh. Chuir sí litir bhrónach chuige agus d'imigh sí go Londain agus tar éis tamaill go dtí Aimerice. Fear uaigneach, aonarach ab ea Fiontán ina diaidh. Chum sé filíocht dhoimhin, dhiamhartha ina taobh; cuireadh cuid di amach ina leabhar – faoi ainm cleite - agus bhí an-trácht ar an leabhar ar feadh scathaimh, ach trácht ná tuairisc ar Eibhlín féin ní bhfuair sé. Tamaillín tar éis teitheadh di d'éag a bhean, agus Créide ina naíonán. Ina dhiaidh sin bhí a shaol ní b'uaigní ná riamh. Cheap a chairde gurbh é bás a mhná a chuir an t-uaigneas agus an dólás thar meán air. Is annamh a chonaic éinne acu é taobh amuigh dá oifig, agus rinne a bhformhór dearmad air, nach mór, le himeacht aimsire. Rinne corrdhuine, mar an Dochtúir Ó Dúda, an-iarracht chun é a bhrostú, ach theip orthu dubh is dubh i gcónaí.

Bhí sé cliste ar an bhfo-eagarthóireacht, cé nach raibh a chroí san obair, ní nárbh ionadh. Bhíodh sé ciúin, croíúil san oifig, agus bhí meas ag a chomhoibrithe air. Níorbh eol d'éinne acu go raibh smaointeoir ná údar ann, ná go raibh iontaoibh aige in aon rud seachas fo-eagarthóireacht. Nuair a thráchtaí ar údair agus fealsúin na haimsire seo ní chuimhnítí ar Fhiontán ar chor ar bith.

Bhíodh áthas air de bhrí go raibh Créide chomh gleoite síúil meanmnach agus a bhí sí ó aimsir a hóige. Mheasadh sé go raibh sí cosúil le hEibhlín Ní Dhónaill ar shlite. Shocraigh sé go mbeadh togha oideachais le fáil aici, agus bhí. Ach níorbh eol d'éinne go mbíodh a chroí ag cur thar maoil le gean is grá dá iníon.

Fear caol, meánard, lách, smaointeach a bhí ann. Bhí a shúile go soilseach cé go mbíodh rian an uaignis orthu de ghnáth. Bhí a ghruaig agus a fhéasóg ag éirí liath, cé nach raibh sé ach timpeall le ceithre bliana is daichead d'aois um an am seo.

Le himeacht aimsire d'éirigh Eibhlín Ní Dhónaill ina mheanma mar a bheadh Deirdre nó Eimhear. Samhlaíodh dó go mbíodh sí ní ba ghiorra dó ná a bhíodh sí roimh imeacht as Éirinn di. Bhíodh ardaoibhneas air ach a bheith ag smaoineamh uirthi. Ach anois agus arís d'éiríodh sé mífhoighdeach leis an saol agus leis an bhfo-eagarthóireacht agus leis an bhfealsúnacht féin; ansin ba mhian leis éirí as an obair ar fad agus triall i gcéin ar lorg Eibhlín. Dúirt sé leis féin go minic go ndéanfadh sé amhlaidh chomh luath agus a bheadh Créide oilte aige. Bhí Eibhlín óg fós – bhí sí deich mbliana ní b'óige ná é féin – agus bheadh saol sona acu fós. Uaireannta eile shamhlaítí dó nach raibh brí ná buanas in aon ní ach smaoineamh agus spiorad agus gur mhór an dearmad é duine a bheith ag brath ar rud ar bith a bhaineas leis an saol coiteann. Ná bíodh ceist oraibh mar gheall arna mhárach,' mar gheall ar nithe coiteanna: is é sin, éirígí agus bígí in éineacht le hardbheatha rúnda na cruinne …

D'airigh sé Créide ag teacht isteach tar éis an mheánoíche. Bhain sí a hata agus a clóca di. Chuaigh sí chun na cistineach. Chuir sí citeal ar an tine. Rinne sí crónán deas aerach di féin.

I gceann tamaillín tháinig sí chun na leabharlainne, agus thug cupán caife dá hathair. '"Caife chun suain agus tae chun faireacháin",' ar sise.

Rinne sé miongháire. 'Is aisteach an rud é Gaeil a bheith tugtha do sheanfhocla i gcónaí,' ar seisean leis féin. 'Is trua gur furas iad a shásamh.'

'Bhíos ag caint leis an Dochtúir Ó Dúda anocht,' ar sise agus a hathair ag ól an chaife. 'Tá brón an domhain air faoi nach mbíonn tú i measc na nGael, ag déanamh na hoibre móire ab fhuras duit a chur chun críche.'

'Is ait an fear é,' ar Fiontán. 'Ní bhíonn obair gur fiú trácht uirthi á déanamh ag formhór na nGael inniu. Ní bhíd ach ag caint agus ag rince, an Dochtúir féin chomh maith le cách. Sea, ag caitheamh aimsire nó ag clamhsán a bhíos na Gaeil inniu. Tá na laochra agus na saoithe imithe.'

'Ach, a athair, má chreideann tú nach mbíonn na daoine beoga agus fuinniúil go leor nach ceart duit dul chucu lena ngríosú?'

'Bheadh sé fánach agam a leithéid sin de ghnó a chur romham, a Chréide. Na daoine atá le feiscint in Éirinn anois – nó a bhformhór pé scéal é – tá siad cosúil le cranna agus clocha ar shlite. Tá a n-anamanna as feidhm. Bím ag obair ar son na nGael dofheicthe. Ach is fada an scéal é, agus ní furas é a mhíniú. Beidh sé soiléir duit, áfach, lá éigin, a Chréide, a chroí.'

'Tuigim go maith, anois féin, gur féidir linn a bheith ag obair ar son na nGael dofheicthe. Go deimhin bíonn gach uile fíor-Ghael dofheicthe i gcónaí; is é sin le rá, bíonn a n-intleacht, a n-anamanna, agus gach a bhaineas leis an tsíoraíocht dofheicthe ó thús deireadh. Bhíomar ag trácht ar an gceist chéanna anocht, ag teacht abhaile ón gcéilí dúinn, agus mar a dúirt Ruairí –'

Stad sí go hobann, agus las a gnúis. 'Tá an caife ólta agat,' ar sise, agus thóg sí an cupán uaidh. 'Tá sé ródhéanach le díospóireacht dhiamhartha. Táim ag éirí tuirseach, agus is mithid dom dul i gcodladh.'

Rinne sí miongháire. 'Slán leat, a athair' agus amach léi.

D'éirigh Fiontán go smaointeach.

Tá athrú tagtha ar Chréide, ar sé leis féin. Is léir an méid sin gan aon agó. Bean atá inti, dá óige í – agus is cosúil go mbeidh sí ag imeacht uaimse gan rómhoill. Cé hé "Ruairí?" Duine faoi leith go cinnte. An seanscéal! – an seanscéal ar a mbíonn cosúlacht nua gach uair! Agus nuair a imeos Créide le "Ruairí" cad mar gheall ormsa? Beidh an-uaigneas orm ina diaidh ... Ach – bead saor faoi dheireadh! Ní bheidh éinne ag brath orm. Bead in ann slán a fhágáil ag an bhfo-eagarthóireacht agus triall ar lorg Eibhlín!

Tháinig ardáthas air. D'oscail sé an fhuinneog bheag agus d'fhéach sé amach. Thíos os a chomhair bhí an fharraige álainn faoi shoilse na gealaí. Rud draíochtach ab ea í, dar leis, ag dul go díreach go Tír na nÓg. Ar bhord loinge iontaí ar bhóchna na háille ba cheart dósan agus d'Eibhlín a bheith. Bhí rúncheangal síúil sprioradálta idir anam an duine agus anam na farraige. Thuig saoithe agus ardscéalaithe na sean-Ghael an fhírinne rúnda sin. B'fheasach dóibh an ollsacht, an draíocht, an naofacht a bhíos i mBóchna an Iarthair – fíor-Bhóchna an Iarthair, rún-Bhóchna a chíonn an tsúil spioradálta. Ní dhearna na Gaeil riamh gníomhartha ná litríocht gur fiú a chur i gcomórtas leis na scéalta a bhain le bóchna agus oileáin an Iarthair. Bhí draíocht agus diagacht iontu.

Dhún sé an fhuinneog faoi dheireadh. Shuigh síos agus dhearc ar na leabhra a bhí ina ranga thart timpeall air.

'Faoistiní' ab ea a lán acu: Augustine, *La Vita Nuova* le Dante, *Dichtung und Wahrheit* le Goethe, Rousseau, *Apologia pro Vita Sua* le Newman, 7rl. Ní raibh sé sásta leo; bhí sé tuirseach dá bhformhór, cé gur mhór a gclú. Mheas sé go mbíonn scéal anama duine i bhfad ní ba dhoimhne ná mar a chuir na scríbhneoirí sin i gcéill.

I bhfad roimhe sin rinne seisean iarracht ar fhaoistin a scríobh – scéal a bheatha agus a bhróin – ach d'éirigh sé míshásta léi sa deireadh.

Dhearc sé ansin ar leabhra móra a bhí á gcumadh ag a n-údair ar feadh fhormhór a saoil liteartha: *An Aenéis* le Virgil, An *Divina Commedia* le Dante, *Gerusalemme Liberata* le Tasso, *Faust* le Goethe, agus tuilleadh. Cheapadh sé i laethanta eile gur mhór an rud é údar a bheith tugtha d'aon mhórcheist nó d'aon mhóraidhm amháin. Rinne seisean an-iarracht ar *épopée* nua a dhéanamh ar scéal Chú Chulainn, agus ansin ar an bhFiann, agus ina dhiaidh sin ar na draoithe agus Naomh Pádraig. Ach theip air gach uair. D'airigh sé beatha ann féin nach raibh freagrach dóibh san. Faoi dheireadh dhearc sé ar ardleabhra an Domhain Thoir: an *Bhagavad Gita*, an *Dhammapada*, agus a lán eile. B'iad ab fhearr leis. Ach cén fáth go mbeadh Gael mar eisean chomh tugtha do leabhra agus d'fhísíocht an Oirthir? Agus duine a bhí chomh tugtha dá leithéid sin d'fhealsúnacht agus de naofacht cad chuige go dtabharfadh sé an oiread sin taitnimh d'aon bhean faoin ngréin agus a thug seisean d'Eibhlín? Ceisteanna iad ba dheacair dó a réiteach.

Ba mhinic dó ag nochtadh a smaointí ar nós saoithe na nIndiacha agus na hÉigipte. Aon tráchtas amháin a bhí scríofa aige bhí sé cosúil leis an *Bhagavad Gita*; ceann eile bhí sé cosúil le cuid den *Pistis Sophia*; agus mar sin de. Ina dhiaidh sin is uile ní raibh sé sásta; ar shlí ní raibh sé ach ag tosnú fós, dar leis.

Shíl sé nach raibh leath na fírinne ins na gnáthbharúla – ná barúla na bhfealsamh féin – faoin 'duine' agus an 'stát' agus an 'aois.' Gan amhras bhí saghas ceangaltais eatarthu, ach bhí cúrsa áirithe le triall ag gach duine, bhí baint aige le domhan dofheichte chomh maith leis an domhan sofheicthe, agus ba cheart dó a shaol rúnda a chur ar aghaidh go dúthrachtach cibé staid ina mbeadh a 'thír' agus a 'chomharsana' agus lucht comhaimsire. Dá bhrí sin d'oibríodh Fiontán ar chroí a dhíchill ar son nithe agus smaointí nár chuir Éireannaigh suim ar bith iontu; scríobhadh sé leabhra nach raibh súil aige lena gcur amach go brách. Ba é a dhualgas agus a dhúchas é. Bhí sé cinnte gur cheart é agus bhí sé sásta …

D'oscail sé an fhuinneog arís agus d'fhéach sé chun na farraige agus chun na spéire. B'iontach é, a dúirt sé leis féin, chomh fada i gcéin agus a bhí duine in ann a fheiscint leis an tsúil bheag chorpartha. Ach an méid a bhí le feiscint aige sa gcruinne ba bheag é i gcomórtas leis an méid nach raibh le feiscint: réalta gan teorainn gan áireamh. Agus an méid a bhí os comhair a shúl (dar leis) ní fhaca sé ach blúire de. Ní fhaca sé aon réalt ná aon phláinéad – grian nó domhan mór – ach ponc solais. Agus an bheatha agus an saol – cibé iad féin – a bhí i ngach ceann acu, níorbh fheasach dó, beag nó mór, iad. Mar sin, ba bheag den chruinne nithiúil féin a bhí le feiscint aige. Sa tslí chéanna ba bheag den chruinne spioradálta go raibh eolas aige uirthi. Ní raibh sa gcine daonna ach tosnaitheoirí, aos óg ag dul chun scoil na cruinne. Ní raibh i bPlato, i bPlotínus, in Eriugena, i nDante, i Shakespeare, i nGoethe ach foghlaimeoirí a bhí beagán ní ba chliste ná an slua. Bhí an mhórfhoghlaim, an tsaíocht dháiríribh, le teacht fós. Nach mór an dearmad ag Gaeil a bheith ag caoi agus ag clamhsán agus ag ceapadh go raibh na haoiseanna iontacha thart. Bheadh na milliúin acu rompu: sa ndomhan so agus ar stada eile.

Ba léir dó ansin an fáth nach mbíodh sé sásta le haonra dár scríobh sé ó bhliain go bliain.

V

An turas chun an tsléibhe tráthnóna an Domhnaigh d'éirigh sé leis go geal. Tionóladh na céadta Gael ann, idir óg agus sean. Bhí an aimsir go soineanta, agus de réir dealraimh bhí croí an tslua go soineanta leis. D'éiríodh ceol agus amhránaíocht, rince agus seanchas ar thaobh cnoic, an fharraige ghrianmhar go ciúin, sítheach i gcéin, an ghrian ag taitneamh go gluair, agus an spéir mar dhíon de mhórtheampall sollúnta síoraí – b'in é an smaoineamh a bhí in aigne Chréide agus í ag siúl go mall le Ruairí ar iomaire álainn. Bhíodar tar éis óráid a chloisint ón Dochtúir Ó Dúda.

'Labhrann an Dochtúir go díreach mar a labhrann a lán Gael eile,' bhí Ruairí á rá. 'Ceapann seisean, agus ceapann siadsan, nach dtigeann athrú ar an rud ar a nglaoitear "Gaelachas" ó aois go haois. Ba mhaith leo sinne a bheith mar a bhí ár sinsir in aimsir Chormaic Mhic Airt nó in aimsir Phádraig Naofa. Ní féidir é, agus dá mb'fhéidir níor mhaith é.'

'Conas san?' ar Créide.

'Bíonn athrú ag teacht ar gach uile ní sa gcruinne gach uile nóiméad –'

'Deirtear go mbíonn,' ar Créide. 'Tá na healaíontóirí deimhnithe de. Ach is dócha nach dtigeann athrú ach ar chrot agus chumhdach. Sílim go mbíonn brí agus anam go seasmhach pé scéal é. Ach bíodh san mar atá sé, is geal liom bheith i measc na nGael ins na laethanta so. Bíonn an saol go hálainn; agus b'fhéidir gur fearr dúinn a bheith sásta agus aoibhneach mar gheall ar áilleacht an tsaoil ná bheith ar lorg mínithe an tsaoil.'

'Ach cuimhnigh air seo. Níl in áilleacht an tsaoil ach ceapadh agus smaoineamh. Ba dhóigh leat anois go bhfuil an "spéir" go han-álainn. Ach tá a fhios againn go maith nach bhfuil "spéir" ar bith ann. Samhlaítear dúinn go bhfuil, ach –'

'Ó!' ar Créide go haerach, 'cuireann tú an spéir as feidhm! Cuirfidh tú an fharraige agus na sléibhte as feidhm gan mhoill. Cá mbeimid ansin? Cuireann tú Fearghas Ó Ruanaí i gcuimhne dhom. Dúirt sé ag Cumann Réalta an Eolais an oíche faoi dheireadh –'

'Tá aithne agat ar Fhearghas?'

'An-aithne. Dúirt sé go bhfuil an dorchadas níos sine, níos iontaí, agus níos rúndiamhraí ná an solas.'

'Is dócha nach raibh sé ag trácht ar dhorchadas coiteann saolta, ach ar dhorchadas ina chiall phréamhach, ina staid absalóideach,' ar Ruairí. 'Ins na staideanna sin, de réir saoithe áirithe, spiorad glan is ea an "Dorchadas." Ina staid absalóideach, mar an gcéanna, spiorad glan is ea an "Solas." Ní fheiceann an tsúil chorpartha solas ná dorchadas mar a bhíd iontu féin. Ní furas an cheist a mhíniú. Maidir le dorchadas saolta agus solas saolta, cuimhnigh air seo: is minic a bhíos an oíche níos iontaí agus níos spioradálta ná an lá.'

Rinne Créide miongháire.

'Tá an ceart agat san méid sin,' ar sise. 'Is ionadh liom nár airíos féin é.'

Leanadar ag trácht ar Chumann Réalta an Eolais agus ar

Fhearghas Ó Ruanaí, a chuid filíochta agus a shaíocht, ar feadh tamaill.

'Is mór an rud é,' ar Créide, 'a bheith ag trácht ar shárfhear mar Fhearghas, ar phríomhsholas, agus ar staid absalóideach an dorchadais, ach ba mhaith liom ceist a chur ort faoi rud níos saolta. Bhíos ag smaoineamh go minic le déanaí ar obair na múinteoirí taistil. Céard é do mheas uirthi? Tá fáth agam leis an gceist.'

Chuir sé in iúl di a raibh in aigne aige le fada i dtaobh na múinteoirí céanna: an léann agus an fhealsúnacht go mbeidís in ann a chraobhscaoileadh i measc aos óg na tíre, an spionnadh a chuirfidís ar lárchroí na hÉireann, dá mbeadh an bhrí cheart iontu féin. Ord nua ab ea iad, agus b'fhéidir leo aigne na ndaoine d'fhairsingiú, agus anam na ndaoine a chur ar lasadh, dá mb'áil leo é. Bhí ábhar aspal intleachta iontu. Bhí cuid acu ar aon intinn leis, ach ní raibh modh oibre socraithe acu fós.

Ansin dúirt Créide:

'Is é an fáth go raibh eolas ag teastáil uaim ar shaol na múinteoirí taistil: go bhfuilim ag ceapadh nár mhiste dhom cromadh ar an obair chéanna.'

'Tusa! Nílir dáiríribh –'

'Táim, gan amhras. Cén fáth nach mbeinn?'

'Bheadh an obair róchrua ort. Bíonn sé crua go leor ar na fir féin sa ngeimhreadh. Agus ní gá dhuitse a leithéid sin de ghnó a dhéanamh. Táir an-fhoghlamtha, agus –'

'Dar ndóigh tá "leabhareolas" agam, cuid de gan mórán maitheasa,' ar sise. 'Ach ní mheasaim go mbeadh post le fáil agam in Áth Cliath, agus dá mbeadh féin ní bheinn sásta fanacht ann: ní bheadh mo chroí san obair. Is mian liom bheith i measc na ndaoine dea-chroíocha faoin tuath. Teastaíonn Tír na nÓg uaim. Táim chomh haidhmeach le daoine eile.'

Bhí cosúlacht bhuartha ar Ruairí. Bhí sé go mór in aghaidh Créide dul ina múinteoir taistil, ach ba dheacair dó a mhíniú cén fáth. Mheas sé nach mbeadh aon áit ach Tír na nÓg fíoroiriúnach di.

'Deirtear a lán faoi léann,' ar sise. 'Bím aoibhneach agus bím míshásta san am céanna mar gheall air. Is geal liom go bhfuaireas méid maith de féin. Ach a lán daoine óga atá gan é sílim go bhfuil sé tuillte acu níos mó ná agamsa. Tá sé de dhualgas orm, ar shlí éigin, an t-oideachas céanna a riaradh ar na daoine óga breátha bochta nár leag súil ar choláiste riamh; agus conas is féidir liom a leithéid a dhéanamh níos fearr ná trí mhúinteoireacht taistil? Ach tá taobh eile leis an scéal. Táim im Bh. E., ach airím nach bhfuil mo chuid oideachais ach tosnaithe agam. Tá m'aigne ullmhaithe agus curtha in ordú, mar a déarfá, i gcomhair fíorfhoghlama. Agus cá bhfaighinn an fíorléann céanna ach in obair agus saothar i measc na ndaoine?'

'Tá sin go maith,' a dúirt Ruairí. 'Admhaím nach mbíonn in oideachas scoile ach ullmhú. As smaointí agus saothar ina dhiaidh sin faightear fíorfhoghlaim go cinnte. Agus ní foláir dúinn bheith ag obair ar son ár gcomharsan agus ár gcine ar shlí éigin. Gan chómhothú agus chomhoibriú bímid caillte. Ach tá a lán slí ann leis an obair a dhéanamh, seachas múinteoireacht taistil.'

'Ní léir dom slí ar bith eile,' ar Créide.

Tháinig daoine eile ina dtreo ansin: Pádraic Mac Éanna agus buachaillí óga, agus d'éirigh seanchas eatarthu faoi oideachas na n-úrghas Gaelach. Dúirt Pádraic nach mbeadh sé sásta go dtí go bhfeicfí ollscoil Ghaelach ansin ar thaobh an tsléibhe, í chomh gluardha ina slí féin agus a bhí an ghrian san iarthar. B'fhearr leis a tógáil ina hathbheochan na Teamhrach.

Sular fhágadar slán ag a chéile um thráthnóna dúirt Créide le Ruairí go mba ghnaoi dó bheith ina bhall de Chumann Réalta an Eolais, agus aithne a bheith aige ar Fhearghas Ó Ruanaí agus a chomhoibrithe. Ní raibh uaidh ach an focal.

VI

Maidin Chéadaoin tar éis an turais bhí Ruairí ag siúl cois na Bóinne in aice na hUaimhe le héirí gréine. Shíl sé go raibh blianta imithe ó bhí sé ag caint le Créide ar thaobh an tsléibhe lámh le Baile Átha Cliath. Shíl sé san am céanna gurbh amhaidh a bhí sí lena chois ar bhruach na Bóinne.

Ba mhinic a mheas sé le déanaí go raibh rúncheangal idir a mheanma féin agus an Mhí, dá uaigní "an Mhí" dofheicthe. Samhlaíodh dó go minic go raibh spiorad san áit, brí dhiamhartha, nach raibh i sléibhte Átha Cliath ná ina bhaile dúchais féin faoin tuath. Cén fáth a bhí leis sin? Théadh an cheist i ndaingean air i gcónaí.

An mhaidin seo, de réir mar a smaoinigh sé ar Chréide is ea a chuaigh an mothú san i ndoimhneacht. Agus shíl sé leis go raibh ceangal sonrach idir ise agus an Mhí mar an gcéanna.

B'fheasach dó gurbh 'áit naofa' gleann na Bóinne anallód, de réir scéalta áirithe, scéalta a bhí imithe as cuimhne an tslua le cianaibh. Ba bheag Éireannach a chreidfeadh go raibh aon difríocht eatarthu agus finscéalaíocht; nach raibh san Daghda agus Aonghus Óg ach ainmneacha. Ach má bhí na déithe úd fíorga! –

rúnchumhachta ar a raibh eolas ag saoithe agus draoithe: daoine go raibh radharc síceach, nó fís spioradálta féin, acu. Agus má bhíodh na rúnchumhachta san i ngleann na Bóinne anallód bheidís ann inniu chomh maith céanna: bhí an Mhí chomh naofa agus a bhí sí riamh – do dhaoine a bhí freagrach don rún-naofacht. Ach cén ceangal atá idir Créide agus an Mhí! Bhí sé cinnte go raibh an ceangal ann, ach chinn sé air duth is dath é a mhíniú.

Bhí sé ag siúl go mall faoi na cranna idir an chanáil agus an abhainn um an am seo, agus ag féachaint suas dó chonaic sé an tAthair Micheál Ó Gadhra ag teacht ina ghar ó dhroichead na Bóinne. Bhí leabhar beag ina láimh aigesean agus bhí sé á léamh.

Sagairtín lách ciúin dathúil ab ea an tAthair Micheál. Bhí sé ina oide i gColáiste na Fairche. Bhí sé an-fhoghlamtha agus bhí an-dúil i gceol agus i bhfilíocht aige. Is é an leabhar a bhí aige *La Vita Nuova* a chum Dante, agus d'éirigh trácht idir an mbeirt faoi chomh dílis agus a bhí Dante do Bheatrice ó aimsir a óige. Smaoinigh Ruairí ar Chréide ó thús deireadh. Dá mb'fhéidir leis a bheatha rúnda, a shaol spioradálta, a cheangal léi sa tslí chéanna!

'Ach táimid ag dul amú, a Ruairí,' dúirt an sagairtín. 'Táimid ag caint ar Dhante agus na meánaoiseanna agus ag déanamh dearmaid ar ghleann na Bóinne agus ar dhraíocht na maidine. Mar sin a bhíos an scéal i gcónaí ag Gaeil, agus b'fhéidir ag formhór an chine dhaonna. Bímid i gcaisleán draíochta, nó i dTír na nÓg féin, agus ní thig linne ár súile a choimeád ar na hiontais a bhíos inár dtimpeall. Anseo anois ar bhruach na Bóinne is cosúil go bhfuil Spiorad na Maidine ag gáire fúmsa agus fútsa. "Féach!" ar sise, "chomh dall neamhaireach agus atá an bheirt acu! Ní léir dóibh an ríocht neamhaí ina bhfuilid! Tá an tsúil fhileata, an tuiscint dhiamhartha, imithe glan ó Ghaeil".'

Chuimhnigh Ruairí ar a smaointí féin faoi bhrí rúnda na Mí, agus rinne sé iarracht lena mhíniú don Athair Micheál.

Ba é tuairim an Athar Micheál nach raibh an rúndiamhaireacht chéanna (*le mysticisme*) ach i meanma Ruairí féin. B'fhearr leis féin bheith ar lorg 'áilleachta,' a dúirt sé. D'fhreagair Ruairí gurbh ionann 'áilleacht' agus *le mysticisme* – toradh radhairc agus saothair spioradálta. Bhí áilleacht agus áilleacht ann, arsa an sagairtín, agus ba dhual do Ghaeil a bheith dílis d'áilleacht faoi leith, cé go ndearnadh dearmad uirthi le fada faoi chomh crua agus a bhí an saol ar mhuintir na Fódla. Bhíodar ag éirí arís, áfach, agus ag teacht chucu féin, agus nuair a bheadh a gceart acu, agus an tír dá réir, bhí sé cinnte go n-éireodh leo 'Oileán na hÁilleachta' a dhéanamh d'Éirinn. An iomarca daoine ar fud an domhain bhíodar ag éirí mífhoighneach, rócheistiúil, ag síorthrácht ar a bhfuil i gcinniúint don duine, agus ar bhrí na cruinne go léir. Ní mar sin a bheadh an scéal ag Gaeil. Leanfaidís ar fhilíocht shíúil, ar cheol draíochta, ar litríocht na háille. B'iad ab fhearr.

'Tá imní orm i do thaobhsa, a Ruairí,' ar seisean, agus rinne sé miongháire. 'Is file thú, agus bíonn do chroí ag cur thar maoil le "*le romantisme*" agus "*l'idéalisme.*" Ach níl tú sásta leis sin, faraor. Éiríonn tú go ceistiúil buartha i dtaobh na beatha. Is é atá uait: an chruinne a mhíniú. Má leanann tú ar an mbealach sin millfear do mheanma agus an fhéith fhilíochta atá ionat. Táir i gcontúirt dearmad a dhéanamh ar thréithe agus ar dhúchas na gCeilteach, agus an iomarca suime a chur i leabhra agus i bhfísíocht an Domhain Thoir. Ní réitíonn Criosna agus na Ceiltigh le chéile.'

'Táir ag dul amú go mór, a Athair Micheál. Dúirt Criosna féin: "Is mé an Áilleacht féin i measc nithe áille." Ní admhaím go bhfuil neamhchosúlacht idir físíocht an Domhain Thoir agus fíorfhealsúnacht an Domhain Thiar. Ach ní ó leabhra an Oirthir ná leabhra an Iarthair a fuaireas mo chuid smaointí.'

'Ach, a Ruairí, bír ag léamh agus ag scrúdú leabhar i

gcónaí beagnach,' arsa an tAthair Micheál.

'Dar ndóigh, ní bhíonn. Gan amhras bhí dúil i leabhair agus i léann agam ó thosach, ach ní bhfuaireas iad ach ar shlí shuaraigh in aimsir m'óige. Bhí mo mhuintir an-bhocht. Cuireadh amach iad as feirmeacha compordacha dhá uair, agus i ndeireadh na dála b'éigean dóibh bheith sásta le paiste talún a bhí cosúil le riasc. Ansiúd a oileadh agus cothaíodh mé. Ní raibh aon teanga mháthartha agam! – Ach saghas Gaeilge agus saghas Sacs-Bhéarla measctha le chéile. Ba shuarach an méid oideachais a fuair mé sa scoil "náisiúnta," ach d'éirigh liom bheith im fhomhúinteoir, agus bhí an scéal ní b'fhearr agam ar feadh tamaill, an dúil i léann ag dul i méid i gcónaí, cé nach mbíodh leath mo dhóthain de leabhra le fáil agam. D'éiríos as an múinteoireacht agus chuas chuig an gcathair mar chléireach. Luíos isteach go dúthrachtach ar leabhra agus ar léann ins na hoícheanta. Ar shlí bhí an Ghaeilge, an Sacs-Bhéarla, an Laidin, an Fhraincis, agus an Ghearmáinis foghlamtha agam sa deireadh, agus thosnaíos ar an nGréigis –'

'Ba mhór an méid sin,' arsa an tAthair Micheál. 'Cuireann tú ionadh orm.'

'Léas a lán litríochta i ngach teanga díobh, ach fágaim le huacht nár chuireas suim faoi leith i bhfealsúnacht. Ansin tháinig Conradh na Gaeilge agus d'éiríos im dhúiseacht, mar a déarfá. Ach tar éis teacht don Mhí dhom mar mhúinteoir taistil, d'airíos "duine" eile ionam nach raibh aithne agam air riamh roimhe sin. Samhlaíodh dom gurbh áit naofa é gleann na Bóinne. Samhlaíodh dom go raibh Rúnchumhachta Móra (ghlaoití an Daghda, Aonghus Óg, ⁊l. orthu anallód) ní ba ghiorra dhom ná na daoine sofheicthe. Samhlaítear dom anois é.'

'Cuireann an méid sin crot nua ar an scéal,' arsa an tAthair Micheál. 'Téann sé i ndaingean orm é a mhíniú. Is iontach an rud í an mheanma. Ar shlí eile tá spiorad nua ag corraí i measc na sagart óg anseo agus ansiúd. Ceapann siadsan go bhfuil an Eaglais in Éirinn rófhoirmiúil agus róshaolta, agus go mba cheart do na heaspaig agus do na sagairt a bheith náireach faoin staid ina bhfuil a lán daoine. Is é ár gcara an tAthair Dónall Ó Dálaigh an duine is láidre díobh san. Tá trioblóid á tuar agus is trua liom é. B'fhuras don Eaglais agus d'Éirinn an-áilleacht agus ard-Ghaelachas a bheith acu san am atá romhainn. Ina ionad san is amhlaidh atáimid i gcontúirt troda agus buartha.'

'Is fearr troid agus trioblóid ar son na fírinne ná lagbhrí agus neamhaireachas,' ar Ruairí.

Chroith an tAthair Micheál a cheann agus bhí cosúlacht imní agus bróin air. Dúirt sé ansin gur mhithid dó dul abhaile. Bheadh an chéadphroinn ullamh, agus i ndiaidh na céadphroinne bheadh obair an lae roimhe.

'Is ea,' ar seisean agus iad ag dul ar ais go droichead na Bóinne, 'tá beomheanma agus éirí intleachta ár ndóthain againn in Éirinn inniu, agus ní fheadar cad a thiocfas astu. Le linn na maidine áille bíonn dóchas agus aoibhneas agam, ach ar feadh an lae agus i rith na hoíche is minic a bhíonn amhras agus eagla orm.'

'Múscail do mhisneach,' ar Ruairí. 'Tá ríocht Neimhe ionainn, agus buann an t-anam i gcónaí.'

Ansin d'fhágadar slán ag a chéile.

Chuaigh Ruairí go dtí an tigín ina raibh sé ag cur faoi. Bhí litir ann ó Chréide roimhe.

Dúirt sí go raibh sí ag caint ina thaobh le Fearghas Ó Ruanaí an oíche roimhe sin. B'aoibhinn le Fearghas é a bheith ina bhall de Chumann Réalta an Eolais. Ba mhaith le Fearghas fós dá dtiocfadh Ruairí chun a thí féin oíche Dhomhnaigh ina dhiaidh sin – thigeadh filí agus fealsúna ar cuairt ann gach Domhnach i rith na bliana.

'Tar, más féidir é,' ar Créide. 'Is iontach an duine é Fearghas; cuireann sé an oiread suime i bprátaí agus i bhfísíocht, i gcuraíocht agus sa gcosmos, i mbeacha agus i mBrahma. Airím agus mé ag éisteacht leis gurb uasal an cine daonna agus gur fial fairsing spioradálta an tír í Éire. Airím go mbím in aice le Tír na nÓg.'

Bhí aoibhneas ar Ruairí. Níor bhaol nach rachadh sé go tigh Fhearghais. A bheith ag éisteacht le Fearghas agus in aice le Créide san am céanna –!

Ansin chrom Ruairí ar nótaí a scríobh i gcomhair an *Herald*, ceann de pháipéiri na Mí. Ba ghnách leis a leithéid a scríobh gach seachtain, agus bhíodh an-trácht orthu, ní amháin ar fud an chúige ach i mBaile Átha Cliath féin. Chuidíodh sé leis an eagarthóir – seanfhear lách leisciúil – ar an iomad slí nuair a bhíodh am aige. (Scríobh sé sraith aistí faoi leith ar stair agus seanchas na Mí.) Bhíodh ionadh ar an eagarthóir faoi go mbíodh sé fíorchúramach fá snas agus ordú na bhfocal, i Sacs-Bhéarla chomh maith agus i nGaeilge. 'Fad' an-mhór ab ea é sin, dar leis.

VII

Oíche Dhomhnaigh, agus é ag dul go tigh Fhearghais Uí Ruanaí, chuimhnigh Ruairí ar an gcéad uair a léigh sé filíocht Fhearghais. Bhí sé tar éis teacht don chathair mhór an uair sin. Bhí sé uaigneach go leor, agus fonn air a bheith ar ais arís ina bhaile dúchais dá iargúltacht é. Níor thuig sé an fhilíocht ar chor bith an t-am sin. D'admhaigh sé go raibh sí go ceolmhar, ach chuaigh sé thar a dhícheall na smaointí a thuiscint. Anseo agus ansiúd sa leabhar beag bhí trácht ar nithe Gaelacha, nithe a bhain leis an tseanaimsir, ach ní raibh aon chosúlacht, dar leis, idir an trácht sin agus trácht na seanchaithe faoin tuath. Dá mba rud é go raibh ciall ann chinn sé air í a fháil.

D'imigh sin agus tháinig seo. Anois – b'aoibhinn lena chroí an fhilíocht chéanna.

Ba léir as sin go raibh an-athrú tagtha ar a mheanma ó d'fhág sé slán ag a bhaile dúchais, ach níor airigh sé mórán athruithe ó lá go lá agus ó bhliain go bliain. Ba mhór an difríocht, áfach, a bhí idir é féin agus an Ruairí óg ar a raibh ionadh faoi fhilíocht Fhearghais. An Ruairí úd bhí sé tugtha d'fhilíocht Eoghain Rua Uí Shúilleabháin, d'amhráin Roibeaird Burns, do scéalta Chathail Cicham, do sheanchas na ndaoine. Um an am seo ní raibh teora lena dhúil i litríocht dhiamhartha, agus cheap cairde Gaelacha, mar an tAthair Micheál agus an Dochtúir Ó Dúda, go raibh sé ag dul ar fán.

Ach, dúirt sé leis féin agus é ar an mbóthar ag dul go tigh Fheargħais – an raibh mórán bundifríochtaí idir filíocht Eoghain Rua agus fealsúnacht Fhichte, idir scéalta Chathail Cicham agus barúla Bhergson? Bhaineadar go léir le saothar agus le cinniúint an chine dhaonna. Úlla den chrann céanna ab ea iad. Bhí an crann ní b'iontaí ná mar a thaispeáin éinne díobh. Bheadh sí ag fás, agus faoi bhláth as an nua, i ngach aois. Bheadh tuilleadh úll sármhilis le fáil air go brách.

Mar sin féin tháinig amhras ar Ruairí. De réir mar a chuimhnigh sé ar a shaol faoin tuath in aimsir a óige is ea a d'éirigh an t-amhras agus an t-uaigneas leis. 'Raibh sé dílis don dúchas? Arbh fhiú é a bheith ceistiúil i dtaobh na cruinne? Nárbh fhearr dó bheith sásta le cluichí agus scéalta a chumadh faoi ghreann agus faoi ghrámhaireacht a bhaile agus a mhuintire féin? Mac na tuaithe ab ea é. Nárbh fhearr dó bheith ag obair faoin tuath i gcónaí gan bacadh le saol na cathrach ar aon chuma?

D'éirigh seanchuimhní; thángadar mar thaoide na farraige. Stad sé ar an mbóthar san oíche uaigneach. Shíl sé go raibh sé i bhfad ó Bhaile Átha Cliath, i bhfad ó na sléibhte, i bhfad ón bhfarraige; go raibh sé ar ais ar an bpaiste talún ar ar oileadh agus ar cothaíodh é. Chonaic sé seanchomharsana cois na tine ar cuartaíocht. Chuala sé ceol agus amhráin agus seanchas. Samhlaíodh dó go raibh sé i mbaile aoibhinn ina mbeadh ceol agus amhránaíocht agus seanchas ar siúl go brách.

Ógánach ab ea é arís, dar leis.

Nárbh aoibhinn an rud é, a dúirt sé leis féin, éirí as an múinteoireacht taistil, imeacht leis abhaile don phaiste talún, agus saol simplí nádúrtha a bheith aige! ...

Ansin chuimhnigh sé ar Chréide. Phreab sé, agus

chuaigh sé ar aghaidh i gcomhair tigh Fhearghais. Ach shíl sé go raibh an paiste talún os comhair a shúl, chomh maith le Créide, le gach céim den bhóthar dár chuir sé de as san amach.

D'fhéach sé chun na spéire, é ag smaoineamh ar na réalta gan áireamh gan teorainn. Chuireadar áthas agus saghas scanraidh air san am céanna.

Is iltaibhse í an chruinne, ar seisean leis féin. Agus is é an t-ionadh amuigh is amach nach mbíonn eagla orainn roimh an iltaibhse céanna. Téimid ar aghaidh agus bród nó buairt orainn faoi phaiste talún, nó faoi litríocht, nó faoi bhean, nó faoi 'náisiún', agus gan pioc suime a chur i dtaibhse ná taibhsí! Sáraíonn sé ar an scéal is iontaí. Buann sé ar na 'heachtraí' go léir!

VIII

Ar shroichint tigh Fhearghais do Ruairí bhí a lán daoine ann roimhe, ins an dá sheomra (a bhí mar aon seomra amháin) ar an 'urlár' ab ísle. Bhí cuid acu ina suí, cuid eile ag scrúdú pictiúr a bhí ar crochadh ar na ballaí, cuid eile fós ina seasamh anseo agus ansiúd, ina mbeirt nó ina dtriúr, iad ag caint agus ag caitheamh tobac ar a sástacht. Bhí corrbhean féin agus gailín ina béal aici. D'airigh Ruairí ar ball go raibh 'spiorad' faoi leith ann. Níorbh fhéidir a thuilleadh grinn agus croíúlachta a bheith i gcéilí faoin tuath, cé go mbeadh ionadh ar na 'daoine' faoina lán den seanchas.

Bhí Fearghas ina sheasamh in aice an dorais ar theacht isteach do Ruairí. Bhí Créide i ngar dó. D'éirigh sí agus chuir sí Fearghas agus Ruairí in aithne dá chéile. Ansin d'iompaigh sí agus lean sí ag éisteacht le bean lách sholas-súileach a bhí ag cur síos ar thaibhreamh diamhartha (dar léi féin) a tharla di cúpla oíche roimhe sin.

Chuir Fearghas togha fáilte roimh Ruairí, agus d'airigh Ruairí an chéad nóiméad gurbh an-chara é. Duine ní ba lái níor casadh air riamh roimhe sin. Bhí sé cosúil le gruagach, ach bhí sé cineálta, greannmhar, súilaibí agus aerach, agus bhí a ghuth go ceolmhar: ba dhóigh leat gach nóiméad go raibh filíocht á rá aige.

'Is aoibhinn liom aithne a chur ort, a Mhic Uí Dhuibhir,' ar seisean. 'Táir i do mhúinteoir taistil, agus bír i do chónaí i ngleann na Bóinne. Is sonasach an staid í. Ní bhíonn saothar níos tábhachtaí ná múineadh na Gaeilge á dhéanamh ar fud na Fódla. Sáraíonn sé ar an gcomhoibriú féin. Ní thuigimid chomh tábhachtach agus atá sé ach tuigfear in aois eile é – i gceann míle bliain, b'fhéidir.'

Bhí fear liteartha darbh ainm Eagleton in aice le Fearghas. Dúirt seisean nach léir dó an gá a bhí leis an nGaeilge ar chor ar bith.

'Anois agus arís,' ar Fearghas, 'bíonn ár n-anamanna níos freagraí d'fhilíocht Whitman nó do smaointí Emerson ná do rud ar bith atá scríofa sa nGaeilge. Ach ní hionann sin agus a rá go mbíonn Whitman agus Emerson – nó filí agus saoithe an domhain mhóir go léir – níos tábhachtaí dúinn ná an Ghaeilge féin. Tá gá an-mhór againn léi; gá diamhartha agus gá saolta.'

Chuir an méid sin ionadh ar Eagleton.

'Is spiorad gach éinne againn, agus dar ndóigh ní bhíonn teanga ag teastáil ó spiorad inti féin,' ar Fearghas. 'Ach nuair a thigeann spiorad ar ais chun an domhain chorpartha bíonn a mhalairt de scéal aige. Tógann sé gléas síceach agus gléas corpartha – is é sin "colainn" – air féin, i dtreo is go mbeidh sé in ann a chuid úroibre ar an saol seo a dhéanamh. Bíonn a bheatha nua mar chaibidil i scéal fada, agus bíonn ceangal idir an chaibidil nua agus na caibidlí roimhe sin – gach "beatha" a chaith an spiorad ar an saol so anallód, agus ar stada eile. Dá mbíodh an Ghaeilge mar ghnáth-theanga ag an "nduine" – nó "duine" i ndiaidh "duine" – inar colnaíodh an spiorad anallód, nach ceart an Ghaeilge a bheith ag an "nduine" nua ina gconaíonn sé arís?'

Bhí Eagleton ina bhall de Chumann Réalta an Eolais, agus bhí sé an-doimhin ar na ceisteanna a bhíodh á bplé ann. Ba ghnách leis aontú ar dtús le gach barúil nach mór dár chuala sé; ina dhiaidh sin théadh an-amhras air. Anois réitigh sé le Fearghas chomh fada agus a bhí Fearghas ag caint. Ansin dúirt sé, 'Is cosúil go bhfuil an ceart agat – b'fhéidir gurb amhlaidh atá an scéal – ach fan go fóill – tá amhras orm mar gheall air –'

Rinne Fearghas gealgháire.

'Sin mar a bhíos an scéal ag Eagleton i gcónaí,' ar seisean. 'Bheadh sé faoi chlú mór sa tseanaimsir. Siúlann sé le leathbhróg na deimhne agus le leathbhróg an amhrais gach lá dá shaol.'

Ba ghnaoi le Ruairí an díospóireacht agus an greann. Ach b'fhearr leis trácht Fhearghais ar an gceangal a cheap sé a bheith idir anam agus teanga, agus rinne sé tagairt don cheist chéanna.

'Is ea,' ar Fearghas. 'Nuair a bhíodh tusa agus mise agus ár gcairde ag obair in Éirinn na céadta bliain ó shin bhíodh an Ghaeilge á cleachtadh againn, agus ar an ábhar sin tá brí inár nádúr, inár ngléas síceach, atá freagrach don Ghaeilge. Ní féidir lenár nádúr a bheith fíoréifeachtach, ní féidir linn ár n-obair a chur chun críche muna mbíonn an Ghaeilge againn anois. Ach maidir le Eagleton, an uair dheireanach a bhí sé ar an saol, i gcolainn eile, is dócha gur Sasanach nó Francach a bhí ann. Dá bhrí sin níl an Ghaeilge ag teastáil chomh géar uaidh agus atá sí ag teastáil uainne.'

Rinne an triúr acu miongháire.

'Tá sin go maith,' ar Eagleton. 'Réitím leat – ar shlí – ach tá amhras agam – tá. Éist liom anois. Is mór, cumhachtach, síoraí é an spiorad. Is beag, suarach, aimseartha í an cholainn. Is aimseartha í teanga. Nach féidir leis an spiorad a ghnó a dhéanamh trí theanga ar bith? Ní bhíonn sé ag brath ar theanga faoi leith.'

'Ní admhaím gur rud suarach í an cholainn,' d'fhreagair Fearghas. 'Ina ionad san is rud an-iontach í. Agus seachas an cholainn bíonn gléas síceach ag an spiorad: spiorad, anam, agus colainn a bhíos ionainn. Agus mar thoradh na mbeatha go léir a bhí againn san domhan roimhe seo, tá brí áirithe inár ngléasanna intleachta, inár n-anamanna, agus bíonn an bhrí sin freagrach don Ghaeilge ar shlí iontach. Tá sé réasúnta go leor go mbeadh teanga faoi leith ag teastáil i gcomhair oibre an spioraid, chomh réasúnta agus go dtiocfadh an spiorad go pláinéad faoi leith nó go tír faoi leith.'

Bhí Eagleton ar tí rud eile a rá, ach d'iompaigh duine a bhí in aice leis, duine a chuir an-suim i gcomhoibriú, agus chuir sé ceist ar Fhearghas faoi uibheacha, agus ar an éileamh a bhí orthu agus rudaí eile a bhain leo.

'Fán fada chuige!' ar Ruairí os íseal. 'É féin agus a uibheacha! Agus sinne ag trácht ar an anam!'

Ach d'fhreagair Fearghas an cheist go lách. Chuir sé síos go cliste agus go bríomhar ar uibheacha, agus ar ar bhain leo in Éirinn an lae inniu. Ba dhóigh leat gur mheas sé iad a bheith chomh huasal agus chomh hiontach le pláinéid. I gceann tamaill bhí mo dhuine lánsásta leis an méid eolais a fuair sé, agus d'iompaigh Fearghas chuig Ruairí – bhí Eagleton ag caint le daoine eile um an am sin.

'Bí i do shuí,' ar Fearghas. 'Ba mhian liom a chloisint conas mar a éiríonn an saol leat cois na Bóinne.'

Shuíodar síos.

'Is beag Éireannach a thuigeas brí agus draíocht na Bóinne inniu,' ar Fearghas.

'Is fada an scéal é agus ní furas é a mhíniú,' d'fhreagair Ruairí. 'I gcois na Bóinne dom istoíche buailtear isteach im aigne gurb áit naofa é an gleann go léir.'

Ansin d'inis sé an scéal d'Fhearghas díreach mar a d'inis sé don Athair Micheál é. Las súile Fhearghais. Ba léir gur thaitnigh an insint go mór leis.

'Is deimhneach go bhfuil an ceart agat,' ar seisean. 'Is áit an-naofa, dhiamhartha é an gleann céanna. Is naofa gach uile áit inti féin, ach baineann rúndiamhra faoi leith le háiteacha áirithe, díreach mar a bhaineann draíocht agus síúlacht faoi leith le háiteacha áirithe eile. Tá beatha rúnda sa bpláinéad seo againne: is spiorad í díreach mar gach aon phláinéad eile sa gcruinne. Is é sin, is spiorad an fíorphláinéad, an Talamh inti féin – an talamh ar a mbíonn aithne ag ár gcéadfaí coitiana níl inti san ach "corp." Is páirt d'Anamanna na Cruinne ár bpláinéad inti féin. Ón bpláinéad spioradálta sin tigeann taoidí rúnda – mar is léir do dhuine go mbíonn radharc síceach aige – agus bíd níos láidre in áiteacha áirithe (cnoic, rátha, 7l.) ná in áiteacha eile. Cuimhnigh ar Olumpos, Sinai, agus sléibhte naofa eile. I mBíoblaí, i seanscéalta agus i mbéaloideas bíonn a lán le rá faoi naofacht agus síúlacht a bhain le háiteacha speisialta. Daoine go raibh fís síceach, nó radharc spioradálta acu, a chraobhscaoil an t-eolas ar dtús. Maidir leis an mBóinn, agus le Brú na Bóinne, agus le Cnoc na Teamhrach –'

Ansin tháinig seanfhear chuig Fearghas agus thaispeáin dó an duilleog dheireanach a chuir an 'Dipeartment' amach. 'Rud chomh hamaideach ní fhacas le fada an lá,' arsa an seanfhear.

'Ba mhaith liom tusa agus an "Dipeartment" a bheith faoi Chuan Átha Cliath,' ar Ruairí os íseal. 'Duilleog an "Dipeartment" an ea! Agus sinne ag smaoineamh ar rúndiamhra na Bóinne!'

Ach maidir le Fearghas léigh sé an duilleog ó thús deireadh, agus ansin thosnaigh sé ag caint uirthi go sámh croíúil dúthrachtach go dtí gur thuig an seanfhear 'dhá thaobh na duilleoige.' Ansin d'iompaigh Fearghas chuig Ruairí.

'Maidir leis an mBóinn,' ar seisean, 'ní gá dom a rá leat go bhfuil dhá Bhóinn ann: an Bhóinn shofheicthe agus an Bhóinn dhofheicthe, is é sin an fhíor-Bhóinn. Thuig saoithe na hÉigipte fadó go raibh Nílus neamhaí ann agus nach raibh sa Nílus a bhíodh os comhair a súl de ghnáth ach macasamhail shaolta. Mar sin leis an mBóinn, mar sin leis an bhfíor-Bhóinn. Tá Anam na Cruinne agus a taoidí go buan. Bíonn na Cumhachta Naofa ar a dtugtar an Daghda agus Aonghus agus Dian Ceacht i gcois na fíor-Bhóinne i gcónaí. Airímid iad, beag nó mór, de réir mar a bhíos ár bhfís shíceach lag nó láidir. Na nithe a chonac agus a chualas i mBrú na Bóinne –'

'Ná habair focal eile den saghas sin leis an mbithiúnach seo!'

Cuireadh lámh ar ghualainn Fhearghais go hobann. Phreab seisean agus Ruairí. D'fhéachadar tharstu. An Dochtúir Ó Dúda a bhí ann, é ag gáire.

Shuigh an Dochtúir síos.

'Tá an bithiúnach seo dona go leor cheana féin,' ar seisean le Fearghas. 'Féach a bhfuil scríofa aige in *Herald* na seachtaine seo. Má ghríosfar é, le do scéalta míorúilteacha faoi Bhrú na Bóinne, beidh an mí-ádh ar fad orainn. Ag scaipeadh págántachta is ea a bheidh sé ó sheachtain go seachtain agus beidh an tóir ar ár mullach dá bharr.'

Rinne Fearghas gáire.

'Seo an treoraí gur mian leis Éire a bheith "fíor-Ghaelach" arís,' ar seisean: '"Nósa agus saíocht na sean" a bheith aici. Agus féach! Tá sé critheaglach roimh –'

'Ó, is furas do shaoithe agus d'fhealsúna bheith ag caint,' arsa an Dochtúir, 'ach ní chónaíonn siadsan in Éirinn: bíd ina gcónaí i dtír ionaidh faoi leith.'

'Tá go maith, a Dhochtúir,' ar Ruairí. 'Ach má chónaíonn dream áirithe i dtír na n-iontas nach ceart dóibh an t-ionadh a chur in iúl don slua?'

Leig an Dochtúir osna as.

'Bíonn ionadh agus ionadh ann,' ar seisean. 'Na Gaeil atá san iarthar agus sa deisceart inniu táid go han-simplí: is iad na daoine is simplí san Eoraip iad. Is iad a choimeádas beo na smaointí agus na nósa a bhí ag Gaeil chomh fada siar agus a bhí ann. As saol agus smaointí na ndaoine bochta céanna tuigtear saol agus smaointí na hEorpa nuair a bhí sí ina hóige.'

'Sin dearmad mór ar fad, a Dhochtúir,' ar Ruairí. 'Gaeil an iarthair agus Gaeil an deiscirt is beag an chosúlacht atá eatarthu agus Gaeil a bhíodh in Éirinn anallód. Tá sibhialtacht na nGael ag meath leis na céadta bliain agus tá sí beagnach imithe ón domhan sofheicthe inniu. Níl an seanspiorad ná an tseanmheanma ag na daoine bochta faoin tuath. A gcuid scéalta, a gcuid smaointí níl iontu ach iarsma. Chomh fada agus a cheaptar gurb iad súd "na Gaeil" amach is amach ní féidir leo ná linne dul ar aghaidh. Bheadh sé chomh maith duit bheith ag déanamh amach gurb í an bhreoiteacht an tsláinte.'

'Réitím leis an méid sin,' ar Fearghas. 'Ní daoine faoi leith iad Gaeil na tuaithe. Tá daoine sibhialta simplí mar iad san le fáil ina lán náisiún ar fud na hEorpa. Tá seanscéalta agus béaloideas acu súd chomh maith agus atá ag na Gaeil. Iarsma, *débris* is ea na scéalta agus an béaloideas úd: nó eireaball de *cycle mythologique*, mar a déarfá. Is ceart agus is cóir ardmheas a bheith againn ar na daoine sin go léir, ach ní ceart ná cóir dúinn a bheith ag ligint orainn gurb é toradh na seansibhialtachta iad. Níl iontu – i bhfeidhm iontu pé scéal é – ach beagán di. Síolraíonn brí seansibhialtachta ar an iomad slí: trí fhuil, trí intleacht, trí anamanna, chomh maith agus trí theanga. Bíonn brí an tsean-Ghaelachais in Áth Cliath – agus in Aimerice – inniu chomh maith agus i nGaillimh agus i gCorca Dhuibhne. Tá an Ghaeilge ag teastáil, agus ag teastáil go géar uainn: tá gá mór léi ar fud na tíre; is cóir dúinn í a dhéanamh níos beoga, níos bríomhaire. Ach tá a lán nithe eile ag teastáil uainn, agus ag teastáil ó Éirinn. Tá intleacht agus neart meanman ag teastáil uainn. Tá mór-Ghaeltacht nua agus mór-Ghaelachas nua ag teastáil uainn. Ach ní féidir iad a fháil chomh fada agus a cheapaimid gurb ionann "Gaelachas" agus dramhaíl scéalaíochta, seanfhocla, agus piseoga. Ní foláir dúinn go léir creidiúint gur spiorada a bhíos ionainn, agus go mbímid anseo ar an saol le mórlaochas a thaispeánadh agus le mórshaothar a chur ar aghaidh.'

D'éirigh guth Fhearghais gan fhios dó féin, agus bhí na daoine go léir ag éisteacht leis um an am seo.

'Maith an fear, a Fhearghais' a dúirt sagart óg ard dathúil a tháinig isteach tamaillín roimhe sin. 'Is geal liom a bheith ag éisteacht le soiscéal den saghas sin. Gan drochní ar m'anam is aoibhinn an rud é an fhírinne a chloisint ó "phágánach" de do leithéid – agus Éire beagnach caillte ag *les pessimistes* agus *les matérialistes*, gan trácht ar *les rigoristes*. *Gaelachas* an ea! Tá an oiread de Ghaelachas in Éirinn inniu agus atá d'fhíor-Chríostaíocht. Is dual do Chríostaí bheith ina laoch chomh maith céanna. Níl bundifríocht idir fíor-Cheilteachas agus fíor-Chríostaíocht. Seasann siad araon ar laochas agus spioradáltacht an fhíordhuine. Ach ceapann *les matérialistes* agus *les rigoristes* nach mbíonn spioradáltacht ná laochas ar bith ins an duine, nach mbíonn ann ach "peacaí direoil dona dearóil deoranta." Is mithid dúinne, na hÉireannaigh, críoch a chur lenár mbaothchaint agus lenár síorchlamhsán agus filleadh ar fhíor-Ghaelachas agus ar fhíor-Chríostaíocht.'

Sin mar a labhair an tAthair Dónall Ó Dálaigh – ollamh le diagacht agus le fealsúnacht a bhí ann. Sin díreach mar a thráchtadh sé go minic.

'Cuireann sibh ionadh orm agus cuireann sibh scanradh orm,' arsa an Dochtúir Ó Dúda. 'Is aoraí cineálta ón tuath mé, gan suim in aon rud agam ach mo chaoirigh shimplí Ghaelacha –'

'Óch, ag an diabhal go raibh sé mar scéal, a Dhochtúir,' ar Ruairí. 'Tá a fhios againn go léir gur fear léannta ealaíonta atá ionat. Is follas duit go bhfuil an ceart ag an Athair Dónall agus Mac Uí Ruanaí. Ba chóir d'Éirinn a bheith beoga in ionad a bheith lagbhríoch. Ní oiriúnach di *débris* agus dramhaíl; is dual di laochas a oiliúint agus toghashibhialtacht a shaothrú – a bheith ina "banaltra shéimh le féile is fíoreolas".'

Leanadar leis an díospóireacht ar chroí a ndíchill. Tháinig ardáthas ar Ruairí. In oll-Ghaeltacht, in oll-chompánacht spioradálta síoraí is ea a bhí sé, dar leis.

IX

Sa deireadh dúirt Créide le Fearghas nárbh fhéidir léi fanúint ní ba dhéanaí. Bhí Ruairí i ngar di, agus cheap seisean gurbh amhlaidh a bhí an scéal aige féin. Bheadh sé in éineacht léi go dtí áit na riancharr.

Bhí go maith. D'imíodar leo. Ach ar shroichint an chrosbhóthair dóibh bhí an riancharr deireanach tar éis imeacht.

'Níl leigheas air,' a dúirt Ruairí. 'Is aoibhinn go bhfuil oíche bhreá ghealaí ann. Ní fada an bealach go Cill Iníon Léinín thar bhóthar an chnoic. Rachaidh mé leat. Cad eile? An amhlaidh go mbeifeá ag dul id aonar? Dar Fionn ní féidir é. Sea, rachaidh mé leat. Is geal liom bheith ag siúl anocht.'

Chuadar ar aghaidh i gciúnas na hoíche; iad ag caint go beoga ar an sárthrácht a bhí ar siúl le linn an chéilí i dtigh Fhearghais.

'B'iontach é,' ar Ruairí. 'Céilí agus seanchas mar iadsan taispeáinid rúnsaibhreas na hÉireann dúinn. Is draíochtach an tír í.'

'Agus seo é an rud a chuireas ionadh orm,' ar Créide. 'Bhí ard-díospóireacht ann, bhí daoine áirithe go mór in aghaidh daoine eile, ach bhí aoibhneas orainn go léir, de réir dealraimh.'

'Bhí, gan aon agó. Le linn cuarta agus céilithe dá leithéid – nó féilte ba cheart dom a rá – samhlaítear dom nach bhfuil mórbheatha agus ardobair an domhain ach ag tosnú, agus nach raibh i saothar na n-aoiseanna uile roimhe seo ach saghas ullmhaithe. Agus maidir le nithe a chuireas romham a dhéanamh samhlaítear dom go rabhadar róbheag ar fad, nach rabhadar leath chomh hálainn ná leath chomh doimhin agus ba cheart dóibh a bheith.'

'Mar sin díreach a bhí an scéal agam féin anocht,' ar Créide, 'nuair a bhí Fearghas agus an tAthair Dónall' ('agus tusa,' bhí sí ar tí a rá freisin) 'ag trácht ar dhúchas agus ar dhualgas.'

Mar sin féin bhí smaoineamh eile in aigne na beirte. Samhlaíodh dóibh ar shlí iontach go rabhadar ag siúl leis na cianta, go raibh an tsiúlóid seo cosúil lena lán siúlóidí eile a bhí acu anallód agus ó shin i leith – go deimhin gur pháirt de thuras síoraí í. Agus nuair a bhuaileadar faoi dheoidh ar bhóthar na farraige, agus na gealuiscí glórmhara os a gcomhair, b'éigean dóibh bheith ina dtost nach mór: bhí an oiread sin rúnríméid orthu.

Thángadar go dtí casadh an bhóthair, áit atá i ngar don fharraige. B'fhíorálainn an radharc é. Stadadar. Dhearcadar ar dhromchla na mara, soir go Brí Chualann.

'Baineann rúndiamhair iontach éigin leis an bhfarraige, go mór mór san oíche,' ar Ruairí, i mbriathra a bhí cosúil le cogar. '"Aghaidh an Aigéin" – "aghaidh na n-uiscí" – is ansin a bhíos an diamhaireacht agus an ollsacht dáiríribh. Ár seanscéalta faoi eachtraí i "mbóchna an iarthair" ní hionadh go gcorraíonn siad go mór sinn.'

'Shíleas go minic go mbíonn draíocht thar barr ins an mbóchna agus go mb'aoibhinn liom a bheith i long bheag sí i gcónaí,' ar Créide agus í ag féachaint go grámhar ar an bhfarraige.

B'fhada ó Ruairí an gnáthshaol an uair sin. Idir áilleacht na farraige agus draíocht na hoíche agus scéimh Chréide d'éirigh sárbhród ina mheanma nár airigh sé inti riamh.

'Is ea,' ar seisean, go háthasach ciúin, 'b'aoibhinn liomsa fós a beith i long bheag sí i gcónaí, ach tusa, agus tusa amháin, a bheith in éineacht liom.'

Agus chuir sé lámh lena muineál agus phóg sé í.

Chuir sí lámh ar a ghualainn, rinne sí miongháire, agus ansin tháinig cosúlacht deor ina súile, agus ina dhiaidh sin dhearc sí air go bródúil agus go scáfar san am céanna.

Shíl Ruairí go rabhadar i gcoillte draíochta, chois farraige síúla, in oileán úrnua, álainn, ceolmhar; nach raibh tús leo riamh agus nach mbeadh deireadh leo choíche. Ba naofa an chruinne í, dar leis.

'Cuireann tú an-ionadh orm,' ar sise go ciúin, tar éis tamaillín. 'Bhíos cinnte gur smaointeoir agus fealsamh thú féin. Ach, féach anois –'

Thóg sé a dhá lámh ina lámha féin, ach níor labhair sé focal.

Shíleadar agus iad ina seasamh ansin go ciúin, sonas agus ionadh orthu, go raibh aithne acu ar a chéile le haoiseanna thar chomhaireamh, ach ar shlí eile nach raibh fíoraithne acu ar a chéile go dtí gur thángadar ansin go casadh an bhóthair in aice na farraige san oíche shoineanta. Bhain a ngrámhaireacht le meanma agus le hanam. D'aithnigh a n-anamanna a chéile. Níor léir don ghnáthintleacht conas mar a tharla sé sin: is rúndiamhrach iad cúrsaí an anama. Ach sin mar a bhí, agus níor ghá dóibh trácht air.

Faoi dheireadh d'fhágadar slán ag a chéile ag geata an gharraí bhig os comhair tí Chréide.

Bhí Ruairí i bhfad ón tigh ósta ina gcuireadh sé faoi ar theacht go Baile Átha Cliath dó. Ach ba chuma leis é sin. Ní raibh dúil aige dul ann ná i dtigh ar bith eile. Chuaigh sé go barr Chill Iníon Léinín, shiúil sé anonn is anall, ag dearcadh ar an bhfarraige agus ar shléibhte Átha Cliath, agus chun na spéire. Bhí a fhios aige go mbeadh Cill Iníon Léinín mar áit naofa draíochta dó go brách. Ba dhóigh leis go raibh laochra agus spéirmhná na sean-Éireann ina thimpeall: Cú Chulainn, Naoise, Diarmaid, Deirdre, Eimhear, is Gráinne, agus na céadta eile nach iad. Bhí Eamhain Mhacha agus Taillte agus an Teamhair go bríoch gleoite; bhí Aonghus agus an Dághdha le feiscint cois na habhann neamhaí; d'éirigh salmcheadal go glórmhar i mBrú na Bóinne. B'eol dó ansin an talamh agus an chruinne go léir a bheith beo, meanmnach, rúndiamhrach, agus an grá a bheith mar réalt eolais lena dtaispeánfaí tuilleadh dá mbrí agus dá mbeatha dó.

Nárbh iontach é, a dúirt sé leis féin, conas mar a casadh Créide agus é féin ar a chéile agus chomh luath agus a thuigeadar an cairdeas croí agus an ceangal anama a bhí eatarthu. Go dearfa, ar seisean, ní bhíonn i mbeatha duine ach aon chaibidil amháin de mhórscéal gan chríoch. I 'gcaibidlí' eile bhí Créide agus mise in aontíos. Is ea agus b'fhéidir go mbímid ag obair le chéile agus in aontíos de ló is d'oíche ar staid anama, staid rúnda, nach mbíonn eolas ná cuimhne ag ár ngnáthmheanma uirthi. Níl ins an ngnáthshaol ach macasamhail dhoiléir den domhan spioradálta – an fhíorchruinne. Ní i bhfad uainn, ní os cionn na spéire an fhíorchruinne úd. Páirteanna di is ea ár spiorada.'

Le héirí gréine chuaigh sé ar ais go Baile Átha Cliath.

X

Casadh Cathal Ó Cinnéide agus Ruairí ar a chéile sa tigh ósta. Bhí Cathal ar tí dul ar ais go Loch Garman agus bhí cosúlacht bhuartha air. Ba dheacair do Ruairí aireachas a thabhairt dá raibh le rá aige – bhí rian taibhrimh air féin.

'Bhí saghas troda idir mé féin agus Eilís Ní Anracháin aréir,' ar Cathal. 'Bhíos i Halla na Saoirseachta um thráthnóna, i measc na ndaoine bochta lácha, agus nuair a thugas cuairt ar Eilís ina dhiaidh sin mholas obair an Lorcánaigh. M'anam ón diabhal! Phreab sí agus dúirt sí go mba cheart dom suim a chur sa "náisiún" in ionad í a chur i "gcineál" ar bith. Ní díospóireacht go dtí sin. Thug sí fúm de bhrí nach mbím im "Shinn Féiní" dáiríribh, dar léi, agus de bhrí go bhfuilim ag géilleadh do "bharúla iasachta" i dtaobh na ndaoirseach agus an lucht oibre. "Barúla iasachta," mhuise! Táim liath ag a lán de na "Gaeil." Níl blúire den sean-Ghaelachas acu; i dtaobh na bhfear oibre go háirithe.'

'Sin rud a chuir ionadh orm go minic le déanaí,' ar Ruairí. 'Ach ní cóir dúinn bheith cáinteach nó mífhoighneach. Tá laetha na sároibre agus na háilleachta romhainn agus roimh na Gaeil go léir. Táim cinnte de sin.

Bí misniúil meanmnach. Ní éisteod le focal bróin uait ná ó Ghael eile arís. Is aoibhneach an rud a bheith beo agus tír álainn le saothrú againn.'

'Tá sin go maith, a fhealsamh na Bóinne, ach ní bhíonn na Gaeil i gcoiteann leath chomh láidir, leath chomh tuisceanach agus ba cheart dóibh a bheith, agus tá a rian orthu. Éist liom anois. Fuaireas seoid eile i bhfoirm leabhair an Satharn seo a ghabh tharainn: *Mirèio* a chum Fredéric Mistral. D'aistríos píosa breá de go Gaeilge agus ligeas orm agus mé ag caint le hEilís aréir gur úramhrán ina taobhse é, agus bhí síocháin eadrainn as sin amach. Cuireann scéal Mhistral an-áthas orm: chomh sona, dúthrachtach a bhíos an seanfhile ar a fheirm álainn, an grá a thugas sé do spiorad agus nósa a dhúchais, an saol féileach fileata a bhíos ina thimpeall i bProbhence an aoibhneasa –'

'Is ea,' ar Ruairí. 'Is breá a bheith ag smaoineamh ar an scéal. Cuireann Mistral comaoin mhór orainn go léir. In ionad cúis ghearáin a bheith agat, is amhlaidh –'

'Is é atá ag cur buartha orm: nach mbímid, na hÉireannaigh, in ann ár saol agus ár saothar a chur chun críche ar nós Mhistral agus mhuintir na Probhence. Tír na mbarúlacha bréagacha, tír na cainte móire is ea Éire, faraor.'

'Ní chreidir an méid sin, a Chathail. Níl ann ach néal aigeanta. Tuigeann tú maitheas agus mórgacht na nÉireannach chomh maith agus a thuigimse féin iad. Gan amhras tá cuid againn inár gcodladh agus ag caint inár gcodladh le fada, ach táimid ag dúiseacht. Beidh ár spiorada ár dtreorú san am atá romhainn.'

Ansin d'fhágadar slán ag a chéile.

Ar dhul ar ais don Mhí dó smaoinigh Ruairí ar a mbeadh le déanamh aige féin agus Créide leis an tsaorshliocht a ghríosú, agus d'éirigh ardáthas air.

XI

D'éirigh Ruairí an-ghnóthach, óir bhí mórfheis na Mí ag druidiúint leo, ach dá ghnóthaí é bhí am aige le smaointí a chroí a chur in iúl do Chréide. Chuir sé litir fhada chuici Dé Luain féin. Níorbh fhada go bhfuair sé freagra. Ba dheas an freagra é ar shlí, ach níorbh é an freagra go raibh sé ag feitheamh leis.

Scríobh sí ar dtús ar a saol in aice le Cill Iníon Léinín, ar leabhra a bhí á léamh aici, agus ar a dúil i múinteoireacht taistil agus i 'dTír na nÓg faoin tuath.' Ansin dúirt sí go raibh a lán nithe ina litir féin a chuir ionadh uirthi.

'Tá an trácht i dtaobh an ghrá go fíorfhileata,' ar sise. 'Ach cén bhaint atá aige liomsa? An amhlaidh a rinne tú dearmad? 'Raibh úrscéal á scríobh agat, agus ar chuiris isteach beart leathanach de i do litir? Munab é seo an míniú, cad eile? Dar ndóigh bhís beagán aisteach agus sinn ag teacht abhaile oíche Dhomhnaigh, go mór mór sa deireadh. Ba chosúil go rabhais ag taibhreamh. De réir na bhfilí is iontach a mbíonn le feiscint le linn aislinge. Ach nár thángais chugat féin fós?'

Lean sí mar sin ar feadh i bhfad, agus ansin chuir sí síos ar Fhearghas Ó Ruanaí, ar chomhoibriú, agus ar chumannachas. Dúirt sí fós gur aontaigh sí a bheith ina moltóir sna comórtaisí liteartha ag mórfheis na Mí, agus b'fhéidir go mbeadh draíocht na Bóinne le fáil aici chomh maith agus ag daoine eile.

Lá arna mhárach fuair sí litir an-fhada ó Ruairí.

'Dearmad mór eile!' ar sise ina freagra. Is dócha gur chuiris an t-úrscéal go léir isteach an taca seo! An é mo bhreithiúnas atá ag teastáil uait? Tá súil agam go mbeidh sé léite agam roimh dheireadh na míosa! Tá cuid mhaith de léite agam cheana. Feicim go mbaineann sé go mór leis an ngrá, agus, mar is ceart i gcúrsa scéil, tá trácht ann faoi phósadh. Ach dá mba mise an cailín chuirfinn rudaí faoi leith in iúl don "laoch." Rudaí den saghas seo: "Deireann tú gur spéirbhean mé, agus sárionadh ionam a bhíos do do ghríosú chun gníomhartha móra. Ní foláir duit é a dhearbhú. Ná habair focal eile faoi phósadh go dtí go mbeidh gníomh mór – i bhfoirm leabhair nó laochais – déanta agat ar son do thíre agus do mhuintire. Creidfidh mé ansin thú." Sea, a chara mo chroí, is mar sin a bheinn ag caint. Ba cheart do gach cailín in Éirinn an smaoineamh céanna a bheith ina meanma aici, agus a bheith chomh láidir ina thaobh agus a bhímse.'

'Is ea, go díreach. Is mian liom cumann cailíní a chur ar bun. Gach ceann acu a bheith faoi gheasa gan pósadh le fear go dtí go ndéanfadh sé mórghníomh – mórghníomh intleachtach nó eile – ar son na hÉireann, nó ar son dreama áirithe de mhuintir na hÉireann. Faighim locht mór ar spéirmhná na Gréige, spéirmhná na Fódla, agus eile a mhair sa tseanaimsir. Chuiridís an iomarca suime ina ngráthóirí, agus iontu féin, agus sa ngrá féin. Ní bhíodh cuimhne acu ar a dtír ná ar an gcine daonna ná ar a ndualgas. Dá mbeidís smaointeach, fadbhreathnaitheach b'fhuras dóibh na fir a ghríosú chun ardghníomhartha.'

'Féach ar Éirinn inniu. Is tír bhocht chráite dhaibhir í. Ach tá cuid dá clann ardsmaointeach; tá mórmheanma rúnda ins na fir óga, ach níl eolas acu ar an ngné is fearr lena cur chun cinn. Ach dá mbeadh ciall ag na cailíní, dá ndúilidís pósadh, díreach mar a mhíníos, gheobhadh na buachaillí an tslí cheart, an modh díreach atá ag teastáil. Scríobhfadh ceann acu leabhar mór, dhéanfadh duine eile timireacht bhreá i measc na bhfear oibre, chuirfeadh cinn eile páipéar neamhspleách ar bun: agus mar sin de. Ní bheadh eagla orthu roimh aon namhaid, ná roimh aon duine cumhachtach dá bhfuil in Éirinn. Is mithid do na cailíní Gaelacha a gcumhacht agus a ndualgas a bheith soiléir dóibh. Cuirimse romham an t-eolas a chraobhscaoileadh.'

Chuir Ruairí litreacha chuici gach uile lá. Bhí a freagartha go haerach: go mór mór i dtaobh an ghrá. Chuir sí síos go deas magúil mar gheall ar an 'aisling' úd ar bhóthar na farraige in aice le Cill Iníon Léinín dóibh.

'Tá m'athair bocht féin ag taibhreamh anois – nó ba cheart dom a rá, ag taibhreamh níos mó ná riamh,' scríobh sí lá. 'Cuireann sé ina luí orm nár mhiste dom pósadh! Deireann sé go mbeadh sé sásta ina aigne ach mise a bheith pósta. Thar a gcualas riamh! Ní fheadar cad a tharla dó.'

Ní raibh Ruairí in ann triall go Baile Átha Cliath, le chomh gnóthach a bhí sé agus an Fheis ag teacht. B'éigean dó bheith sásta le litreacha in ionad caintí le Créide. Chuir sise litir bhreá bhríomhar chuige lá ar dhileagra a thug Fearghas Ó Ruanaí uaidh os comhair Chumann Réalta an Eolais. Ar an gceangal a bhíos idir Anam na Cruinne agus Anam an duine ó bheatha go beatha (síoroilithreacht anama, *Seelenwanderung*) is ea a thrácht sé ar dtús, agus ansin mhínigh sé brí rúnda chomhoibrithe in Éirinn inniu. Thaispeáin sé go mbíonn rúncheangal idir obair Chonradh na Gaeilge, obair na múinteoirí taistil, obair an I.A.O.S., obair an Lorcánaigh agus a lucht leanúna, obair sagart óg neamhspleách, agus obair a lán daoine eile, cé nach léir an ceangal dóibh féin go fóill. Ní thuigeann a ngnáthmheanma an gnó atá ceaptha ag Anam na Cruinne (ardsearbhóntaí

Dé) ina gcomhair, ach tuigeann a n-anamanna go léir é, agus is iad a n-anamanna a ghríosaíonn iad chun oibre gan a fhios ag a ngnáthmheanma roimhráite.

Scríobh an tAthair Dónall Ó Dálaigh chuig Ruairí. Dúirt sé go raibh sé ag éirí míshásta faoin moill a bhí orthu go léir nach mór. Mheas seisean agus cairde áirithe go mba mhór an rud é irisleabhar spridiúil neamhspleách fealsúnach a chur ar bun gan mhoill. Na daoine a bhí ina ndúiseacht – sagairt óga, múinteoirí taistil, comhoibrithe, muintir Chumann Réalta an Eolais, 7l. – ní baol nach mbeadh fáilte acu roimhe. Bhí a fhios aige go raibh teach clódóireachta ealaíonta i ngleann na Bóinne. Bhí go maith. Bhí súil aige go mbeadh seanchas eatarthu faoin gceist go léir le linn na Feise.

B'éigean do Ruairí dul go dtí a bhaile dúchais lá. Buaileadh a athair breoite, agus ceapadh go raibh sé i mbaol báis. Ní raibh, áfach: tháinig feabhas mór air i gceann seachtaine. Ach ba chosúil nach mbeadh sé láidir go leor i gcomhair feirmeoireachta arís choíche. Bhí sé ag éirí aosta, agus bhí formhór a shaoil an-chrua ar fad. Cén rud ab fhearr a dhéanamh ar a shon? Cad mar gheall ar an bpaiste talún? Cuireadh Ruairí ag géarmhachnamh.

Ba gheal lena chroí an seanbhall. Saol simplí na gcomharsan, chorraigh sé go mór é.

Ar theacht ar ais don Mhí dó chuir sé litir chuig Créide. Thrácht sé go grámhar ar an bpaiste talún agus ar shaol agus nósa na ndaoine. B'iontach an freagra a fuair sé uaithi, chomh lách dílis agus a bhí sé. 'Tá a lán eile le rá agam,' ar sise sa deireadh, 'ach is deacair dom mo smaointí a chur síos go beacht. Fan go gcastar ar a chéile sinn lá na feise. Bíonn taibhreamh agam gach oíche ar shaol ar an bpaiste talún. Bíonn sé cosúil le Tír na nÓg. Samhlaítear dom go bhfuil "an solas ag teacht" faoi dheoidh. Bhís róthugtha do leabhra agus do léann, ach an paiste talún cuireann sé taobh eile den scéal in iúl duit – agus domsa. Is iontach é, a Ruairí a chroí.'

'Róthugtha do leabhra agus do léann!' ar seisean, á freagrú. 'Fágaim le huacht nach mbím. Gan amhras bíonn an-dúil agam i leabhra áirithe go minic, ach tar éis tamaill éirím astu. Éirím mífhoighdeach uair, éirím an-áthasach uair eile. Ach gach uile ócáid, cé acu mífhoighdeach nó áthasach a bhím, deirim liom féin gurb é mo dhualgas a bheith ag déanamh rud úrnua. Sea, mé féin! Ní bhíonn Homer, Platón, Virgil, Plotínus, Dante, Goethe, Emerson, in ann mé a shásamh. Ní foláir dom aigne féin bheith á hoibriú ina slí féin. Agus ba mhaith liom céad údar a bheith ag oibriú agus ag scríobh, agus ag gríosú intleachta na hÉireann. Muna mbímid ag gluaiseacht agus ag cruthú nua-oibre ní bhíonn maitheas ionainn. Airím ionam féin agus in Éirinn brí nach bhfuil a leithéid le fáil in aon leabhar a chonaic an domhan go dtí seo.'

XII

D'éirigh sé go geal le mórfheis na Mí de réir dealraimh. Tháinig na céadta chun na hUaimhe ó bhailte eile sa chúige agus ó áiteacha tuaithe. Tháinig feirmeoirí, sclábhaithe, aoirí, siopadóirí, chomh maith le hoidí scoile agus sagairt. Tháinig lucht ceoil, cuid acu sa maidin, agus shiúladar tríd na sráideanna ag seinm poirt Ghaelacha. Bhí ceol le cloisint gan stad. Bhí bratacha á gcrochadh trasna na sráideanna anseo agus ansiúd; bhí comharthaí féile ar gach taobh. Tháinig suaitheantas daoine ar thraenacha agus ar rothair ó Chill Dara, ón Iar-Mhí agus go mór mór ó Bhaile Átha Cliath, agus bhí ionadh orthu ar shroichint na hUaimhe dóibh. Bhí sé amuigh ar an gcúige é a bheith an-chosúil le fásach; deirtí nach mbíodh suim ag formhór na ndaoine ach i mbeithígh agus in airgead. Agus féach! Ba dhóigh le duine go raibh feis den tseanréim ar bun acu agus í go bríoch.

Agus le linn na gcomórtas, i Halla na bhFear Óg, ins na príomhscoileanna, agus i dtithe na mban rialta, tháinig áthas ar a lán, de bhrí go raibh an-chuid de na foghlaimeoirí go cliste géarintleachtach. D'admhaigh na scrúdaitheoirí go raibh buachaillí agus cailíní áirithe thar barr, agus mholadar na múinteoirí taistil go mór. D'admhaigh Pádraic Mac Éanna go mbeadh sé toilteanach Coláiste Gaelach a chur ar bun i ngleann na Bóinne; dhéanfadh sé an gnó chomh maith ansin is dá mbeadh sé ag bun an tsléibhe os comhair na farraige in Áth Cliath. D'admhaigh Diarmaid Mac an tSuaircis gur airigh sé sprid na nDéiseach féin ar feadh an lae. Dhearbhaigh an Dochtúir Mac Shligigh go raibh cora cainte na gConnachtach acu ansin i rícheantar na Teamhrach. Dúirt Áine Ní Fharaille go rabhadar an-chosúil le cora cainte breátha Bhreifne. Is é a chuir an Dochtúir Ó Dúda ina luí ar a chairde: go raibh gríosach bheag Ghaelachais i ngach Éireannach – i dtréadaí féin – agus gur féidir í a mhúscailt agus í a neartú agus tine a dhéanamh di le himeacht aimsire. Ar an ábhar sin ba léir gur chiallmhar é a shíorordú féin: '*Festina Lente.*'

Sin mar a labhair sé lena chairde anseo agus ansiúd ar feadh an lae. Ag an gcruinniú poiblí sa tráthnóna bhí a mhalairt de phort aige. Labhair sé de ghuth mór, agus mhol sé muintir na Mí amach is amach: Bhíodar ag dul ar aghaidh go dána agus go mórálach mar ba dhual do chlann na Fódla ar fad. Bhí a nGaelachas ag éirí mar mhórthaoide na bóchna, agus le cúnamh Dé ní fada fanacht dóibh go dtí go mbeadh an Uaimh agus Ceanannas agus Áth Troim – gach ceann acu – mar Aithne na nGael. Ina cathracha breátha, beoga, intleachtacha, ina seoda i gcoróin na nua-Ghaeltachta, bheidís. Bheadh Teamhair mar Olumpos na nGael agus mar Helicón na nGael chomh maith céanna. Bheadh áthas ar Éirinn agus ionadh ar an Eoraip mar gheall ar bhreáthacht bheatha agus aoibhneas saoil i gcríoch na Bóinne!

Bhí an tAthair Dónall Ó Dálaigh ina scrúdaitheoir sna comórtaisí liteartha agus d'admhaigh sé go raibh cuid de na foghlaimeoirí cliste go leor. Ach ní raibh bród air dá bharr. Ba mhaith an rud é, ar seisean, daoine óga a bheith in ann Gaeilge a léamh. Ach cad a bhí acu le léamh?

Scéilíní agus seanmóirí, agus bhí na scéilíní níos fearr ná na seanmóirí. Cheap na scríbhneoirí agus na sagairt go n-oirfeadh dramhaíl ar bith do na Gaeil. Maidir leis na céadta a bhí cruinnithe ag an bhfeis ba bheag leis cuid acu: siopadóirí, lucht díolta biotáille, feirmeoirí nach raibh toilteanach an talamh do thochailt ná cothrom na Féinne a thabhairt do na fir oibre. Ní ceart ná cóir ná ciallmhar talamh na hÉireann a bheith ag a leithéidí. Dá mbeadh an talamh faoi chúram an náisiúin, mar ba cheart, b'fhuras é sclábhaíocht agus daibhreas a dhíbirt. B'ait an rud é daoine a bheith ag ligint na gaoithe isteach i dtaobh 'Gaelachais' agus gan puinn suime acu i bpréamhacha an Ghaelachais. Ceann acu siúd, gabháilchine: an talamh, nó an chuid ba mhó di, 'leis' an treabh. Ba dhóigh lena lán inniu go ndéanfadh caint agus gramadach 'fíor-Ghael' de dhuine, díreach mar a cheap dream eile go ndéanfadh saghas creidimh agus umhlaíocht do shagairt 'Críostaí' de. Ní bheadh Gaelachas ná saoirseacht sa tír go dtí go mbeadh beomheanma agus misneach i measc an tslua.

Labhair sé mar sin lena lán; dúirt sé nithe den saghas céanna, go breá bríomhar, os comhair an chruinnithe phoiblí.

'Is dána an duine é,' arsa an Dochtúir Ó Dúda le seansagart a bhí lena chois ar an ardán. 'Tá imní orm mar gheall ar smaointí mar iad san –'

'Cuirfear cosc air,' arsa an seansagart. 'Tá sé cosúil le haspal.'

D'inis an tAthair Dónall do Ruairí cad a bhí socraithe aige agus a chairde i dtaobh an Irisleabhair nua.

XIII

Ní minic a bhí seanchas idir Ruairí agus Créide le linn na feise, óir bhí an bheirt an-ghnóthach, ach ar chríochnú don chruinniú poiblí chuadar ag siúlóid dóibh féin trí ghleann na Bóinne. Bhí a fhios acu nach rachadh an traein speisialta ar ais go ceann uair go leith, agus ba mhian le Créide 'abha na n-iongnaí' a fheiscint faoi sholas na gealaí.

'Is deacair a chreidiúint,' ar sise, agus iad sa ngleann, 'nach rabhas ag siúl cois na Bóinne roimhe seo. Measaim go bhfuil seanaithne agam uirthi.'

'Bhí an smaoineamh céanna agam faoi Bhrú na Bóinne, agus faoin Teamhair, agus faoin Mí go léir ar theacht dom ar dtús,' a dúirt Ruairí. 'Is iontach chomh freagrach agus a bhímid don *genius loci* amanta. Ach sílim ar uairibh nach mbíonn ansin ach taibhreamh nó ceapadh aigeanta. Ionainn féin a bhíos an draíocht. Tá an ceart ag Fearghas Ó Ruanaí agus ag an Athair Dónall Ó Dálaigh: is laoch diaga é an fíordhuine; is rí agus saoi é; cónaíonn sé ar staid iontais; agus nuair a ionchollaíonn sé le sealad san domhan gnách is amaideach an rud dó a bheith ag ceapadh gur peacach direoil dona é.'

'Ach bíonn difríocht mhór idir an Athair Dónall agus

Fearghas,' ar Créide. 'Bíonn an tAthair Dónall mífhoighneach, casaoideach féin. Is é atá uaidh aois fhorórga, daoine intleachtacha, mór-réim spioradálta in Éirinn láithreach bonn. Ní bhíonn meas aige ar nithe coiteanna. Ach maidir le Fearghas smaoiníonn sé agus oibríonn sé go bríomhar, ach bíonn sé go ciúin réidh lách i gcónaí. Tuigeann sé gach duine agus gach cine agus bíonn meas aige ar nithe suaracha féin.'

'Táir beagán crua ar an Athair Dónall,' ar Ruairí. 'Is breá an fear é, agus ní hionadh go mbeadh sé mífhoighdeach mar gheall ar an iomad rud in Éirinn. Tá "eachtra" mór ceaptha aige agus ag cairde áirithe –'

'Tá a fhios agam go bhfuil. Bhíos ag caint leis inniu. Tá eagla orm, a Ruairí, go bhfuilir féin ar thaobh an Athar Dónall in ionad a bheith ag seasamh le Fearghas.'

'Is ionadh liom é sin. Tá meas thar meán agam ar Fhearghas –'

Rinne Créide miongháire.

'Ach ní bhíonn tú sásta a bheith chomh sítheach agus chomh foighdeach le Fearghas,' ar sise. 'Féach anois. Is duine de rífhir an domhain é. Is saoi diamhartha é. Tá tuiscint spioradálta faoi leith aige.'

'Admhaím an méid sin óm chroí amach. Is aoibhinn an rud é fear mar eisean a bheith in Éirinn inniu.'

'Ach cuimhnigh air seo, a Ruairí. Oibríonn sé go dúthrachtach ó lá go lá, ag scríobh nótaí ar im agus ar uibheacha, ar churaíocht agus ar chearca – i gcomhair feirmeoirí agus ban tí. Bíonn sé sásta ach obair shaolta úsáideach den saghas sin a dhéanamh ó sheachtain go seachtain. Gan amhras déanann sé pictiúir shiúla – le linn a laethanta saoire sa samhradh – ceapann sé píosaí filíochta anois agus arís; tráchtann sé uair sa tseachtain ag Cumann Réalta an Eolais. Sin é an méid. Níl a fhios ach ag corrdhuine go bhfuil sárfhear dá leithéid in Éirinn.'

'Is ionadh liom mar a fhanas sé chomh ciúin sin. Is mór

an chailliúint d'Éirinn é –'

'B'fhéidir go bhfuil míniú eile ann,' ar Créide. 'Tuigeann sé nach bhfuiltear ullamh roimh theagasc níos doimhne ná obair níos bríomhaire go fóill. Dá bhrí sin bíonn sé sásta a bheith réidh simplí "gnách" ach ar uairibh.'

'Gan drochní ar m'anam,' ar seisean, 'tá athrú mór ag teacht ar d'aigne, a Chréide. Ní chreidfinn go mb'fhéidir é.'

Stad sí, agus mar a stad rinne Ruairí amhlaidh. Bhíodar i ngleanntán álainn uaigneach, ar bhruach na habhann, an spéir go glan soiléir, an ghealach le feiscint thar bharr na gcrann (mar a samhlaíodh dóibh) a bhí in aice leo.

'Dar ndóigh tá mórathrú tagtha orm le déanaí,' ar sise. 'Bhí ionadh agus scanradh orm ar dtús mar gheall ar an athrú céanna. An chaoi mar a thugas grá duitse ón gcéad uair beagnach – déarfaí go rabhas as mo mheabhair nó gur cailín gan náire mé –'

Phóg sé í.

'Ná bíodh ceist ort mar gheall air sin,' ar seisean, 'nó cuirfidh tú brón agus buairt uafásach orm. D'aithnigh ár n-anamanna a chéile –'

'Níl ceist ar bith orm anois,' ar sise. 'Creidim go rabhamar inár mbeatha in Éirinn go minic roimhe seo, agus go rabhamar – ár n-anamanna – in éineacht agus in aontíos. Dá bhrí sin níorbh aon ionadh é gur aithníomar a chéile chomh hobann sin. Ach anois, an obair atá romhainn sa mbeatha nua, san aois nua.'

'Is ea,' ar Ruairí, 'sin í an mhórcheist –'

'Feictear dom go bhfuil sí go han-simplí. Le linn beatha ar bith ní bhíonn mórán maitheasa i bhfealsúnacht munar féidir í a chur i bhfeidhm agus in úsáid.'

Chuir sé lámh fána muineál, agus shiúladar ar aghaidh go mall.

'Tuigeann tú go maith mé,' ar sise. 'Bhíos ag géarsmaoineamh ar do chás agus ar mo chás féin le déanaí. Ba ghnaoi liom tú a fheiscint ar an staid is dual duit. Sea, a

Ruairí dhil. Mar sin iarraim ort gan bacadh leis an obair seo atá ar siúl ag an Athair Dónall agus a chairde; agus rud níos mó ná sin –'

'Rud níos mó ná sin! Tá "sin" dona go leor; ag iarraidh orm gan páirt a bheith agam i dtroid ar son saorintleachta agus spioradáltachta! Cad é an rud uafásach eile?'

'Beidh ionadh ort ar dtús mar gheall air. Ach deirim, agus deirim go láidir é, go mba cheart duit éirí as an múinteoireacht taistil, imeacht abhaile don phaiste talún, agus –'

'Gan bréag a rá is tusa an tíoránaí críochnaithe, a Chréide. Mise imeacht abhaile, a bheith im fheirmeoir beag: agus an Bhóinn, an chúis, an litríocht, agus, mar bharr donais, tusa féin a fhágáil! Ní dáiríribh ataoi!'

'Ní bheadh ort an chúis ná an litríocht a fhágáil, agus maidir liomsa, b'fhéidir go mbeinn in éineacht agus in aontíos leat ansiúd – i gceann tamaillín.'

'Ach, a Chréide, a chroí, ní léir duit chomh crua agus a bhíos an saol faoin tuath. Táir fileata foghlamtha, agus –'

'A Ruairí, táim liath ag na focla sin, "foghlaim" agus "foghlamtha." Gaeil go bhfuil beagán foghlama acu, faoin tuath atáid ag teastáil. Sna "bailte móra" bímid mar phríosúnaigh de ghnáth: i bhfad ó shibhialtacht, ó na taoidí síoraí, ó anam na cruinne.'

'Admhaím gurb ionúin liom an tuath – gurb aoibhinn le mo chroí an "paiste talún." Ach tusa, a Chréide! I ngleann na Bóinne, ar shléibhte Átha Cliath, is cosúil le sióg nó spiorad thú. Ach ar riasc –'

'Tá Baile Átha Cliath i bhfad níos measa ná riasc,' ar sise. 'Is fásach é. Bíonn áilleacht i bhfíor-riasc. Cheapas gur file thú! Ach tá eagla ort roimh aontíos leat in aice le riasc!'

Ansin thrácht sí ar na brionglóidí faoi shaol ar an bpaiste talún a bhí aici gach oíche le tamall. Ba shiúil an scéal é.

Faoi dheireadh chuir sé a lámha lena muineál agus phóg

sé í.

'Ar riasc nó i bhfásach, in uaimh, ar dhroim sléibhe, in oileán fiáin i bhfad sa bhfarraige, nó i gcarcar féin, bheinn go sona ach tusa a bheith in éineacht liom,' ar seisean go grámhar.

'Is ea,' ar sise. 'Tá an margadh déanta againn anois. Is iontach an saol a bheas againn ar an bpaiste talún le cúnamh Dé.'

B'éigean dóibh dul ar ais don Uaimh ansin, óir ní fhanann traenacha speisialta nóiméad ar bith le lucht an ghrá seachas daoine eile. Ar dhul ar ais dóibh thrácht Créide go haerach ar an saol a bhíodh ag filí faoin tuath ó na laethanta inar mhair Theocritos agus Virgil go dtí aimsir Mhistral féin.

XIV

Ar luí ina leaba do Ruairí i bhfad d'éis an mheán oíche b'fhada uaidh fonn codlata. Ag smaoineamh ar an bhfeis, agus ar Chréide, agus ar an seanchas cois na Bóinne, agus ar an bpaiste talún is ea a bhí sé. Saol ansiúd in aontíos léi, b'aoibhneach é. Agus an t-áthas a bheadh ar a athair agus ar a mháthair, agus ar na comharsana! D'fhan sé ar feadh i bhfad ag cuimhneamh ar a mbeadh le déanamh aige faoin seantigh. Ba riachtanach, gan amhras, seomraí beaga eile a chur leis. Bheadh ceann acu mar leabharlann dheas cheolmhar. Smaoinigh sé ar na leabhra go mba mhaith leis a bheith ann. Sa gcéad áit: gach uile leabhar agus leabhrán a bhí le fáil i nGaeilge. B'fhéidir go mbeadh seisean in ann, in éineacht le Créide, togha leabhair, *épopée* dáiríribh, a chumadh sa nGaeilge. Shíleadh sé go minic, go mba mhór an rud é, *épopée* a dhéanamh ar eachtraí, ionadh, agus ollsacht a bhain le hoileáin agus le bóchna an iarthair: barr smaointí na gCeilteach, barr dhraíocht an Ghaelachais iad siúd, dar leis.

Agus an saol a bheadh acu faoin tuath ó ló go ló agus ó shamhradh go samhradh! Agus Baile Átha Cliath – an Bhóinn – an litríocht – Cumann Réalta an Eolais – ina dhiaidh sin is uile – bheadh uaigneas air ina ndiaidh – do b'aisteach an saol – ar réitigh sé le Créide slán a fhágáil ag – ag – ag – chuaigh sé a chodladh ...

Go moch sa mhaidin d'éirigh sé go hobann ina lándúiseacht. Chuimhnigh sé láithreach bonn ar an seanchas cois na Bóinne. Bhí ionadh an domhain air faoi nach ndeachaigh sé go mór in aghaidh Chréide mar gheall ar shaol na tuaithe. Ní raibh an scéal leath chomh simplí agus a shíl sí. Ní raibh na cathracha mar a dtuairisc ach an oiread. Bhí a lán le déanamh acu mar a rabhadar cheana féin. Agus cad a bheadh le rá ag an Athair Dónall dá rithfeadh sé abhaile? An chúis mhór intleachtach a thréigean! Agus imeacht go háit iargúlta! Cad do bhí air cois na Bóinne in aon chor? Tháinig ionadh agus buairt air.

D'admhaigh sé go raibh dúil mhór aige i saol faoin tuath – ar shlí. Ach ba bheag í i gcóimheas leis an dúil a bhí aige i saol liteartha, i dtaoidí smaointí. Agus cónaí ar an bpaiste talún iargúlta – b'ionann é agus deoraíocht ón saol intleachtach. Agus bheadh a mhuintir féin míshásta dá bhfilleadh sé ar obair feirmeoireachta.

Ach bheadh Créide leis! Bheadh draíocht sa tuath mar gheall air sin. Bheadh gan aon agó. Ach nach mbeadh saol ar an bpaiste talún róchrua uirthi? An ceart ligint di dul ann ar aon chuma?

Agus an pósadh! Tháinig amhras air ina thaobh. Bhí Créide cosúil le sióg, le spiorad. Agus sióg mar bhean i seantigh i lár riasca! 'Gile na Gile ar shlí in uaigneas!'

Sin mar a smaoinigh sé ar feadh an lae: go himníoch uair, go hamhrasach uair eile, aoibhneas nár thuig sé air anois agus arís. San Uaimh san oíche scríobh sé an-litir agus chuir sé chuig Créide í. Nochtaigh sé a chroí agus a smaointí ar fad. Dúirt sé sa deireadh gur follas nach rabhadar ach ag taibhreamh an oíche roimhe sin. Ní bheidís sásta le saol ar an bpaiste talún. Bhí a mhalairt de shaol agus de shaothar i ndán dóibh.

Ach nuair a bhí an litir imithe tháinig amhras eile agus

síoruaigneas air!

Maidin lá arna mhárach casadh an tAthair Micheál Ó Gadhra air, agus shiúladar cois na Bóinne ar feadh uaire. Bhí imní mhór ar an sagairtín. Dúirt sé go raibh na seanchléirigh ar buile mar gheall ar an Athair Dónall Ó Dálaigh, go mór mór an óráid a thug sé uaidh ag an gcruinniú poiblí lá na feise. Dúradh i gColáiste na Fairche go gcuirfí cosc ar an Athair Dónall gan mhoill.

I gceann seachtaine fuair Ruairí litir ón Athair Dónall féin. Bhí sé ar tí dul go dtí an tOileán Úr! – le hairgead a bhailiú ar son scoileanna áirithe gur mhian leis an easpag a bheith acu san bhfairche. Bheadh sé thar sáile ar feadh cúpla bliain.

'Tá eagla orthu roimh an irisleabhar,' ar seisean. 'Anois tá sé curtha ar athlá – níos mó ná dhá bhliain. Hélos! Ach b'fhéidir gurb amhlaidh is fearr é. B'fhéidir nach bhfuil an t-aos óg ullamh fós. Lean leat, a chara! Scaip na smaointí. Cuir an síol ins an talamh fónta. Beidh ár *Renaissance* féin againn in am is i dtráth.'

An tAthair Dónall ag imeacht thar sáile! Á dhíbirt as Éirinn! Bhí an lá leis 'les *rigoristes*.'

Ní raibh ach fíorbheagán múinteoireachta eile le déanamh ag Ruairí um an am sin: bhí an téarma caite nach mór, agus ní bheadh buíonta eile ar siúl roimh an bhfómhar. Chuir cairde in iúl dó nach raibh an Coiste Ceantair ar aon intinn faoina atoghadh mar mhúinteoir taistil: níor mhaith le daoine áirithe é: bhí a smaointí agus a bharúla 'róbhaolach.' Ach bhí daoine eile den choiste go mór ar a thaobh, agus ba chosúil go mbeadh troid ar siúl ar theacht an fhómhair.

Smaoinigh sé go géar ar an bhfadhb. Níorbh fhéidir é a réiteach. Seachas an mhúinteoireacht (sa Mhí nó in áit éigin eile) cad a bhí le déanamh aige taobh amuigh den phaiste talún? Dá mba Francach nó Gearmánach nó Sasanach é bheadh an saol liteartha roimhe. Faraor ní raibh ach tús saoil liteartha in Éirinn.

Casadh fear an *Herald* air san Uaimh tráthnóna. Dúirt sé gurbh eol dó conas mar a bhí an scéal ag an gCoiste Ceantair. 'Tá daoine móra áirithe ag obair sa tseanslí,' ar seisean. 'Ach anso sa Mhí ní bhímid chomh critheaglach agus a cheapann siad. Ba cheart dóibh cuimhneamh ar ar thit amach nuair a d'éirigh sinn ar son Pharnell. Ná bíodh ceist ort, a mhic ó! Muna dtoghfaidh an Coiste Ceantair sa bhfómhar thú beidh post le fáil agat ar an *Herald,* agus geallaim duit go mbeidh spórt againn. Ní fear liteartha mé, agus is maith liom saol réidh, ach má bhagraíonn duine orm nó ar chara liom beidh troid eadrainn láithreach bonn. Sin é a fhad is a leithead acu.'

Bhí Ruairí an-bhuíoch de, agus ba gheal leis go raibh an seanfhear chomh dána sin. Ach, dar leis, ba bhocht an rud é a bheith mar thuairisceoir ar pháipéar tuaithe – nó, go deimhin, ar pháipéar na cathrach. Sclábhaithe bochta ab ea tuairisceoirí – agus fo-eagarthóirí, agus eagarthóirí, chomh maith leo. Is é a bhí uaidh: saol smaointeach, neamhspleách, liteartha – d'airigh sé ar uairibh go raibh ábhar céad leabhar ina mheanma. Ach dúirt sé leis an eagarthóir go ndéanfadh sé machnamh ar an gceist ar fad agus go mbeadh trácht acu uirthi in am is i dtráth.

Mhínigh sé an scéal do chairde áirithe, mar Chathal Ó Cinnéide. Scríobh Cathal chuige go cineálta, ach dúirt sé nach raibh ionadh air. Bhí naimhde na smaointí róláidir, agus formhór na nGael ró-chritheaglach aineolach.

'Táim liath ag na Gaeil,' ar seisean. 'Níl misneach ná meanma ná tuiscint iontu. Táim ag ceapadh go mbeadh sé chomh maith dom féin éirí as an múinteoireacht taistil, agus a bheith im thimire i measc na bhfear oibre – bunchloch an náisiúin. B'fhearr duitse an rud céanna a dhéanamh. Táimid go léir ag taibhreamh le fada. Ní bheidh Gaelachas in Érinn go dtí go gcuirfear deireadh le sclábhaíocht agus le daibhreas.'

Bhí gach rud socraithe aige sa Mhí, agus bhí sé ag súil le dul go Baile Átha Cliath, nuair a tháinig litir chuige ó

Chréide – bhí uaigneas air faoi nár scríobh sí roimhe sin.

Chuir an litir an-ionadh air:

'Tá an ceart agat, a Ruairí. Bhíomar ag taibhreamh cois na Bóinne an oíche úd. Ní thuigim an scéal. Ní thuigim an domhan, ní thuigim mé féin. Bhíos cráchroíoch tar éis do litir a fháil. Ach is é an t-ionadh go dtigeann na brionglóidí gach uile oíche, agus bíd níos áille ná a bhíodar cheana. Samhlaítear dom go mbímid go sona ar an bpaiste talún. Bíonn tusa ag déanamh feirmeoireachta go réidh, bímse in éineacht leat, chomh sona le sióg. Ach san am céanna bíonn an fharraige os ár gcomhair – agus dar ndóigh tá an paiste talún i bhfad ón mbóchna – agus bíonn laochra na sean agus anamanna ár gcarad go léir in aice linn. Bíonn sé cosúil le haois forórga, mar a déarfá. Ní féidir cur síos air.'

'Bhíos gan a beith ar fónamh le déanaí. Táim an-ghnóthach anois. Táim ar tí dul go dtí an Coláiste Gaelach i Maoileann na Mara. Is sítheach síúil an áit í de réir gach tuairisce. Is ionúin liom an bhóchna i gcónaí. Ba mhinic a bhíomar ag trácht ar long bheag sí! An féidir leat teacht? Bhí súil agam go mbeifeá in Áth Cliath i bhfad roimhe seo. Scríobhfad chugat go minic, agus muna scríobhfair chugam gach uile lá ...'

'Ní foláir dom brostú,' ar Ruairí leis féin. 'Bead i mBaile Átha Cliath um thráthnóna ...'

Ní hamhlaidh a tharla. Tháinig sreangscéal chuige. Bhí a athair i mbaol báis arís. B'éigean dó filleadh go deifreach ar an bpaiste talún.

XV

Bhí laetha an bhuartha roimh Ruairí ar an bpaiste talún, ach d'éirigh go geal le gach rud i gceann míosa. Tháinig biseach ar a athair. Tháing deartháir dó abhaile ón Oileán Úr, agus airgead aige. Ba mhian leis cónaí ar an bpaiste talún agus cuidiú leis na seandaoine. Bhí go maith. Bhí gach éinne sásta.

Is é an chomhairle ar ar chinn Ruairí ansin triall ar Mhaoileann na Mara, áit a raibh Créide agus a lán dá chairde Gaelacha. Ba mhór le rá an Coláiste Gaelach agus an chomharsanacht agus na hoileáin bheaga taobh thiar di san mbóchna. Bhí eolas aige ar na seanscéalta síúla a bhain leo go léir. Ní raibh sé sa gceantar riamh, ach b'aoibhinn lena chroí an chomharsanacht chéanna agus an bhóchna agus na hoileáin bheaga chlúitiúla. Agus de bhrí go raibh Créide ansin shíl sé go rabhadar mar Thír na nÓg um an am seo.

Na litreacha a fuair sé uaithi le linn a chuairte don phaiste talún chuireadar aoibhneas air i dtosach agus sárionadh air sa deireadh. Thrácht sí ar dtús ar áilleacht na farraige in aice le Maoileann na Mara, ar a dúil i mbádóireacht, ar dhraíocht na n-oileán. Ba mhian léi a bheith ina cónaí ansin go brách.

'Rinne mé dearmad roimhe seo,' ar sise. 'Níor léir dom "mé féin" go dtí anois. Is iontach an t-athrú aigne atá tagtha orm. Ní féidir cur síos air. Measaim go mbíonn an bhóchna sárdhraíochtach naofa. Bím in aice le Tír na nÓg agus mé ag bádóireacht. Agus bíonn na brionglóidí úd níos áille ná riamh. Go deimhin ní ceart "brionglóidí" a thabhairt orthu anois. Airím, a Ruairí, go mbímid in aontíos de ló is d'oíche.'

Dúirt sí i litir eile go raibh saol Átha Cliath mar thaibhreamh di um an am sin. Ní raibh sí tugtha don Choláiste Gaelach féin. Bhí an fharraige agus a draíocht á síormhealladh. 'Tuigim anois, a Ruairí, nach réitíonn sinne – tusa agus mise – le hÉirinn an lae inniu. Bíonn sí róshaolta. Dá mbeimis ag obair sa gcathair nó faoin tuath féin ní bheimis sásta sona. Tá staid agus saothar eile i ndán dúinn. Tuigfir go luath é sin, a ghile mo chroí.'

Ní mó ná go maith a thuig sé an méid sin, áfach. Chuir sé gach rud i gcóir go deifreach, agus chuaigh sé ar a thuras go Maoileann na Mara.

Bhí sé tuirseach ar dhul isteach sa traein dó. Um thráthnóna thit a chodladh air go sámh. Samhlaíodh dó gur dhúisigh sé láithreach bonn in oileáinín i bhfad sa bhfarraige. Bhí Créide roimhe ar an trá, í ag féachaint go grámhar sonasach. Shiúladar tríd an oileáinín. Bhí na céadta Gael ann, Gaeil na seanaimsire ag obair go dúthrachtach le Gaeil an lae inniu. Níor chuir sin ionadh ar bith ar Chréide ná air féin … Phreab sé faoi dheo. Bhí an traein ag druidiúint le Maoileann na Mara.

B'ait an scéal a bhí roimhe. Bhí ionadh agus imní ar a raibh sa gColáiste Gaelach.

Ní raibh Créide le fáil. Ní raibh tásc ná tuairisc uirthi le trí oíche is trí lá.

Chuaigh sí amach tráthnóna sa gcuan i mbád beag mar a chuaigh sí go minic roimhe sin. Bhí Cathal Ó Cinnéide, Eilís Ní Anracháin agus buachaillí agus cailíní eile ag bádóireacht an tráth céanna, corrdhuine acu i mbád beag ina aonar, mar í féin, a bhformhór acu ina mbeirt nó ina gceathrar i mbáid eile. Bhí an aimsir go soineanta, an t-uisce go ciúin, agus b'aoibhinn leis na daoine óga an 'céilí sa gcuan.' Chuaigh cuid acu amach i dtreo an chéad oileáin, ach bhíodar go léir ar ais ar thitim na hoíche – ach amháin Créide. Cheapadar go mbeadh sise ar ais gan mhoill, ach d'imigh cúpla uair agus níor tháinig sí. Bhí ionadh orthu ach ní raibh imní ar éinne, mar bhí oíche bhreá ghealaí ann, agus b'fheasach dóibh a clisteacht ar bhádóireacht. Chonaic cuid acu í agus iad féin ag teacht ar ais: ní raibh sí i bhfad ó bhéal an chuain, ina bád beag, ag rámhaíocht go réidh agus ag gabháil amhráin di féin.

Chuaigh uair eile thart, ach bhí sí gan filleadh fós. D'imigh a lán ar a lorg. Timpeall an mheán oíche bhí gach bád dá raibh le fáil amuigh sa gcuan nó i bhfad ar an bhfarraige i ngach treo. Bhí an oíche go geal glórmhar, ach níor leag éinne súil ar Chréide ná a bád beag in aon aird.

Bhí Cathal Ó Cinnéide, Eilís Ní Anracháin agus buachaill agus cailín eile i mbád faoi leith. Um mheán oíche bhíodar cinnte gur chualadar glór Chréide, í ag gabháil amhráin go meanmnach bródúil. D'éirigh a gcroíthe. D'fhéachadar tharstu ar gach taobh. Ní raibh duine ná deoraí le feiscint ina dtimpeall. Bhí na báid eile i bhfad siar uathu. Lean an amhránaíocht ar feadh tamaill, agus ansin stad sí go hobann. Tháinig síorchiúnas ar an bhfarraige. Tháinig uaigneas orthusan.

Níor cuireadh suas don chuardach go maidin. Ach ní raibh tásc ná tuairisc ar Chréide in aon treo. Dúradh ansin go mb'fhéidir go ndeachaigh sí chun an chéad oileáin. Cuireadh an Coláiste ar athlá. Chuaigh na bádóirí i dtreo na n-oileán. Chuadar ó oileán go hoileán ina raibh daoine ina gcónaí. Bhí a dturas in aistear acu. Ní raibh eolas ar Chréide in aon oileán díobh.

Ansin fuarthas amach – nach raibh bád ar bith ar iarraidh! Agus níor chuimhnigh aon bhádóir go bhfuair

Créide bád uaidh an lá deireanach a bhí sí le feiscint.

Chroith na seandaoine a gcinn. Chuimhníodar ar sheanscéalta a bhain le draíocht na farraige agus le hoileán i bhfad thiar, oileán aerach nár chónaigh duine daonna air leis na cianta.

Sin mar a bhí an scéal ar shroichint Mhaoileann na Mara do Ruairí.

XVI

Is annamh a bhí Ruairí le feiscint i Maoileann na Mara ins na laethanta ina dhiaidh sin, agus nuair a casadh a chairde air anois agus arís bhí ionadh orthu faoi chomh ciúin smaointeach brionglóideach agus a bhí sé. Ní raibh comhartha an bhróin ná rian an uaignis air; ina ionad sin is amhlaidh a bhí cosúlacht áthais air, ach theip ar Chathal Ó Cinnéide féin é a mhealladh chun cainte.

Ba mhinic dó ag bádóireacht ina aonar ar an bhfarraige i bhfad ón gcuan; ba mhinice ná sin, tar éis cúpla seachtain, é a bheith ag siúlóid ar fud na n-oileán. Bhí eolas ag na hoileánaigh ar a chás, chomh maith agus ar scéal Chréide, um an am sin, agus bhíodar fíorchineálta dó; ach tar éis tamaill d'imigh sé leis, agus dúradh gur éalaigh sé go hoileán beag thiar iargúlta nár chónaigh duine ná deoraí ann riamh. Bhí sé amuigh ar an oileáinín gur bhall aerach taibhsiúil é agus níor mhaith leis an oileánach ba mhó dánacht teacht i dtír ann. Chroith na seandaoine a gcinn ar chloisint dóibh go raibh Ruairí ann.

'Rachaidh sé níos sia,' a dúradar.

Nuair a bhí deireadh an téarma sa gColáiste ag druidiúint leo chuaigh Cathal Ó Cinnéide agus cairde eile ar a lorg. Bhí sé ag tóch na talún go saothrach dúthrachtach ar dhroim an iomaire in aice leis an trá ar theacht i dtír dóibh. Tháinig sé anuas chun na trá agus chuir sé togha fáilte rompu. Thrácht sé go beo cineálta ar mhaitheas na talún; bhí súil aige go mbeadh a lán den oileáinín ina gharraí breá fónta lá éigin. Chuadar ina dhiaidh sin go bothán deas aerach a bhí aige ar an taobh thall den oileáinín os comhair na bóchna móire. Bhí uamha móra faoi na haillte; dúirt sé go gcaitheadh sé oíche i gceann acu anois agus arís, ach níorbh eol dó fós an doimhne a bhí iontu ná cá raibh deireadh leo; bhí seanchomharthaí agus seanscríbhinní i gcuid acu. Bhí a thrácht go smaointeach agus go croíúil, agus de réir dealraimh bhí a aigne go socair sonasach.

Sular fhágadar slán aige bhí seanchas faoi leith idir Ruairí agus Cathal; na cairde eile ag siúl anseo agus ansiúd, ar na haillte áille, i gcois na trá, nó istigh ins na huamha. Thrácht Ruairí go réidh bríomhar ar an obair a bhí aige le déanamh san oileáinín, agus ar chomh socair saothrach a bhí a aigne.

'Tamall ó shin,' ar seisean, 'ní chreidfinn go mb'fhéidir a leithéid a bheith i ndán dom. Bhíos ag smaoineamh ar throid intleachtach in Éirinn. Ní fiú a leithéid de ghnó ar aon chuma; ní bhíonn ann ach caitheamh anama. Ní foláir dúinn *la vie créatrice* a chur ar aghaidh go ciúin dílis, agus beidh tír an ionaidh agus Ríocht Neimhe againn dá bharr. Bhí a lán le rá ins na seanscéalta faoi Dhomhan na nUiscí. Bíonn draíocht faoi leith in uiscí, agus bíonn ár n-anamanna freagrach don draíocht. An gnáthdhomhan, Domhan na nUiscí, Tír na nÓg: mar sin a bhíos an cúrsa. Chuaigh mé féin ón bpaiste talún agus ó Bhaile Átha Cliath – an gnáthshaol – go dtí an Bhóinn agus ansin tháinig anseo chun na bóchna. Bhí m'anam ag corraí is ag dúiseacht san am céanna. Is í Tír na nÓg an chéad staid eile, agus bím dom ullmhú i gcomhair na sárstaide céanna. Agus maidir le Créide –'

'Ó,' ar Cathal, 'bhí eagla orm trácht uirthi, cé go rabhas ag smaoineamh uirthi ó thús deireadh. Tá an scéal go-go-go –'

'Go haoibhneach glórmhar,' ar Ruairí go ciúin simplí. 'Níor dheacair di dul go Tír na nÓg. Thuigeas cuid den scéal ó na litreacha a chuir sí chugam agus mé ar an bpaiste talún. Is iontach mar a bhíos a réim ins na hoileáin agus sa mbóchna seo – nó ba cheart dom a rá sna hoileáin rúnda, sa mbóchna spioradálta ag a mbíd seo mar chorp agus cumhdach. Bím in aice léi cheana féin – níos gaire di ná ar bheith i nGleann na Bóinne nó ar Chill Iníon Léinín dúinn – agus de réir mar a shaothród an talamh, agus mar a chuirfead mo mheanma agus m'anam chun críche bead in éineacht léi ar shlí níos iontaí agus níos spioradálta. Anois féin tá brí na beatha agus cúrsa an chine dhaonna níos soiléire go mór dom ná ar theacht dom anseo go hOileán Chréide – Is é sin an t-ainm atá againn air. Ach is mithid dom stad, a Chathail, a chroí, nó beidh tú cinnte id aigne go bhfuilim as mo mheabhair ar fad.'

'Is ionadh liom an scéal ar fad,' ar Cathal. 'Ach airím draíocht éigin san oileáinín, sa mbóchna, agus ionam féin, agus chreidfinn a lán nár chreideas roimhe seo. Ach beidh tú uaigneach anseo, agus rud eile: táir ag teastáil in Éirinn.'

'"Go huaigneach" a deirir, a Cathail! Bím i gcuideachta nach bhfuil a leithéid faoin ngréin. "Ag teastáil in Éirinn:" sea, gan amhras; táimid go léir ag teastáil in Éirinn. Ach cá bhfuil Éire nó cad í? An áit úd a mbíonn eagla ar dhaoine roimh intleacht agus smaointí; an áit úd a mbíonn síorchlamhsán faoi phointí gramadaí; áit na santachta, áit an daibhris, áit an dobhróin – níl inti sin ach cuid shuarach d'Éirinn. Is rud intleachtach, meanmach, spioradálta í an mhór-Éire, an fhíor-Éire. Tá sise á taispeáint dom ina mórgacht, ina háilleacht, ina grámhaireacht faoi dheoidh. Tá súil agam go ndéanfaidh mé, in éineacht le Créide, sárobair ar a son. Go dtí anois ní raibh eolas mo cheirde agam i ndáiríribh.'

Bhí Cathal agus a chairde go smaointeach ar theacht ar ais go Maoileann na Mara dóibh. Níor thuigeadar staid Ruairí. Bhí sé cosúil le duine ó dhomhan eile. Ach ba léir dóibh gur shíl seisean go raibh a chás go nádúrtha agus go haoibhneach.

'Bímid, na Gaeil, ag trácht ar iontaí go han-mhinic,' ar Cathal, agus iad ag druidiúint san oíche ghealaí le cuan Mhaoileann na Mara. 'Admhaímid go raibh sáriontaí ann anallód. Cad mar gheall ar ár n-aimsir féin? Cad a bheifear á rá in Áth Cliath faoi scéal Ruairí agus Chréide?'

Bhí duine amháin in Áth Cliath a mheas go raibh an scéal go feiliúnach, glórmhar. Fiontán Ó Conghaile, athair Chréide, an duine sin. Bhí uaigneas ar a chroí ina diaidh, ach bhí áthas ar a anam de bhrí gur éalaigh sí go sítheach síúil ar staid rúnda fhíorbheoga.

Um an am sin fuair sé litir faoi dheireadh thiar thall ó Eibhlín Ní Dhónaill. Phreab a chroí ar dtús. Ón Oileán Úr a tháinig an litir. Litir an-fhada ab ea í. Dúirt Eibhlín go ndeachaigh sí cúpla lá roimhe sin go feis mhór a chuir Gaeil ar bun. Bhí áthas uirthi faoin tuairisc a thug teachtairí uathu ar an mbeocht in Éirinn an lae inniu. Bhí sí saibhir; b'aoibhinn léi cuidiú leis an obair. Mhínigh sí conas mar a tharla an saibhreas ina treo. Blianta ó shin, nuair a bhí sí bocht brónach, phós sí le seanmhilliúnaí. Bhí dó croí aici riamh ó shin faoi go ndearna sí amhlaidh óir bhí a croí tugtha d'Fhiontán féin i gcónaí. D'éag a fear cúpla bliain tar éis an phósta. Dhá shaibhre a bhí sí bhí a saol gan sonas gan suaimhneas ó bhliain go bliain. D'éirigh sí dóchasach ar chloisint scéal nua-Éireann di. Ba gheal léi bheith ina seirbhíseach do Chaitlín Ní Uallacháin. Rachadh sí go hÉirinn dá mba mhian le Fiontán é.

Léigh Fiontán an litir ina leabharlann bheag. Ansin bhí sé ag smaoineamh ar feadh i bhfad. Faoi dheireadh d'éirigh sé go mall. Chuir sé an litir sa tine. D'oscail sé an fhuinneog. D'fhéach sé chun na farraige agus chun na spéire. Dhearc sé ar na réalta gan teorainn gan áireamh …

Tháinig sé ar ais chun an bhoird. Bhí cosúlacht deoir ina shúile ach bhí rian áthais ar a ghnúis. Fuair sé lámhscríbhinn mhór. Lean sé á scríobh go ciúin ...

Casadh Cathal Ó Cinnéide ar Fhearghas Ó Ruanaí oíche fhómhair, agus Fearghas ag dul abhaile tar éis cruinniú de Chumann Réalta an Eolais. Bhí seanchas acu faoi Ruairí agus faoi Chréide.

'Is aisteach an rud é go gcuireann an scéal an oiread sin ionaidh ar dhaoine, ar Ghaeil go mór mór,' a dúirt Fearghas. 'Imíonn "daoine" ar shlí aisteach gach bliain, agus ní bhíonn trácht ar an imeacht. Mar shampla: bíonn fear óg go fileata smaointeach, agus a chroí ag cur thar maoil le grá dá thír agus dá cúis. Ach ar fháth éigin, nó gan fáth ar bith, cailleann sé a fhilíocht, a ardáthas, a ghrá, agus a dhílseacht, agus ní bhíonn le feiscint ach clamhsánaí agus duine gan éifeacht. Is ea, imíonn an mórdhuine fileata cé go bhfanann an cholainn chéanna inár measc. Is uafásach an t-imeacht é, ach ní chuireann sé ionadh ar ár bhformhór. Bíonn Éire ag cailleadh daoine intleachtacha spioradálta gach bliain de bhrí nach mbíonn sí intleachtach spioradálta inti féin – ní féidir léi a gcoimeád ina measc, nó má choimeádann sí a gcolna agus a ngnáthmheanma ní bhíonn a n-anamanna go beoga éifeachtach.'

D'admhaigh Cathal go raibh an ceart aige sa méid sin.

'Maidir le Ruairí agus Créide,' ar Fearghas, 'tá a mhalairt de scéal ann. Bíd araon ar ardstaid, go mór mór Créide. Sin rud nach dtuigeann formhór ár gcarad. Ceapann a lán Gael nach féidir le daoine bheith ag obair ar son na hÉireann muna mbíd le feiscint inár measc anseo ar thalamh na Éireann. Tá *le matérialisme* tagtha orthu gan fhios dóibh.'

Stad sé nóiméad agus ansin dúirt sé:

'B'aoibhinn liomsa a bheith i bhfad in oileáinín aoibhinn i mbóchna an iontais, chomh maith le Ruairí – bím ann ar shlí ar uairibh – ach tá a lán le déanamh agam anseo i mBaile Átha Cliath go fóill. Tá nithe móra le cur chun críche agam ar son comhoibrithe, nithe móra nach bhfuil éinne eile toilteanach a dhéanamh faoi láthair. Dóchas na hÉireann – dóchas an domhain – comhoibriú. Ach bíonn comhoibriú rúnda meanmach spioradálta ann chomh maith le comhoibriú saolta; agus cuidíonn Ruairí agus Créide leis an gcomhoibriú rúnda sin, go mór mór Créide, óir bíonn sise ar an staid is iontaí. Bíd ag obair sa mór-Éirinn – tír níos naofa agus níos doimhne ná a airímid anseo ins an ngnáth-Éirinn.'

'Téann sin thar m'eolas,' ar Cathal. 'Is trua nach féidir le duine bocht brí na beatha a fháil amach gan dua gan deacracht –'

'Ní foláir do gach éinne oibriú go dian – chomh dian agus is féidir leis – lena lámha agus lena mheanma gach lá dá shaol,' ar Fearghas. 'Obair agus smaoineamh, smaoineamh agus obair: is iad na múinteoirí is fearr iad, is iad seirbhísigh an anama iad.'

D'fhéach Cathal chun na spéire, agus chuir na mílte réalta saghas uaignis agus scanraidh air.

'Is áibhéil ilfhillteach an chruinne í,' ar seisean. 'Níl teorainn léi in aon tslí: corpartha, meanmnach, ná spioradálta. Níl aon mhíniú le fáil uirthi – an ceann is doimhne níl ann ach iarracht.'

'Agus nach aoibhinn dúinn a bheith ag obair agus ar oilithreacht i gcruinne atá chomh hiontach san?' ar Fearghas. 'Níl teorainn lenár maoin. Siúlaimid trí dhraíocht agus trí dhiagacht. "Lán de Zeus na cathracha, lán de Zeus na cuanta, lán de Zeus is ea ilslite na ndaoine".'

The Boyne and the Sea

I

On a sunny afternoon in the summer of 19_, a trim and lovely young woman entered the Gaelic League building in Dublin and asked a clerk was Diarmaid Mac an tSuaircis in. If so, she wanted to speak with him for a few minutes. Her name was Créide Ní Chonghaile, she said in a pleasant, musical voice.

The clerk was surprised. He had often heard mention of Créide Ní Chonghaile. People said that she was highly educated, but he didn't think the young woman before him looked highly educated. He thought that a highly educated woman would be haughty and a bit lacking in good cheer. And as for Créide, she was unaffected and modest and looked innocent. She was slender and petite – no taller than five feet or so – and beautiful. Her fair, lovely face was at once both cheerful and pensive and she had elfin eyes. The clerk called to mind a good deal of poetry about goddesses, but he couldn't think of a bit of it that would be appropriate to describe Créide, her eyes in particular. It seemed to him that the poets were too earth-bound.

He jumped up and went to look for Diarmaid.

Diarmaid was very busy, but he came to the door of his room at once and gave Créide a warm welcome. Looking delighted, he asked her to come in. One would have thought that she was a Gaelic princess and that Diarmaid was an hospitable and princely chieftain on whom she was paying a visit.

What she wanted was precise information (numbers, etc.) concerning *feiseanna*, travelling teachers, Irish-language colleges, etc. A friend in America had asked her to get this information for her. It was needed for an article in an American magazine.

Diarmaid gave her the information promptly, clearly and gladly. You would think that was the only thing he had been awaiting for a long time. You would think that he wanted nothing more than to send full information about what the Gaels were doing to America.

Créide was about to leave when the door opened and who should come in but the lord of the West, the poet of the countryside, the noble storyteller from the back country, Dr Mánas Ó Dúda? His eyes lit up when he looked at Créide.

'Well, I'm delighted to see you,' he said. 'It's a long time since we last met. And you're a B.A. now! The youngest B.A. in Ireland and the most beautiful, I'd say, except I'm afraid you'd say I was trying to flatter you.'

'As you always do,' said Créide.

'Oh! Oh! Oh!' said the Doctor. 'Me, a flatterer! Me! Who is vexed and shrunk to a heap of worry with laymen and clergy badgering me and the responsibility for all the rascals like Diarmaid on my shoulders! You're mocking me, fairest flower in the land. But where have you been for so long?'

'I was searching for Ireland and it is hard to find,' said Créide and she smiled. 'Yes, it's very hard to find. Now and again, I think you are doing great harm, Doctor.'

'What?' said the Doctor.

'Yes,' she said. 'You urge us to be Gaelic and to take a deep interest in all things Gaelic. Well and good we say and we read the great old stories until our minds are awash in heroism and magic and we think that Ireland is a heroic and poetic place –'

'And in the name of the League, isn't that –'

'Instead, it is a poor, tormented, unfortunate place, as is clear to us at once. The Ireland of the heroes, the Ireland of Cú Chulainn, is not to be found at all. Therefore we are troubled and sad. We are dissatisfied about everything. You, and people like you, are responsible for that.'

'What you say is clever,' said the Doctor. 'But, fairest flower in the land, you are too hard on me altogether. Without a doubt there is a big difference between the world of your mind and the ordinary world, for that mind is truly delightful and otherworldly. But that is not thanks to either me or to stories in Irish, but rather to God and your heritage.'

'Wasn't I right?' said Créide to Diarmaid. 'The Doctor is a consummate flatterer.'

Diarmaid laughed. He was usually laughing when he was not putting his whole heart into his work.

'How is my old friend and the dear friend of the Gaels, your brave, hero-hearted father?' the Doctor asked Créide.

'To tell you the truth, I know little about him,' said the young woman quietly and affectionately. 'He is a secretive man and it seems that there is usually something worrying him. He comes home from the newspaper – he named it *The Blabberer* long ago – late at night and then he stays in his study for a long time. Who knows what he's doing? He is tired and silent the next day. At any rate, you would think that the world was of no concern to him at all.'

'That's odd,' the Doctor said. 'He used to do great work for literature in Irish years ago when workers were scarce anywhere in Ireland. He used to discuss the storytelling and the lore of the ancients cogently in the *Irisleabhar*. It's an odd thing and a great pity that he is not in our midst these days, with the Gaels feeling young at heart.'

After that Créide said that she had to leave, but immediately the door opened and a young man looked in. He was startled.

'Excuse me,' he said. 'I thought Diarmaid was alone.'

'Come in, Ruairí,' said Diarmaid. 'Don't worry. There are only friends here before you.'

The young man came in. He was slender and good-looking, shy and pensive. But if he was shy and pensive, it was clear that he was also energetic and independent, although his eyes were a bit dreamy. You'd think he combined in himself shyness, bravery and poetic force.

'You've known the Doctor for a long time,' said Diarmaid, 'and you probably know Miss Ní Chonghaile also. "Créide" of the *Claidheamh* who wrote those poetic articles you praised so highly when we were talking the other day.'

'I know "Créide" very well,' said the young man, 'but I never saw Miss Ní Chonghaile before now.'

'That's odd,' said Diarmaid. 'I heard you praising the poetic articles she wrote and I heard her praising the philosophical articles you wrote. You might say that you were close in the intellectual world but did not know each other at all in the ordinary world until now.'

He looked from Ruairí to Créide and from Créide to Ruairí.

'Créide Ní Chonghaile, a goddess and a B.A. – Ruairí Ó Duibhir, travelling teacher, poet of Tara and philosopher,' he said gallantly.

Everyone laughed. Ruairí liked laughter. He couldn't say a word to Créide. He was overcome with shyness and wonder and joy. He thought that in some way he could not understand he had known Créide for a long time. Images of old *feiseanna* and of ancient gatherings appeared before his eyes. He and she were there. Delightful music was being played and unusual voices could be heard around them. It seemed to him that his ordinary memory was being extended in a wonderful way.

The Doctor put his right hand on Ruairí's shoulder and looked at Créide.

'Since you're acquainted with each other now,' he said, 'I ask you, fairest flower, never to pay too much attention to what this Ruairí says.'

Créide laughed.

'It's no laughing matter,' said the Doctor. 'A couple of years ago, he was as unaffected and natural as a young priest, except that he believed in fairies, something never said of a priest. But he went to the province of Meath as a travelling teacher and an extraordinary magic took hold of him in the Boyne valley. You would think that the Dagda and Aengus Óg were his neighbours. He doesn't believe that the visible world is real and substantial. It's a philosophical illusion. And some of his opinions about the world are frightful. The Gaelic notes he writes for a local paper in Meath scare me. And the fact that travelling teachers and other Irish speakers are following his example augurs trouble. We will have a big new problem to deal with. We will have another *dies crisimus* in Gaelic Ireland.'

'I'm glad to hear that,' said Créide. 'I'm delighted that there are people – even one single person – who believe that the world is not as it seems to be. I have often read in books that "the Gael recreates the world" until he is living in a separate universe, a spiritual universe, an otherworldly universe, but I'm afraid that that is just flattery. If Mr. Ó Duibhir believes that the world is not real and substantial, he is the first true Gael who ever came my way.'

She looked at Ruairí and smiled again.

'Oh! Oh! Oh!' said the Doctor. 'The first true Gael is it! According to you, neither I myself nor our brave and jovial Diarmaid is a true Gael. "Oh, that is what sickened and tormented me!" Now I would like for the world to be unreal because then your bad opinion would not be real either.'

They kept up a joking conversation for a while, the Doctor and Diarmaid saying that the 'universe' and eternity were fine for philosophers, but simple, honest people had to be satisfied with their own country and today's work.

'You two are witty as usual,' said Ruairí, 'but my opinion is that the Gaels are becoming too worldly and that they take too much interest in the "nation" and in the "world," and in everything common. I've thought for a long time that the "world" and "time" and "body" and "ordinary life" are false gods and the greatest tyrants to be found. We have a great deal to say about revival and about freedom. The real revival and the real freedom would be in ourselves if we truly understood and had the courage. Today's Gaels don't know the road to *Tír na nÓg*.'

'And where is that road?' Créide asked calmly. 'I would like to travel it. The roads by Dublin Bay and the roads to the mountain are nice, but they don't satisfy my heart. The road to *Tír na nÓg*! Where is it? Where is it? Or is it a mystery?'

Ruairí smiled. It would be delightful, he thought, to show her the road to *Tír na nÓg*. But what he said aloud was: 'I'm afraid you're joking. At any rate, the story of that road is a long one.'

'That's a pity,' said Créide. 'If that is so, I'll have to be content with the road to Killiney. And it's time for me to go now.'

She bid them goodbye and left.

Ruairí felt a profound loneliness. For a couple of minutes he was about to start out after her. He almost forgot the Doctor and Diarmaid.

Then he remembered where he was. I'm a big fool, he said to himself.

He did the business he had to do with Diarmaid and left. He knew that Créide would be gone, but still he felt sad and lonely that she was not to be seen. Even so, there was happiness mixed with the sadness and loneliness.

He used often think in the days before that that there were many 'people' in himself: one that craved solitude, another that wanted to do great work in the world, yet another that was very literary and so on. He would be poetic at one time. Philosophic at another. He had sensed by now that there was another 'person' in him, a person with whom Créide had a mystical bond. What was the unifying factor among all these people? What was the explanation for human life itself? It was like the sea. It changed every hour and there was no limit to its depth or its wonder. He remembered a line from a French poet:

L'océan éternel où bouillone la vie.

Yes, but it was a pity that one could not learn more about the meaning of the 'sea' during his 'life.'

As he was going along O'Connell Street, he looked from side to side hoping to see Créide. Alas, he did not.

It is very strange, he said to himself. I never before believed in the enchantment of women and enjoyed only a few love stories in any language. May love stay far from me! It is usually a worldly and dangerous thing. It does not suit Créide. She has nothing to do with the ordinary world. She is a being from the otherworld, a spirit. I would love to find out what she thinks of people and the world, the heart and the universe.

II

Near O'Connell Bridge, Ruairí met another travelling teacher, Cathal Ó Cinnéide, who had been working for a while in Wexford. As usual, he had books old and new under his arm. He came to Dublin almost every Saturday, browsed through bookshops of every sort and bought what attracted him – old things in particular – if he had the money.

'Let's have tea, philosopher of Tara,' he said after a couple of minutes. 'I'm as tired as a man who has been listening to the minutes of the League's Executive Committee.'

Ruairí would have preferred to be walking alone and thinking about Créide. But he and Cathal were great friends and he couldn't refuse him.

They went to a hotel nearby. Cathal was a young, lighthearted man, but however lighthearted, he could be quite bold, particularly about intellectual things. He loved to debate, about history, psychology and art. He called himself the 'enemy of common opinion.' He wasn't as tall or slender as Ruairí, but he was good-looking and powerfully built, with a clear complexion, a hero's cheek, lively eyes and a well-formed head of curly black hair. He looked like a good-hearted warrior.

'There are two men in me, Ruairí,' he said when they were drinking their tea. 'They fight each other every day. One of them wants a sword and supremacy. He wants to resurrect the Fianna and overthrow and drive out the bad Irish people and the enemies of Ireland. He would banish most of the farmers and the shopkeepers. He would leave the odd teacher like Pádraic Mac Éanna in charge in the country to establish true education – especially for the children of the poor – as well as priests like Father Dónall Ó Dálaigh and Father Micheál Ó Gadhra, of whom there aren't many. There would be armed warfare and a war for the exploited labourers in Ireland. But the other man in me has a longstanding love of esoteric literature –'

'Perhaps there is a link between the two of them,' said Ruairí. 'True literature is a kind of heroism –'

'Perhaps, but I'm getting impatient with literary men. Fighting is far more appropriate for the Ireland of today than even the most profound literature. If Fionn were among us he would put his seven curses on literature and storytelling and ideas until we had beaten our enemies. I'm ashamed of my love for books. Still, I have a couple of gems here.'

He took *La Tentation de Saint Antoine* by Flaubert and showed it to Ruairí.

'I don't like Flaubert,' said Ruairí. 'He had a beautiful "style," but that's all.'

'I was of the same opinion before I found this book,' said Cathal. 'I've been reading it all afternoon, even in the streets. I now know that there were two Flauberts and the Flaubert who wrote *La Tentation de Saint Antoine* was a poet and a philosopher. From a book like this one understands the beauty and the magic of language. Indeed language is itself a poet, a spirit. And the theme that is the basis of this book! *La Tentation* deals with all of the *penchants naturels*; it deals with beauty, with knowledge, with power, with the highest form of love. It is a universal story, or a universal poem. Isn't it high time for us, the Gaels, or for the majority of us at any rate, to bid farewell to the potato and the boreen and to make an attempt at real ideas and good writing?'

Ruairí laughed.

'I like even potato prose and boreen poetry, if they are natural and fitting. The potato is a fine component of the universe and boreens go to the Land of Wonders in their own way. But I agree with you about noble thoughts and great mental effort. I do my best myself! I begin on a new *épopée* every week. *La Tentation* reminds me that I once tried to see a mystical poem in the story of St Kevin –'

'It wasn't worth the effort,' said Cathal. 'The murder of Kathleen! It was a terrible thing.'

'The story was most likely a parable. "Sanctity" against the "Feminine" –'

Cathal smiled wryly.

'We should all understand the sanctity of women,' he said, 'but most Irishmen since the time of the Fianna have not understood it. Ireland has been full of false ideas for hundreds of years and the worst of those ideas was the foul opinion of fine, righteous, charming women. Wait until I write my book about *The True Sanctity of Women*. The poets will be amazed by my poetry and the philosophers by the force of my philosophy, but I vow that the priests will be even more amazed by the range of my theology and mysticism.'

'You're still young, Cathal,' said Ruairí, 'and you are brave and poetic and you take a great interest in what the poets have said about women –'

His cheek flushed a bit. He remembered Créide Ní Chonghaile. As for writing, he did not think he would have any trouble with it. 'You are a witty philosopher,'

Cathal answered. 'But remember this. Although I am very much on the side of the women, that is not to say that I favour a particular woman or girl. I do not, any more than I favour a particular being from the otherworld. That would be dangerous and foolish – in my case. One's nature cannot be sound unless he has a heartfelt friendship, an affection even, for women. That is as necessary for him, as beneficial for him, as are art and literature and philosophy. But it would be a strange thing for a person to be obsessed with only one picture or one book. In the same way –'

'Poetic joking, Cathal! There is a great deal of difference between women and books! It is possible to avoid them all or to love one of them, but the way of doing things you're talking about is a comical dream.'

'We are too given to rules and to opinions, Ruairí. One should travel his own road. The proverb says "To each his own," but it is usually forgotten. I'm not interested in marriage. In the first place I don't have a real livelihood and I like freedom. But I find women as delightful as I do literature. I now have a nice and easy intellectual love for seven separate girls. I need not say that none of them is aware of the situation. That love is a source of great satisfaction to my heart. It is like otherworldly music or like a view of the sea at sunrise on a summer morning.'

'Of all the things I've ever heard!' said Ruairí. 'But by Aengus it's a nice story. There's nothing can beat it, not even in all the stories of the middle ages. It beats *les troubadours* and *die Meistersinger* altogether. Good luck to you and the Seven Girls. But don't be too satisfied, too dreamy, too complacent. We should all encourage Ireland and the young. Much depends on us travelling teachers. We do not understand our duty or half of our power either –'

'What other great deeds, what else big or small, can we do?'

'Many other things, Cathal. I have no doubt at all about

that. I think that there is in everyone a soul that comes into the world with a particular job to do and that when it has done that it goes into another state of being to do another job. If it doesn't finish the work, or doesn't do it right, I think that it must come back to finish it – in another body. I am not yet entirely certain about the real work for me, but I think it involves being a travelling teacher and reviving the mysteries of ancient Ireland – I have understood that since coming to Meath. The two things go together. The travelling teachers are a special new order. If we were learned, knowledgeable, independent and zealous, we would be able to spread ideas and awaken strength of mind in a wonderful way. And then –'

'Despite all that, it is not clear to me that the travelling teachers can do anything heroic,' said Cathal. 'There is, alas, a great difference between us and the Fianna, or between us and –'

'Let's leave it like that. We don't need the Fianna or other heroes of ancient times. I'm glad that the Fianna are not to be seen or found in today's Ireland. I'd rather have them in stories than in the real world. They were always fighting and hunting. In some ways they were fine in their own day, but there is a more profound and intellectual spirit in us. For that reason we must advance and bring into existence a fine, generous, special and purposeful world. It is a great mistake to be looking backwards as we are. We incorporate all that there was in the past – we have it all or it is in us in a mystical way – and it is our duty to advance and be constantly creating. The reason we are distressed and miserable is that we do not usually have *la Vie Créatrice* in us.'

'That is true and poetic advice, my dear philosopher,' said Cathal cheerfully. 'But it is time for us to act. It is all very well to be arguing back and forth about fate and about the universe, but the Central Branch's *céilí* will be happening soon. Liam and Art and Críostóir told me that it would beat the best festival ever. Dr Ó Dúda and many other leaders will be there and, something even more delightful than that, one of the Seven Girls will be there: Her Majesty, Créide Ní Chonghaile, Goddess, B.A.'

He got up suddenly, as did Ruairí.

Cathal continued speaking lightheartedly as they went out. Ruairí did not fully understand at first. He was overcome with loneliness and sorrow. Créide! Cathal! If they were ever in love –

Cathal gripped his shoulder.

'Wake up, philosopher,' he said cheerfully. 'You're in O'Connell Street now, not in the wilds of Meath. What is the difficult question troubling you! What's wrong with the universe?'

Ruairí smiled. He told himself it was a strange thing to forget the universe because of a girl.

III

When Cathal and Ruairí reached the big hall, the *céilí* was in full swing. There were many people talking here and there and every one of them was to all appearances merry and happy. It was a kind of *feis,* and people who weren't much interested in dancing – like Ruairí himself – were happy just to be there. People were joking over here and discussing points of grammar over there. They were talking about literature in one corner and arguing about education in another. You would think from all the talking that there was no limit to the intellectual life of Ireland, that it was full of force and energy, that it was at once both sociable and independent. There were teachers there as well as a good number of clerks, shop attendants, craftsmen and many others. It appeared that there were no distinctions at all among them. No one felt anything but cordiality and kindliness.

During the *céilí* – as was usual in gatherings of that kind – it was easy for Ruairí to think that the reign of the Gaels and Gaelic culture had never been broken. One would think, he told himself, that there had always been a fine, mystical race in the country and that members of that race would go to the Gaelic gatherings. It was not hard to imagine that the Tara of the ancients and the Dublin of today were somehow connected, or, indeed, that it was people of the ancient times who were present, as alive as they ever were.

Before he became aware of it, his mind was filled with joy; even his body felt light. It seemed to him that music and poetry were rising easily and freely and wonderfully in his mind, but there were no notes to the music and there were no words in the poetry; they were like the raw material of music and poetry. Where is the true origin of poetry? What is the mysterious state from which it arises? Was he nearer to it then? He felt that he was.

The fact of the matter, he told himself after a while, is that we are not usually truly awake, we are not usually living our true life. Our souls are hidden from us. We move through a desert. Yes, but now and then we come to *feiseanna* like this one and in some strange way the deep powers and the mysterious tides of the universe are clear to us. It is a mystery and cannot be explained. There are people here talking about grammar and other people talking about love, yet other people talking about education, nationality, books, art, life in the country and so on. None of them are talking about life itself or about the most wonderful significance in the gathering and in themselves. But everyone feels it, it kindles every heart, big or little, and it changes every mind. It seems that little happens during gatherings of this kind, but in fact we have beautiful adventures, adventures of the mind – spiritual adventures.

He spoke with many people. He spoke with Dr Ó Dúda about storytelling in the countryside, with Pádraic Mac Éanna about education in the distant past and today, with Dr Mac Shligigh about grammar, with Taidhgín the Poet about ancient poetry, with Diarmaid Mac an tSuaircis about elegant writing, with Eoghan Ó Niallagáin about the religion of the Celts, and with other people about music and about the co-operative movement. The discussion was always lively, but he felt that there was something more alive in every person there, something that he could not express clearly and that it was exactly the same with himself. 'People' were talking and spirits in them were watching and listening.

Cathal Ó Cinnéide came towards him at last.

'I'm worn out from all this dancing and laughing,' said Cathal. 'A *céilí* is an amazing thing. It takes away one's sense and memory. The modern *céilí* is a kind of intoxication. Everyone here is out of his ordinary mind. A *céilí* is an excellent part of *l'illusion universel*. There is magic in gatherings. St Anthony, St Kevin and all the holy hermits were right. Learning and solitude, sanctity and deserts suit each other.'

'I have a different opinion now,' said Ruairí. 'I discovered tonight that the poetry and the divinity of the people emerge during cheerful gatherings. It is clear to me that there was a mystical reason for the festivals of the Greeks and the *feiseanna* of the Gaels long ago. It is also clear to me that there is some meaning that our intellect does not understand in modern *feiseanna* and *céilithe*. The Gaels understand more than they realise. When they are enjoying themselves in each other's company, if only just dancing, they are preparing themselves for some beautiful world; they are on a mystical road without their knowing it –'

'I am delighted to hear it,' said Cathal cheerfully, 'because I very much want to dance and have fun tonight and it is a fine thing that there is a mystical meaning in that. This is a great night. I thought only one of the Seven Girls would be here, but three of them came – Yes, three! Now one of them is waiting for me, as the long dance is about to begin.'

He went away in good spirits.

A little while after that Ruairí saw that he was dancing up a storm with Créide. She was looking lovely and she danced in a lively and artful way. Ruairí only watched her and the dancing for a couple of minutes. He was overcome by loneliness and a kind of fever. He moved to the door. He told himself that he would have to leave, but when he reached the door he didn't want to go. He stayed there, pensive and troubled.

He heard two men talking. It was Dr Ó Dúda and Dr Mac Shligigh. They were going home and they were debating a difficult question of grammar. Dr Mac Shligigh was saying in a loud voice that everyone was wrong about this question except himself and Windisch and Laoide. Dr Ó Dúda was convinced that every old woman in Conamara understood it properly. He called to Micheál Mag Tuireadh, the jovial gardener, who was near them. He explained the question to him. Micheál's eyes lit up. He began to make a speech, his face alight, his arms waving. People gathered all around him. Some of them had no interest in the question, but they were very interested in Micheál and they gave a great shout of praise and appreciation.

Micheál was often a subject of discussion. Ruairí knew many of his stories. He was amazed by the force and fluency of his oration was about a minor question of grammar! He thought that there was not another country under the sun in which the like would be heard from a gardener. His heart rose. Without a doubt Ireland was a fine country!

The *céilí* was over. People were coming out from the hall talking and laughing; you would think from listening to them that there had been a hundred *céilithe* going on at the same time.

'I was afraid you'd gone,' said Cathal Ó Cinnéide to Ruairí, coming up to him suddenly. 'There are two goddesses here and they would like to talk to you. They've heard that you hate women and therefore you will be a marked man. A word to the wise,' he said in a low voice, 'they are two of the Seven Girls.'

It was Créide and a friend of hers, Eilís Ní Anracháin.

'I was talking to Mr. Ó Duibhir this afternoon,' said Créide cheerfully. 'I thought that he was a normal Gael, but he took no interest in me during the *céilí*.'

'Oh, shame on you,' said Cathal to Ruairí. 'You will give all of the travelling teachers a bad reputation. I will write to the Executive Committee complaining about you. But I have no time to argue with you now. We have to go to the Pillar. Ordinary life is grim and mean and the last tram will not wait, even for lovely goddesses.'

Cathal and Eilís went ahead. Ruairí and Créide walked behind them.

Ruairí was blissful. But he was unable to say a word at first. Then he asked Créide whether she had enjoyed the *céilí*.

'I enjoyed it very much in some ways,' she said, 'but in one way I did not. It did, however, seem to me that it was a remarkable *céilí*. I am not usually happy during gatherings. In fact I am usually lonely. But I found out tonight, or so it seemed to me at any rate, that there is a great, secret meaning to the gatherings of the Gaels.'

'That's strange,' he said. 'I myself thought that. The same idea was in my mind throughout the night.'

'But if it's true,' she said, 'it's no wonder that two people would think it. The wonder is that many do not realise it.'

Still, Ruairí thought that it was wonderful that the two of them had the same idea during the night.

'Now and again during the *céilí* there was in my mind a mixture of great joy and a kind of fear,' said Créide. 'I thought I had lived in Ireland many times in past ages. I believed that I had been in Eamhain Mhacha and after that in Tara and in many other places. Then I thought that there had been just one age – one great mystical age – since the beginning of the world – that we, the people of today, are the same people who lived in the time of Cú Chulainn, in the time of the Fianna, and so on. I thought that every ordinary life, or every ordinary age, was, you might say, just a tide of the same sea. How do you explain that?'

'I am hard pressed to explain it,' he said. 'It is easy to think that the thing we call real "time" is only relative, *relatif*. Perhaps we have always been in eternity unbeknownst to ourselves – or to our ordinary intellect – and that "time" and the ordinary mind and the ordinary world are just diminishments, concepts.'

'Yes,' she said 'that reminds me – ah, we're near the Pillar now. I love to think that that Pillar – and Dublin itself – are temporal, transient: that they have nothing to do with "the timeless world".'

They stopped.

'I'll have to say goodbye now,' said Créide. 'I'd like to stay to settle that great question, but the last tram is about to leave and the driver is not interested in the universe. The poor man is thinking about the road to Dalkey. Oh yes, now I remember. We were talking about another road this afternoon – the road to *Tír na nÓg*.' She spoke easily, calmly, lightheartedly. 'When will you show me that wonderful road?'

She reached out her right hand. Ruairí took it in his own right hand.

'It is always the goddess, Niamh of the Golden Hair, who points out the road,' he said. 'It is she and her like who have the choicest knowledge. You are no exception. You are already at the heart of *Tír na nÓg*.'

'There's flattery hiding behind the philosopher's teaching. Shame on you!' she said.

'Many of the Gaels of the city will be going on an excursion to the mountain tomorrow afternoon,' he said.

'In a way the road will be very like the road to *Tír na nÓg*.'

'If so, I'll go,' she said, 'and –'

'We'll meet each other,' he said happily.

The driver rang the bell. They parted, laughing.

In a few more minutes, Créide and her friend were in the tram and it was moving off.

'This was a great night,' said Cathal to Ruairí, as they were walking to their hotel. 'Even so, it didn't satisfy Eilís. We had a big quarrel. She criticised the travelling teachers and all the young Gaels. She said we aren't as strong and daring as were the Gaels in almost every other age. She is an out and out Sinn Féiner. The goddesses have changed greatly. I was thinking of Eoghan Rua Ó Súilleabháin and other great poets during the argument. If they were alive now they would have different dreams and about their visions. The "Goddesses" would have new things to report.'

Ruairí agreed and he began talking rapidly and enthusiastically about Eoghan Rua and those like him and their visions. Cathal was surprised by what he had to say about them. Ruairí spoke like that to avoid talking about Créide. But it was she he was thinking about the whole time.

'I admit that I get tired of the "visions" and the "goddesses",' said Cathal. 'They have nothing to do with the world or with humanity. The Gaels are too concerned with the moon. I would rather have a simple stanza from the true poets of love, like Catullus, or Burns, or those who created the love songs of Connacht, than all of the vision poems put together. "We live in earnest, my Lesbia, we will love and we will love passionately. We mock all the sermons of the gloomy old people … give me a thousand kisses" … and so on. Catullus was in some ways a Gael.'

'He didn't understand the otherworldly nature and the spirituality of love,' said Ruairí.

Cathal became a bit pensive.

'I told you that there are two men in me,' he said at last. 'A literary man and a man with a sword. After my talk with Eilís, the man with the sword has the upper hand. A young man cannot run his life in his own way. When he thinks that he has everything settled, a girl comes and rearranges everything in spite of his best efforts. It is oppressive work, but it is not without delight.'

Ruairí gave a good-humoured laugh, but nevertheless he knew Cathal was right.

IV

While Créide was at the *céilí,* her father Fiontán Ó Conghaile was sitting in his study in his cottage near Dalkey below Killiney. He had been there since morning. Because it was a Saturday he did not have to bother with the newspaper office, and he spent the day exactly as he had spent every Saturday – and any other free time he had – for twenty years – reading and looking through books and writing down his thoughts when he wanted. The books dealt with the mysticism of the ancient world and the druidism of the Celts, with visionary knowledge and with wisdom. In a way he had two lives in those years: the life of a sub-editor in the office – an empty life, he felt, although pleasant enough – and a life among the mystical books. He had no interest at all in any art or science that dealt with corporeal, concrete things, or in contemporary literature in general. He liked the great stories of ancient Ireland – or their mystical meaning I should say – and as for present-day Ireland, he didn't think it was worth a mention: its life had been withering for a long time and not even a druid or a sage could revive it. When he came home from the office every night – or early in the morning – he would go to the study and stay there for a long time instead of going to bed. Essays he wrote under a pen-name would appear from time to time in philosophical journals little-known in Ireland, but the majority of what he wrote was not yet in print. And at any rate, no one but himself and the odd person abroad knew that someone like him existed. He had opinions of his own about life and literature and scholarship; they got stronger from year to year. Many people would, he thought, be amazed and frightened by them. He was absolutely convinced that no one would publish what he had written in Irish and, if it were published, few people would be ready for it. Another thing: he had no interest in fame or recognition. He delighted in thinking and writing and silence.

His life had not been without trouble and very great trouble too. After coming to Dublin as a young man, he had married a young woman from his home place. After a while it was clear to him that he had made a big mistake. The couple were not compatible and Fiontán was dissatisfied and miserable for a long time. Then he chanced to fall in love – a pure and poetic love – with a pretty, intellectual, warm-hearted girl, and that girl – Eibhlín Ní Dhónaill was her name – loved him in the same way. But Eibhlín finally became frightened. She sent him a sad letter and she went off to London and then after a while to America. Fiontán was a lonely, solitary man after she left. He composed profound, mystical poetry about her; some of it was published in a book – under a pen-name – and the book was much discussed for a while, but he never heard a single word about Eibhlín herself. A little while after she went away, his wife died while Créide was still an infant. After that his life was lonelier than ever. His friends thought that it was his wife's death that caused him so much loneliness and sorrow. Rarely did any of them see him outside the office and most of them all but forgot him as time passed. The odd person like Dr Ó Dúda made a considerable effort to rouse him, but they always failed entirely.

He was a skillful sub-editor, although his heart was, predictably enough, not in the work. He was quiet and pleasant in the office and his co-workers respected him. None of them knew that he was a thinker or an author, or that he was serious about anything but sub-editing. When there was discussion of contemporary authors and philosophers, no one at all thought of Fiontán.

He was happy that Créide had been so lovely, otherworldly, and spirited ever since childhood. He used to think that she was like Eibhlín Ní Dhónaill in some ways. He arranged for her to have the finest education and she did. But no one knew that his heart was overflowing with affection and love for his daughter.

He was a slender, affable, pensive man of medium height. His eyes were bright, though they were usually marked by loneliness. His hair and his beard were turning white, although he was only forty-four or so years of age.

With the passing of time, Eibhlín Ní Dhónaill was becoming like Deirdre or Emer in his mind. It seemed to him that she was closer to him than she had been before she left Ireland. He was happy just thinking about her. But now and again he would become impatient with life and with the sub-editing and with philosophy itself; then he wanted to throw over the work altogether and journey afar in search of Eibhlín. He often told himself that he would do so as soon as he had raised Créide. Eibhlín was still young – she was ten years younger than himself – and they would have a happy life yet. At other times, it seemed to him that there was no meaning or permanence in anything except thought and spirit and that it was a great mistake for a person to rely on anything at all having to do with ordinary life. 'Don't ask questions about tomorrow, about ordinary things: that is, arise and join in the mystical noble life of the universe ...'

He heard Créide coming in after midnight. She took off her hat and her cloak. She went to the kitchen and put a kettle on the fire. She hummed a nice, cheerful tune to herself.

After a little while she came to the study and gave her father a cup of coffee. 'Coffee for sleep and tea for staying alert,' she said.

He smiled. It's a strange thing that the Gaels have always been so given to proverbs, he said to himself. It's a pity they are so easy to satisfy.

'I was talking to Dr Ó Dúda tonight,' she said while her father was drinking the coffee. 'He is very sorry that you do not join the Gaels and do the great work you could easily achieve.'

'He's an odd man,' said Fiontán. 'Most of the Gaels today are not doing work worth speaking of. They're just talking and dancing, the Doctor as well. Yes, the Gaels today are always just passing the time or complaining. The heroes and the sages are gone.'

'But father, if you believe the people are not alive and energetic enough, shouldn't you go and inspire them?'

'It would be useless for me to set out to do work like that, Créide. The people you see in Ireland today – the majority of them at any rate – are in a way like trees and stones. Their souls are not functioning. I am working for the invisible Gaels. But it's a long story, one not easy to explain. It will, however, be clear to you some day, Créide dear.'

'I understand well, even now, that we can be working for the invisible Gaels. Indeed all true Gaels are always invisible; that is to say their intellects, their souls, and everything related to eternity are entirely invisible. We were discussing this very question tonight as we were coming home from the *céilí* and as Ruairí said –'

She stopped suddenly and blushed. 'You've drunk your

coffee,' she said taking the cup from him. 'It's too late for a debate about mysticism. I'm getting tired and it's time for me to go to sleep.'

She smiled, said 'Good night, father,' and left the room.

Fiontán grew pensive.

Créide has changed, he said to himself. That much is clear beyond doubt. She is a woman now, however young she is – and it's likely she will be leaving me fairly soon. Who is 'Ruairí?' Someone special obviously. The old story! The old story that always seems new! And when Créide goes off with 'Ruairí,' what about me? I'll be terribly lonely after she goes ... But – I will be free at last! No one will be depending on me. I will be able to take my leave of sub-editing and set off in search of Eibhlín!

He felt very happy. He opened the little window and looked out. The sea below was beautiful in the light of the moon. It was a magical thing, he thought, leading straight to *Tír na nÓg*. He and Eibhlín should be on a wonderful ship on the beautiful sea. There was an otherworldly, spiritual, mystical bond between the human soul and the soul of the sea. The sages and the great storytellers of the ancient Gaels understood that mysterious truth. They knew the wonder, the magic, the sanctity that is in the 'Western Sea' – the true Western Sea, the true Sea that the spiritual eye sees. The Gaels never performed deeds or created literature that was worthy of comparison with the stories that dealt with the sea and the islands of the West. There was magic and divinity in those stories.

Finally he closed the window. He sat down and looked at the books on the shelves around him. Many of them were 'Confessions': Augustine, *La Vita Nuova* by Dante, *Dichtung und Wahrheit* by Goethe, Rousseau, *Apologia pro Vita Sua* by Newman, etc. They didn't satisfy him. He thought that the story of a person's soul was far more profound than those writers suggested.

He had once tried years earlier to write a *confessio* – the story of his life and his sorrow – but ultimately he grew dissatisfied with it.

He looked then at the great books their authors had spent their whole lives creating: Virgil's *Aeneid,* Dante's *Divina Commedia,* Tasso's *Gerusalemme Liberata,* Goethe's *Faust* and more. He had once thought that it was a great thing for an author to devote himself to one big question or one big theme. He had striven to write a new *épopée* based on the story of Cú Chulainn, then on the Fianna, and after that on the druids and St Patrick. But he failed every time. He felt that the life in him was not in tune with theirs. At last he looked at the great books of the East: the *Bhagavad Gita,* the *Dhammapada* and many others. It was those he preferred. But why would a Gael like himself be obsessed with the books and visionary wisdom of the East? And why would someone so fascinated by philosophy and sanctity like those of the East be as infatuated with any woman under the sun as he was with Eibhlín? These were questions he found difficult to answer.

He often expressed his thoughts in the manner of the sages of India and Egypt. One treatise he had written was like the *Bhagavad Gita*; another was like some of the *Pistis Sophia* and so on. Nevertheless he was not satisfied; it seemed to him that in a way he was still just a novice.

He thought that the accepted opinions – and the opinions of the philosophers themselves – weren't even half true with regard to the 'person' and the 'state' and the 'age.' No doubt they were somehow connected, but everyone had to travel his own particular road; everyone had a connection with an invisible world as well as with the visible world and should develop his mystical life, no matter what state his 'country' and his 'neighbours' were in. Therefore Fiontán worked zealously for things and ideas in which Irish people had no interest at all and he wrote books he never expected to publish. It was his duty and his nature. He was certain he was right and therefore he was content.

He opened the window again and looked towards the sea and the sky. It was strange, he thought, how far one could see with his little corporeal eye. But what he could see of the universe was negligible compared to what he could not see: stars without limit or number. And what he saw before his eyes was only a bit of what existed. He didn't see any stars or any planets – suns or great worlds – just points of light. And he knew nothing at all about life and the conditions of life – whatever they were – on any one of them. Thus he could see little of even the material world. Likewise, there was little of the spiritual universe he knew anything about. Human beings were just beginners, children going to the school of the universe. Plato, Plotinus, Eriugena, Dante, Shakespeare, Goethe, were just learners who were a bit cleverer than the mass of the people. The great learning, the real wisdom, was yet to come. Weren't the Gaels making a big mistake lamenting and complaining and thinking that the ages of wonder were over? There would be millions of such ages ahead of them in this world and in other states of being.

It was clear to him then why he had never been satisfied with anything he had written over the years.

V

The excursion to the mountain on the Sunday afternoon was a great success. Hundreds of Gaels both young and old were gathered there. The weather was pleasant and judging by appearances the hearts of all present were pleased as well. There was music and singing, dancing and conversation on the hillside, the sunny sea quiet and peaceful in the distance, the sun shining brightly and the sky like the ceiling of a great solemn and eternal temple – that is what was in Créide's mind as she walked slowly with Ruairí along a beautiful ridge. They had just heard a speech from Dr Ó Dúda.

'The Doctor says the same things as do many other Gaels,' Ruairí was saying. 'He thinks, as do they, that what is called Gaelic culture does not change from age to age. He would like us to be as our ancestors were in the time of Cormac mac Airt or in the time of St Patrick. It's not possible and if it were it would not be a good thing.'

'How so?' said Créide.

'Change affects every single thing in the universe every single moment –'

'So they say,' said Créide. 'The scientists are certain of it.

But most likely it is only the appearances and the exterior that change. I think that the vitality and soul are constant at any rate. But be that as it may, I am delighted to be among the Gaels in these days. Life is beautiful; and perhaps we would be better off being content and happy because of the beauty of life rather than searching for the meaning of life.'

'But think about this. The beauty of life is just a concept and an idea. You think that the "sky" is very beautiful now. But we know very well that there is no such thing as "sky." There seems to be but –'

'Oh!' said Créide lightheartedly, 'you do away with the sky! You will do away with the sea and the mountains soon. Where will we be then? You remind me of Fearghas Ó Ruanaí. The other night at the Society of the Guiding Star he said –'

'You know Fearghas?'

'I know him well. He said that the darkness is older, more wonderful and more mysterious than the light.'

'Most likely he was not speaking of ordinary, mundane darkness, but about darkness in its root sense, in its absolute state,' said Ruairí. 'In that state, according to certain sages, "Darkness" is pure spirit. In the same way, in its absolute state "Light" is pure spirit. The corporeal eye does not see light or darkness as it really is. It isn't easy to explain. As regards mundane darkness and light, think of this: often the night is more wonderful and spiritual than the day.'

Créide gave a little laugh.

'You're right there,' she said. 'I'm surprised I never noticed it myself.'

They continued for a while discussing the Society of the Guiding Star and Fearghas Ó Ruanaí, his poetry and his erudition.

'It's a great thing,' said Créide, 'to be discussing an

extraordinary man like Fearghas, the primeval light and the absolute state of darkness, but I would like to ask you a question about something more mundane. Lately I have often been thinking about the work of the travelling teachers. What do you think of it? I have a reason for the question.'

He told her everything he had been thinking about the travelling teachers for a long time: the education and the philosophy that they would be able to spread among the young people of the country, the way they would vitalise the heart of Ireland if they themselves had the right energy. They were a new order and it would be possible for them to broaden the mind of the people and to set alight the soul of the people, if they wanted to. They had the potential to be apostles of intellectuality. Some of them were of the same mind as he was, but they had not yet agreed on a methodology.

Then Créide said, 'The reason I wanted information about the life of the travelling teachers is that I think that I may take up that work.'

'You! You aren't serious –'

'I certainly am. Why wouldn't I be?'

'The work would be too hard for you. It's hard enough even for the men in the winter. And there is no need for you to do that kind of work. You are highly educated and –'

'Of course I have "book learning," not all of it of much use,' she said. 'But I don't think there would be a position available for me in Dublin and, even if there were, I would not be content to stay with it: my heart would not be in the work. I want to be among the goodhearted folk out in the country. I want *Tír na nÓg*. I am as ambitious as other people.'

Ruairí looked worried. He was very much opposed to Créide's becoming a travelling teacher, but it was hard for him to explain why. He thought that nowhere but *Tír na nÓg* would truly suit her.

'A great deal is said about education,' she said. 'I am at one and the same time happy and dissatisfied about it. I am happy that I got a good deal of it. But I think that many young people who lack it have earned it more than I have. In a way, it is my duty to provide the same education to the fine young poor people who never laid eyes on a college; and how better can I do that than by being a travelling teacher? But there is another side to the story. I am a B.A., but I feel that my education has just begun. You might say that my mind has been prepared and organised for true education. And where would I get that true education except by working and toiling among the people?'

'That's all very well,' said Ruairí. 'I admit that academic education is just a preparation. Certainly it is from ideas and exertion afterwards that one gets a true education. And we must work for our neighbours and our people in some way. Without fellow-feeling and co-operation we are lost. But there are many ways to do the work apart from being a travelling teacher.'

'I don't see any other way,' said Créide.

Other people approached them then. It was Pádraic Mac Éanna and some other young men, and a conversation started up among them about the education of the new generation of Gaels. Pádraic said that he would not be satisfied until they saw a Gaelic university on the side of the mountain, as resplendent in its own way as the sun in the west. He would like it to be built as a revival of Tara.

Before they took leave of each other in the evening, Créide told Ruairí that he would enjoy being a member of the Society of the Guiding Star and getting to know Fearghas Ó Ruanaí and his co-workers. He only needed to hear the word.

VI

On the Wednesday morning after the excursion Ruairí was walking by the Boyne near Navan at sunrise. It seemed to him that years had passed since he talked to Créide on the mountainside near Dublin. At the same time, it seemed that she was beside him on the bank of the Boyne.

He had often thought of late that there was a mystical connection between his mind and Meath, however mysterious the invisible 'Meath' might be. It often seemed to him that there was a spirit in the place, a mysterious energy that did not exist in Dublin or in his own native place in the country. Why was that? The question was always too hard for him to answer.

As he thought about Créide on this morning, that feeling grew more profound. And it also seemed to him that there was in some way a special connection between her and Meath.

He knew that according to stories long forgotten by most people the Boyne valley had been a holy place long ago. Few Irish people would believe that those stories were anything but fables, that the Dagda and Aengus were not just names. But if those gods were real! Mystical powers that sages and druids knew about, people who had a psychic aspect or even a spiritual vision. And if those mystical powers were in the Boyne valley long ago, they would be there today as well: Meath was as holy as it ever had been – for people who were responsive to mystical holiness. But what connection was there between Créide and Meath! He was certain that there was a connection, but he could not explain it.

He was walking slowly beneath the trees between the canal and the river when, looking up, he saw Father Micheál Ó Gadhra approaching him from the Boyne bridge. He had in his hand a little book that he was reading. Father Micheál was an affable, quiet, good-looking young priest. He was a teacher in the Diocesan College. He was highly educated and had a great love for music and poetry. The book he had was Dante's *La Vita Nuova,* and the two of them began to discuss how faithful to Beatrice Dante was from the time he was a young man. Ruairí was thinking of Créide the whole time. If he could link his mystical life, his spiritual life, with her in the same way!

'But we are going astray, Ruairí,' the young priest said. 'We are talking about Dante and the middle ages and forgetting the Boyne valley and the magic of the morning. That is how it always is with the Gaels and perhaps with most of the human race. We spend our time in magical castles, or even in *Tír na nÓg,* and we cannot keep our eyes on the wonders around us. Here now on the bank of the Boyne, the Spirit of the Morning is probably laughing at me and you. "Look!" she says, "how blind and heedless the two of them are! They do not see the heavenly realm they are in! The poetic eye, the mystical understanding, have passed from the Gaels entirely".'

Ruairí remembered his own thoughts about the mystical energy of Meath and he tried to explain them to Father Micheál. Father Micheál's opinion was that that mysticism (*le mysticisme*) existed only in Ruairí's mind. He would rather search for 'beauty,' he said. Ruairí answered that 'beauty' and *le mysticisme* were the same – the result of vision and spiritual effort. There was more than one kind of beauty, the young priest said, and it was natural for Gaels to be faithful to a particular kind of beauty, although it had been long forgotten with how hard life had been for the people of Ireland. They were, however, coming alive again and regaining consciousness and when they had their rights and control of the country as a result, he was certain that they would be able to make Ireland 'the Island of Beauty.' Too many young people throughout the world were losing patience, asking too many questions, talking constantly about the fate of humanity and the meaning of the universe. The Gaels would be different. They would stay with otherworldly poetry, magical music and the literature of beauty. And they would be the better for it.

'I'm worried about you, Ruairí,' he said smiling. 'You are a poet and your heart is overflowing with *le romantisme* and *l'idéalisme*. But alas, you are not content with that. You become suspicious and troubled about life. What you want is to explain the universe. If you go on like that your mind and your gift for poetry will be ruined. You are in danger of forgetting the qualities and the heritage of the Celts and taking too much interest in books and in the visionary beliefs of the East. Christ and Krishna and the Celts are in conflict with each other.'

'You are greatly mistaken, Father Micheál. Krishna himself said "I am Beauty itself among beautiful things." I will not admit that there is any dissimilarity between the visionary beliefs of the East and the true philosophy of the West. But I did not get my ideas from the books of the East or the books of the West.'

'But Ruairí, you are almost always reading and poring over books,' Father Micheál said.

'Indeed I am not. Without a doubt I have always had a

love for books and learning, but I had very few of them when I was young. My family was very poor. They were evicted from comfortable farms twice and, in the end, they had to be satisfied with a bit of bogland. There I was born and raised. I had no mother tongue! Just a kind of Irish and a kind of English mixed together. I got a negligible education in the "national" school, but I managed to become a teacher's assistant. Things were better for me for a while. My love for learning was constantly growing, although I could never get half as many books as I wanted. I gave up teaching and went to the city as a clerk. At night I worked hard at the books and educated myself. Somehow I ended up learning Irish, English, Latin, French and German and began on Greek –'

'That's no small achievement,' said Father Micheál. 'You amaze me.'

'I read a good deal of literature in every one of those languages, but I took a special interest in philosophy. Then the Gaelic League came along and you might say I woke up. But after coming to Meath as a travelling teacher, I sensed there was in me another "person" I had never known before. It seemed to me that the Boyne valley was a holy place. I felt that the Great Mystical Powers (they were called the Dagda, Aengus Óg etc. in ancient times) were closer to me than people I could see. I feel that now.'

'That puts things in a different light,' Father Micheál said. 'I find it hard to explain. The mind is a strange thing. On the other hand, there is a new spirit stirring among the young priests here and there. They think that the Church in Ireland is too formal and too worldly and that the bishops and the priests should be ashamed of the condition in which many people find themselves. Our friend Father Dónall Ó Dálaigh is the most active of them. There are ominous signs of trouble and I regret that. The Church and Ireland could easily have great beauty and a great Gaelic culture in the future. Instead of that we are in danger of quarrels and trouble.'

'Quarrels and trouble for the sake of the truth are better than enervation and apathy,' said Ruairí.

Father Micheál shook his head and looked anxious and sad. Then he said that it was time for him to go home. Breakfast would be ready and after breakfast he would have the day's work to do.

'Yes,' he said as they were going back to the Boyne bridge, 'we have plenty of lively thought and intellectual excitement in Ireland today, but who knows what will come of it. During the beautiful morning I am hopeful and happy, but throughout the day and during the night, I am doubtful and afraid.'

'Rouse up your courage,' said Ruairí. 'The Kingdom of Heaven is in us and the soul always wins.'

Then they took leave of each other.

Ruairí went to the cottage where he was staying. There was a letter from Créide there.

She said that she had been talking about him with Fearghas Ó Ruanaí the previous night. Fearghas would be delighted to have him as a member of the Society of the Guiding Star. Fearghas wanted Ruairí to come to his house on the following Sunday evening – poets and philosophers came visiting there every Sunday during the year.

'Come if you can,' said Créide. 'Fearghas is a wonderful person. He takes as much interest in potatoes as he takes in visionary knowledge, in tillage as in the cosmos, in bees as in Brahma. When I am listening to him I feel that the human race is noble and that Ireland is a rich and spiritual country. I feel that I am near *Tír na nÓg*.'

Ruairí was delighted. There was no danger that he wouldn't go to Fearghas's house. To be listening to Fearghas and near Créide at the same time –!

Then Ruairí got down to writing notes for the *Herald*, one of the newspapers in Meath. He usually wrote such notes every week and they occasioned considerable discussion, not only throughout the province but even in Dublin. He would help the editor – an affable, easygoing old man – in many ways when he had the time. (He wrote a separate series of articles on the history and the traditional lore of Meath). The editor was surprised that he was extremely careful about the syntax and polish of the words, in English as well as in Irish. He thought that was quite a new 'fad'.

VII

As he was going to Fearghas Ó Ruanaí's house on the Sunday evening, Ruairí remembered the first time he read Fearghas's poetry. He had just come to the city at that time. He was quite lonesome and wanted to be back in his native place again, however remote it might be. He did not understand the poetry at all. He acknowledged that it was musical, but it was beyond him to make sense of the ideas. Here and there in the little book there was mention of things Gaelic, things having to do with ancient times, but what was said there was not at all like what the storytellers out in the country said. If it made any sense, he couldn't find it.

Things changed. Now he took heartfelt delight in that same poetry.

It was clear from that that a great change had occurred in his mind since he had taken his leave of his native place, yet he did not notice many changes from one day to the next and from one year to the next. There was, however, a big difference between himself and the young Ruairí who had marvelled at the poetry of Fearghas. That Ruairí loved the poetry of Eoghan Rua Ó Súilleabháin, the songs of

Robert Burns, the stories of Charles Kickham and the traditional folklore. By now there was no limit to his fascination with mystical literature, and Gaelic friends like Father Micheál and Dr Ó Dúda thought that he was going astray.

But, he told himself as he went along the road to Fearghas's house, was there all that much fundamental difference between the poetry of Eoghan Rua and the philosophy of Fichte, between the stories of Charles Kickham and the ideas of Bergson? They all dealt with the work and fate of the human race. They were fruit of the same tree. The tree was more wonderful than any of the fruit suggested. It would grow and bloom anew in every age. There would always be wonderfully sweet fruit to be found on it.

Even so, Ruairí began to have his doubts. As he remembered his life as a boy in the country, the doubts and the loneliness grew. Was he faithful to his heritage? Was it worth it to ask questions about the universe? Wouldn't it be better for him to be content with games and writing stories about the humour and the warmth of his native place? He was a country boy. Wouldn't it be better for him to still be working on the farm and not bothering with city life at all?

Old memories arose; they came like the tide in the sea. He stopped on the road in the lonely night. He felt that he was far from Dublin, far from the mountains, far from the sea; that he was back on the patch of land where he was born and raised. He saw old neighbours visiting at the fireside. He heard music and songs and storytelling. It seemed to him that he was in a beautiful place in which there would be music and singing and storytelling forever.

He was a boy again, he thought.

Wouldn't it be delightful, he said to himself, to give up being a travelling teacher, to go home to the patch of land and to have a simple, natural life …!

Then he remembered Créide. He came out of his reverie and went on to Fearghas's house. But it seemed that the patch of land was before his eyes, as was Créide, every step of the way from then on.

He looked towards the sky, thinking about the numberless and boundless stars. They made him happy, but also at the same time a bit frightened. The universe is a many-faceted revelation, he said to himself. We carry on proud or troubled about a patch of land or about literature, or about a woman or about a 'nation' and take no interest in a manifestation or manifestations! It beats the strangest story. It beats all of the 'adventures.'

VIII

When Ruairí reached Fearghas's house there were many people there before him in the two rooms that formed a single space on the ground floor. Some of them were seated, others were examining pictures hanging on the walls, still others were standing here and there in twos and threes talking and smoking at their ease. There were a few women with cigarettes in their mouths. Ruairí soon felt that there was a special 'spirit' there. There could not have been more enjoyment and good cheer at a *céilí* in the country, although the 'folk' would have been startled by much of the conversation.

Fearghas was standing near the door as Ruairí entered. Créide was near him. She got up and introduced Fearghas and Ruairí to each other. Then she turned and continued listening to an affable, bright-eyed woman who was describing what she thought was a mystical dream that she had had a couple of nights before.

Fearghas gave Ruairí a warm welcome and Ruairí felt at once that he was a great friend. He had never before met a man more likeable. He looked like a shaggy giant, but he was kind, witty, observant and lighthearted, and his voice was musical: you'd think that everything he said was poetry.

'I'm delighted to meet you, Mr. Ó Duibhir,' he said. 'You're a travelling teacher and you live in the Boyne valley. You're in a fortunate situation. No more important work is being done in all of Ireland than the teaching of Irish. It is more important than even the co-operative movement. We don't understand how important it is, but it will be understood some other time – in a thousand years perhaps.'

There was a literary man by the name of Eagleton near Fearghas. He said that he didn't really see the need for Irish.

'Now and again,' said Fearghas, 'our souls are more responsive to the poetry of Whitman and Emerson than to anything at all written in Irish. That is not, however, the same as saying that Whitman and Emerson – or the poets of the whole world – are more important to us than Irish. We have great need of it, a mystical need as well as a worldly need.'

That surprised Eagleton.

'Every one of us is a spirit and, of course, a spirit by its nature does not need a language,' said Fearghas. 'But when a spirit comes back to the material world, things are different for it. It assumes a psychic and a corporeal aspect – that is a "body" – so that it will be able to do its new work in this world. Its new life is like a chapter in a long story and there is a connection between the new chapters and the preceding ones – that is, all the "lives" that a spirit spent in this world in ancient times and in other states of being. If Irish was the usual language of the "person" – or "person" after "person" – in which the spirit was incarnated in ancient times, isn't it only proper for the new "person" it lives in again to use Irish?'

Eagleton was a member of the Society of the Guiding Star and he was deeply interested in the questions being discussed there. It was his habit to agree at first with almost any opinion he heard; then he would become quite skeptical. Now he agreed with Fearghas as long as Fearghas was talking. Then he said, 'You're probably right – perhaps that is how things stand – but wait a while – I have my doubts about it –'

Fearghas laughed cheerfully.

'That is how it always is with Eagleton,' he said. 'He would have been very famous in ancient times. He walks in one shoe of certainty and one shoe of doubt every day of his life.'

Ruairí liked the debate and the humour. But he preferred Fearghas's discussion of the link he saw between soul and language and he referred to that question.

'Yes,' said Fearghas. 'When you and I and our friends were working in Ireland long hundreds of years ago we were using Irish and therefore there is something in our nature, in our psychic aspect, that responds to Irish. Our nature cannot be truly effective, we cannot accomplish our work, unless we have Irish now. But as for Eagleton, the last time he was on earth, in another body, he was most likely an Englishman or a Frenchman. Therefore he doesn't need Irish as keenly as we do.'

The three of them laughed.

'That's good,' said Eagleton. 'I agree with you – in a way – but I have my doubts – I do. Listen to me now. The spirit is great, mighty, eternal. The body is small, insignificant, temporal. Language is temporal. Can the spirit not do its work in any language at all? It doesn't rely on a particular language.'

'I don't agree that the body is an insignificant thing,' Fearghas answered. Instead, it is a marvellous thing. And besides the body, the spirit has a psychic aspect – we are spirit and soul and body. And as a result of all of the lives we have had in the world before now, there is a certain energy in our intellectual faculties, in our souls, and that energy responds to Irish in a wonderful way. It is reasonable enough that a particular language would be needed for the work of the spirit, as reasonable as that the spirit should come to a particular planet or a particular country.'

Eagleton was about to say something, but someone near him, someone who was very interested in the co-operative movement, turned and asked Fearghas about eggs – what demand there was for them and much else about them.

'May he long wander!' said Ruairí in a low voice. 'Himself and his eggs! And us discussing the soul!'

But Fearghas answered the questions good-humouredly. He discussed eggs and everything relating to them in contemporary Ireland intelligently and enthusiastically. You would think that he felt that they were as noble and as wonderful as planets. After a while this person was entirely satisfied with all the information he had gotten, and Fearghas turned to Ruairí – Eagleton was now talking to other people.

'Sit down,' Fearghas said. 'I would like to hear how things are going with you by the Boyne.'

They sat down.

'Few Irish people understand the significance and the magic of the Boyne today,' said Fearghas.

'It's a long story and not an easy one to explain,' said Ruairí. 'When I'm by the Boyne at night, it strikes me that the entire valley is a holy place.'

Then he told Fearghas the story exactly as he had told it to Father Micheál. Fearghas's eyes shone. It was clear that he liked the story very much.

'You're definitely right,' he said. 'That valley is a very holy, mystical place. Every place is inherently holy, but there are particular mysteries associated with particular places, just as a particular magic and otherworldly quality are associated with certain other places. There is a mystical life in this planet of ours: it is a spirit just like every other planet in the universe. That is the true planet, the land itself – the land our ordinary senses know as nothing but a "body." Our planet itself is part of the Soul of the Universe. From that spiritual planet come mystical tides – as is clear to one who has psychic vision – and they are stronger in certain places (hills, raths, etc.) than in other places. Think of Olympus, Sinai and other holy mountains. In Bibles, in ancient stories, and in folklore, much is said about the holiness and supernatural quality associated with special places. It was people who had psychic or spiritual sight who first spread that knowledge. Concerning the Boyne and Newgrange and the Hill of Tara –'

Then an old man came to Fearghas and showed him the most recent bulletin the 'Dipeartment' had issued. 'I haven't seen anything so foolish for a long time,' the old man said.

'I'd like to see you and the "Dipeartment" at the bottom of Dublin Bay,' Ruairí said in a low voice. 'A bulletin from the "Dipeartment" is it! And us pondering the mysteries of the Boyne!'

But as for Fearghas, he read the bulletin from start to finish and then began to discuss it calmly and cheerfully and earnestly until the old man understood 'both sides of the bulletin.' Then Fearghas turned to Ruairí.

'As for the Boyne,' he said, 'I hardly need tell you that there are two Boynes: the visible Boyne and the invisible Boyne, that is, the true Boyne. The sages of Egypt understood long ago that there was a heavenly Nile and that the Nile before their eyes was just its worldly counterpart. So it is with the Boyne, so it is with the true Boyne. The Soul of the Universe and its tides are permanent. The Holy Powers that are called the Dagda and Aengus and Dian Ceacht are near the true Boyne always.'

'Don't say another word like that to this scoundrel!'

A hand was suddenly laid on Fearghas's shoulder, startling him and Ruairí. They looked around. It was a smiling Dr Ó Dúda.

The Doctor sat down.

'This scoundrel is bad enough already,' he said to Fearghas. 'Look at what he wrote in this week's *Herald*. If he is stirred up by your miraculous stories about Newgrange, it will be a disaster for all of us. He will be spreading paganism week after week and we'll be the ones blamed for it.'

Fearghas laughed.

'Here is the leader who wants Ireland to be "truly Gaelic" again,' he said, 'to have "the customs and culture of our ancestors." And look! He is shaking in fear of –'

'Oh, it's easy for sages and philosophers to be talking,' said the Doctor, 'but they don't live in Ireland. They live in their own separate land of wonders.'

'Very well, Doctor,' said Ruairí. 'But if a particular group of people live in the land of wonders shouldn't they let the multitude know about it?'

The Doctor sighed.

'There is more than one kind of wonder,' he said. 'The Gaels in the west and in the south today are very unsophisticated people; they are the most unsophisticated people in Europe. They are the ones who keep alive the ideas and the customs the Gaels have had for as far back as it is possible to imagine. From the life and thoughts of these poor people one can understand the life and thoughts of Europe in its youth.'

'That is wrong altogether, Doctor,' said Ruairí. 'There is little resemblance between the Gaels of the west and south and the Gaels who were in Ireland in the distant past. The civilisation of the Gaels has been in decline for hundreds of years and has all but vanished from the visible world today. The poor people out in the country don't have the old spirit or the old state of mind. Their stories, their ideas, are just relics. As long as it is thought that they are "the Gaels" pure and simple, neither they nor we can make any progress. It would be as well for you to conclude that sickness is health.'

'I agree with that,' said Fearghas. 'The Gaels out in the country are not a people apart. Civilised but unsophisticated people like them can be found in many nations throughout Europe. Those people have legends and folklore as do the Gaels. Those stories and that folklore are relics, *débris*, or, you might say, the tail end of a *cycle mythologique*. It is proper and fitting that we have great respect for all of those people, but it is neither proper nor fitting for us to pretend that they are the products of a high civilisation. They only have – or at any rate actually make use of – a little bit of such a civilisation. The vitality of an ancient civilisation perpetuates itself in many ways: through blood, through intellect, through souls, as well as through language. The vitality of the ancient Gaelic culture exists today in Dublin – and in America – as well as in Galway and on the Dingle Peninsula. We need Irish and need it sorely. There is a great need for it throughout the country. We should make it more vital, more energetic. But we need many other things, as does Ireland. We need intellect and strength of mind. We need a new greater *Gaeltacht* and a great Gaelic culture. But we will not be able to get them as long as we imagine that Gaelic culture is no more than a useless collection of storytelling, proverbs and superstitions. All of us must believe that we are spirits and that we are here on earth to show great heroism and to promote great work.

Fearghas's voice had gotten louder without his realising it and everyone was listening to him.

'Good man, Fearghas,' said a tall, good-looking young priest who had come in a little earlier. 'I like to hear that kind of sermon. God save me, it is delightful to hear the truth from a "pagan" like you – with Ireland nearly lost with *les pessimistes* and *les matérialistes,* not to mention *les rigoristes.* Gaelic culture, is it! There is as much Gaelic culture in Ireland now as there is true Christianity. It is only right for a Christian to be a hero as well. There is no fundamental difference between true Celtic culture and true Christianity. They both depend on the heroism and spirituality of the true individual. But *les matérialistes* and *les rigoristes* think that there is no heroism or spirituality in anyone, that he is nothing but an insignificant, wretched, lost sinner. It is time that we Irish put an end to our foolish talk and our constant complaining and return to true Gaelic culture and truer Christianity.'

That is what Father Dónall Ó Dálaigh, professor of theology and philosophy, had to say. That is exactly how he often spoke.

'You surprise me and you frighten me,' said Dr Ó Dúda. 'I am a kindly shepherd from the country, interested in nothing but my simple Gaelic sheep –'

'Ah, the devil take that story, Doctor,' said Ruairí. 'We all know that you are an educated and sophisticated man. You know very well that Father Dónall and Mr. Ó Ruanaí are right. Ireland should be vigorous rather than weak. *Débris* and rubbish do not suit her; it is natural for her to foster heroism and to develop the highest civilisation – to be "a gentle nurse of generosity and true knowledge".'

They continued to debate enthusiastically. Ruairí was delighted. He was, he thought, in a great *Gaeltacht,* in a great and eternal spiritual fellowship.

IX

At last Créide told Fearghas that she could not stay any later. Ruairí was near her and he also felt it was time to leave. He would accompany her to the tram stop.

All well and good. That was fine and off they went. But when they reached the crossroads the last tram had left.

'There's nothing to be done,' said Ruairí, 'It's a good thing that it's a fine, moonlit night. It's not that far to Killiney along the hill road. I'll go with you. Why not? Would you go alone? By Fionn mac Cumhaill, that won't do. Yes, I will go with you. I'll enjoy a walk tonight.'

They started out in the quiet of the night, talking animatedly about the excellent conversation that had gone on during the evening at Fearghas's house.

'It was wonderful,' said Ruairí. 'An evening and conversation like that shows us Ireland's secret wealth. It is a magical country.'

'And here is what amazes me,' said Créide. 'There was intense debate, some people were very much opposed to other people, but it seemed that we were all happy.'

'Yes, without a doubt. During such visits and social evenings – festivals, I should say – it seems to me that the great life and chief work of the world are just beginning and that the work of all the ages before now has only been a kind of preparation. And as for things I set myself to do, it seems to me that they were too insignificant altogether, that they were not half as beautiful or half as profound as they should have been.'

'That is just how I felt tonight,' said Créide, 'when Fearghas and Father Dónall ('and you' she was about to say) were discussing heritage and duty.'

Yet there was another thought in both their minds. It seemed to them in some strange way that they had been walking for ages, that this walk was like many other walks they had taken long ago and since – that it was, indeed, part of an eternal journey. And when they finally reached the road by the sea, with the bright, glorious waters before them, they almost had to fall silent they were so filled with a mystical joy.

They came to the bend in the road where there was a beautiful view. They stopped and looked at the surface of the sea, east towards Bray.

'There is something mysterious about the sea, especially at night,' said Ruairí in a near whisper. '"The Face of the Ocean" - "the face of the waters" – that is where the mystery and the marvels really are. It is no wonder that our ancient stories about adventures in "the western sea" stir us so deeply.'

'I have often thought that there is an extraordinary enchantment in the sea and that I would be delighted to be forever in a little otherworld boat,' said Créide, looking lovingly at the sea.

The ordinary world was far removed from Ruairí at that time. With the beauty of the sea, the enchantment of the night, and the beauty of Créide, there arose in his mind an extraordinary joy he had never felt before.

'Yes,' he said, elatedly but quietly, 'I also would like to be forever in a little otherworldly boat, but with you, and you alone, with me.'

And he touched her neck and kissed her.

She put a hand on his shoulder and smiled. Then it seemed there were tears in her eyes and after that she looked at him, both pleased and fearful at the same time.

Ruairí thought they were in an enchanted wood by an otherworld sea, on a newly created, beautiful and musical island; that they had no beginning and would never have an end. It was, he thought, a holy universe.

'You amaze me,' she said quietly after a little while. 'I was certain that you were a thinker and a philosopher. But look now –'

He took her hands in his own but did not say a word.

Standing there quietly, happy and lost in wonder, they thought they had known each other for countless ages, but in another way had never really known each other until they came there to the turn in the road by the sea on a calm night. Their love involved both mind and soul. Their souls recognised each other. It would not be clear to the ordinary intellect how that happened; the affairs of the soul are mysterious. But that is how it was and they had no need to discuss it.

At last they took their leave of each other at the gate of the little garden in front of Créide's house.

Ruairí was a long way from the hotel where he stayed when he came to Dublin. But he did not care. He had no interest in going there or to any other house. He went to the top of Killiney, where he walked back and forth, looking at the sea, at the Dublin mountains and at the sky. He knew that Killiney would forever be a holy place for him. It seemed to him that the heroes and the goddesses of ancient Ireland were around him: Cú Chulainn, Naisi, Diarmaid, Deirdre, Emer, Gráinne and hundreds of others. Eamhain Mhacha and Tailtiu and Tara were alive and beautiful; Aengus and the Dagda could be seen by the heavenly river; choral-singing rose gloriously in Newgrange. He knew then that the whole universe was alive, vital, mystical and that love was the guiding star by which more of its meaning and theirs would be revealed to him.

Isn't it strange, he thought to himself, how he and Créide had met and how quickly they had realised the bonds of heart and soul there were between them. Indeed, he thought, one's life is just a single chapter in a great story with no end. In other 'chapters' Créide and I lived together. Yes, and perhaps we will be working together and living together day and night in a spiritual state, a mystical state of which our ordinary minds know or remember nothing. The ordinary world is just an obscure emblem of the spiritual world – the true universe. That true universe is not far away from us nor up in the sky. Our spirits are part of it.

At sunrise he went back to Dublin.

X

Cathal Ó Cinnéide and Ruairí met each other in the hotel. Cathal was about to go back to Wexford and he looked worried. Ruairí found it difficult to pay attention to what he was saying – he looked as if he hadn't fully wakened from a dream.

'Eibhlín Ní Anracháin and I had quite a fight last night,' Cathal said. 'I had been in Liberty Hall among the friendly poor people during the evening and when I visited Eibhlín after that I praised Larkin's work. God save me! She flared up and said that I should take an interest in the "nation" instead of in any "class." What an argument! She attacked me because I am, in her opinion, not a true Sinn Féiner and because I defer to "foreign ideas" about the peasants and the workers. "Foreign ideas" indeed! I'm sick of a good number of the Gaels. They don't have a bit of the old Gaelic outlook with regard to labourers in particular.'

'That's something that has often surprised me of late,' said Ruairí. 'But we shouldn't be critical or impatient. The days of great work and beauty are ahead of all Gaels. I am certain of that. Be courageous and high-spirited. I will never again listen to a sorrowful word from you or any other Gael. It is a beautiful thing to be alive and to have a beautiful country to develop.'

'That's all well and good, philosopher of the Boyne, but the Gaels in general are not half as strong, half as wise as they should be, and it shows. Listen to me now. I found another gem of a book this past Saturday: *Mirèio* by Fredéric Mistral. I translated a fine piece from it into Irish and when I was talking to Eibhlín last night I pretended that it was a new song about her and there was peace between us after that. Mistral's story gives me great joy: how happy and diligent the old poet is on his beautiful farm, the love he has for the spirit and the customs of his heritage, the festive, poetic life that surrounds him in lovely Provence –'

'Yes,' said Ruairí. 'That's a fine subject to be thinking about. We all owe a great deal to Mistral. Instead of having cause for complaint, it is how –'

'What troubles me is that we Irish are not able to make our lives and our work productive as Mistral and the people of Provence do. Ireland is the land of false opinions, the land of big talk.'

'You don't believe that, Cathal. It's just a bout of depression. You understand the goodness and the greatness of the Irish as well as I do myself. Doubtless some of us have been asleep and talking in our sleep for a long time, but we are waking up. Our spirits will be guiding us in the future.'

They took leave of each other.

As he was going back to Meath, Ruairí thought about what he and Créide would have to do to inspire the noble race and he felt very happy.

XI

Ruairí was soon very busy, for the great Meath *Feis* was approaching. Still, however busy he was, he had time to share his heartfelt thoughts with Créide. He sent her a lengthy letter on the Monday. It wasn't long until he got an answer. In a way it was a nice enough answer, but it wasn't the answer he was expecting.

She wrote first about her life near Killiney, about books she was reading and about her interest in becoming a travelling teacher and in *Tír na nÓg* out in the country. Then she said that there were many things in his letter that surprised her.

'The discussion of love was genuinely poetic,' she said. 'But what does it have to do with me? Did you make a mistake? Were you writing a novel and did you put a bunch of pages from it into your letter? If that isn't the explanation, what else could it be? You were, of course, a bit odd when we were coming home Sunday night, particularly at the end. You seemed to be in a dream. According to the poets, one sees strange things during a dream. But haven't you come to your senses yet?'

She continued in that vein for a good while and then she

discussed Fearghas Ó Ruanaí, the co-operative movement, and socialism. She also said that she had agreed to be an adjudicator in the literary competitions at the great Meath *Feis* and that perhaps she would experience the magic of the Boyne as other people had.

The following day she received a very long letter from Ruairí.

'Another big mistake!' she said in her answer. 'You seem to have put the whole novel in this time! Is it my judgement you want? I hope to have it read by the end of the month! I've read a good deal of it already. I see that it deals mostly with love, and, as is expected in a love story, there is talk of marriage. But if I were the girl I would let the "hero" know a few things in particular. Things like this: You say I am a goddess and that it is what is extraordinary in me that is inspiring you to great deeds. You need to prove that. Don't say another word about marriage until you have done something great for your country and your people in the form of a book or a heroic action. I will believe you then. Yes, my dear friend, that is how I would speak. Every girl in Ireland should have the same idea in her mind and be as firm about it as I am. Yes indeed. I want to set up a club for girls. Every one of them to be bound not to marry a man until he has done a great deed – some great intellectual accomplishment for example – for Ireland, or for a particular section of the Irish people. I find much to blame in the goddesses of Greece, the goddesses of Ireland, and others who lived in ancient times. They attached too much importance to lovers, to themselves, and to the very idea of love. They did not give a thought to their country or to the human race or to their duty. If they had been thoughtful and far-seeing it would have been easy for them to inspire the men to noble actions. Look at Ireland today. It is a poor, tormented, impoverished country. But some of its children are high-minded; there is a great, mystical courage in the young men, but they do not know how best to use it. But if the girls had any sense, if they were willing to marry as I explained, the boys would find the right way, the direct way that is needed. One of them would write a great book, another would be a fine organiser among the workers, others would start an independent newspaper and so on. They would not be afraid of any enemy or of any powerful person in Ireland. It is high time for Irish girls to have a clear idea of their power and their duty. I set myself the task of spreading that message.'

Ruairí sent her letters every day. Her answers were playful, particularly with regard to love. She talked cleverly and mockingly about that 'vision' when they were on the road by the sea near Killiney.

'My poor father is dreaming now – or should I say dreaming more than ever,' she wrote one day. 'He tells me that I should think about getting married! He says that his mind would be content if only I were married. Have you ever heard the like! I don't know what has happened to him.'

Since he was so busy with the *feis* approaching, Ruairí was not able to travel to Dublin. He had to make do with letters instead of talks with Créide. One day she sent him a fine, lively letter about a talk Fearghas Ó Ruanaí gave before the Society of the Guiding Star. First he talked about the link that existed between the Soul of the Universe and the individual Soul from one life to the next (an eternal pilgrimage of souls, *Seelenwanderung*). Then he explained the mystical meaning of the co-operative movement in modern Ireland. He showed that there is a mystical link connecting the work of the Gaelic League, the work of the travelling teachers, the work of the Irish Agricultural Organization Society, the work of Larkin and his followers, the work of independent young priests, and the work of many other people, although that link was not yet clear even to those involved. Their ordinary minds do not understand the job that the Soul of the Universe (the high servant of God) has conceived for them, but their souls understand it and it is their souls that inspire them to work unbeknownst to their ordinary minds.

Father Dónall Ó Dálaigh wrote to Ruairí. He said that he was growing dissatisfied with how slowly they were all proceeding. He and certain of their mutual friends thought that it would be a great thing to begin a spirited independent journal of ideas as soon as possible. There was no danger that the people who were awake – young priests, travelling teachers, co-operators, the people in the Society of the Guiding Star, etc. – would not welcome it. He knew that there was a skilled publishing company in the Boyne valley. So far so good. He hoped that they could discuss the whole question during the *feis*.

That was not to be. One day Ruairí had to go home. His father had fallen ill and it was thought that he was in danger of dying. He was not, however, and he improved greatly in a week's time. But it did seem likely that he would never again be strong enough for farm work. He was getting old and most of his life had been very hard. What would be the best thing to do for him? What about the patch of land? Ruairí had much hard thinking to do.

He had a great love for the old place. The simple life of the neighbours moved him deeply.

After returning to Meath, he sent a letter to Créide. He spoke lovingly of the patch of land and of the life and customs of the people. The answer he got from her was wonderfully kind and affectionate. 'I have much to say,' she wrote in conclusion, 'but it is difficult for me to express my thoughts precisely. Wait until we meet each other on the day of the *feis*. I have a dream every night about life on the patch of land. It is like *Tír na nÓg*. It seems to me that "the light is coming" at last. You were too taken up with books and learning, but the patch of land reminds you – and me – of another side of the story. It is wonderful,

Ruairí dear.'

'"Too taken up with books and learning!"' he said in his reply to her. 'I swear I am not. Without a doubt I am often fascinated by certain books, but after a while I lose interest in them. I become impatient at times; I feel elated at other times. But on every single occasion, whether I am impatient or elated, I tell myself that it is my duty to be doing something new. Yes, myself! Homer, Plato, Virgil, Plotinus, Dante, Goethe, Emerson – none of them can satisfy me. My mind must be working in its own way. And I would like for there to be a hundred authors working and writing and inspiring the intellect of Ireland. Unless we are moving and creating new work we are useless. I feel in myself and in Ireland an energy the like of which is not to be found in any book the world has yet seen.'

XII

To all appearances, the great Meath *Feis* was a brilliant success. Hundreds came to Navan from other towns in the province and from rural places as well. Farmers' labourers, shepherds, shopkeepers came as well as schoolteachers and priests. Musicians came, some of them in the morning, and they walked through the streets playing Irish tunes. There was no break in the music. Here and there flags were hanging across the streets and there were festive signs on all sides. A large number of people came on trains and bicycles from Kildare, from Westmeath and especially from Dublin, and they were amazed when they reached Navan. It had been said that the province was a desert, that the majority of the people were interested in nothing but cattle and money. And look! They had created a vibrant *feis* worthy of ancient times.

And during the competitions in the Young Men's Hall, in the primary schools, and in the convents, many were delighted because a large number of the learners were proficient and sharp-witted. The examiners acknowledged that certain boys and girls were first-rate and they had high praise for the travelling teachers. Pádraic Mac Éanna declared that he would be willing to start a Gaelic college in the Boyne valley, that it would serve as well there as it would at the foot of the mountain above the sea in Dublin. Diarmaid Mac an tSuaircis stated that he felt the spirit of the Decies throughout the day. Dr Mac Shligigh declared that they had the idioms of Connacht right there in the royal kingdom of Meath. Áine Ní Fharaile said that they were very like the fine idioms of Breifne. Dr Ó Dúda impressed on his friends that there was a little ember of Gaelic culture in every Irish person – even in a shepherd – and that it would with time be kindled and strengthened and made to burst into flame. Therefore it was clear that his own constant command – *Festina Lente* – made sense.

That is how he spoke to his friends here and there throughout the day. At the public meeting in the evening he had a message. He spoke in a loud voice and he praised the people of Meath unreservedly. They were progressing boldly and proudly as all the people of Ireland should. Their Gaelic spirit was rising like a great tide of the sea and with God's help they would not have to wait long before Navan and Kells and Trim would be like Gaelic versions of Athens. Fine, lively, intellectual towns – they would be jewels in the crown of the new *Gaeltacht*. Tara would be like Olympus and Helicon for the Gaels. Ireland would be joyous and Europe amazed by the quality of life and life's happiness around the Boyne!

Father Dónall Ó Dálaigh was an examiner in the literary competitions and he acknowledged that some of the learners were clever enough. But he wasn't proud because of that. It was, he said, a good thing for young people to be able to read Irish. But what was there for them to read? Little stories and sermons. The writers and the priests thought that any rubbish at all was good enough for the Gaels. As for the hundreds who gathered at the *feis*, he had little respect for some of them: shopkeepers, sellers of strong drink, farmers who were not willing to cultivate the soil or treat the labourers fairly. It was neither fitting nor sensible for people like that to have the nation's land. If that land were in the care of the nation, as it should be, it would be easy to get rid of serfdom and poverty. It was a strange thing for people to be ranting about Gaelic culture and yet have no interest in the bases of that culture. One of those was gavelkind – that the land, or most of it, 'belonged to' the tribe. Many now thought that talk and grammar would make a 'true Gael' just as another group thought that some kind of faith and subservience to the priests made one a 'Christian.' There would be neither Gaelic culture nor freedom in the country until there was mental vigour and courage in the mass of the people.

He spoke like that to many. He said the same kinds of things very forcefully at the public meeting.

'He is a daring man,' said Dr Ó Dúda to an old priest who was next to him on the platform. 'I am worried about ideas like those –'

'He will be stopped,' said the old priest. 'He is like an apostle.'

Father Dónall told Ruairí what he and his friends had decided about the new journal.

XIII

Ruairí and Créide did not get much chance to talk during the *feis*, for they were both very busy. But when the public meeting was over, they went for a walk through the Boyne valley. They knew that the special train would not go back for an hour and a half and Créide wanted to see 'the river of wonders' in the moonlight.

'It's hard to believe,' she said when they were in the valley, 'that I never walked by the Boyne before now. I feel that I have known it for a long time.'

'I had the same thought about Newgrange and about Tara, indeed about all of Meath when I first arrived,' said Ruairí. 'It is wonderful how responsive we are to the *genius loci* at times. But I sometimes think that that is just a dream or an instinctive response. The magic is in ourselves. Fearghas Ó Ruanaí and Father Dónall Ó Dálaigh are right. The true person is a divine hero, a king and a sage; he lives in a state of wonder and when for a while he becomes flesh in the ordinary world it is foolish to think that he is an insignificant and wretched sinner.'

'But there is a great difference between Father Dónall and Fearghas,' said Créide. 'Father Dónall is impatient, quick to complain even. What he wants is a golden age, people of intellect, a great spiritual realm in Ireland – and all of this immediately. He has no respect for common things. But as for Fearghas, he thinks and he works vigorously, but he is always calm, easygoing and affable. He understands every person and every race and respects even inconsequential things.'

'You're a bit hard on Father Dónall,' said Ruairí. 'He is a fine man and it is no wonder that he's impatient about many things in Ireland. He and certain of his friends have conceived of a great "adventure" –'

'I know that. I was talking to him today. Ruairí, I fear that you are on Father Dónall's side instead of standing with Fearghas.'

'I'm surprised at that. I have enormous respect for Fearghas –'

Créide laughed.

'But you are not willing to be as calm and as patient as Fearghas,' she said. 'Look now. He is one of the great men of the world. He is a mystical sage. He has remarkable spiritual wisdom.'

'I admit all that with all my heart. It is a source of joy that we have a man like him in Ireland today.'

'But remember this, Ruairí. He works zealously day after day, writing notes about butter and eggs, tillage and poultry – for farmers and housewives. He is content just to have mundane useful work of that kind to do from one week to the next. Of course, he creates otherworldly pictures – during his holidays in the summer. He composes poems now and again. He speaks once a week at the Society of the Guiding Star. That's all. Only a few people know that there is a genius like him in Ireland.'

'I am amazed at how he keeps so calm. It is a great loss to Ireland –'

'Perhaps there is another explanation,' said Créide. 'He

understands that people are not yet ready for more profound teaching or more meaningful work. Therefore he is content to be so easygoing, unsophisticated, "ordinary" except on occasion.'

'God save me,' he said. 'Your mind is certainly changing, Créide. I would not have believed it was possible.'

She stopped and so did Ruairí. They were in a beautiful secluded little glen by the bank of the river. The sky was bright and clear and the moon, visible over the tops of the trees, seemed to them quite near.

'Of course, I have changed greatly of late,' she said. 'At first I was surprised and frightened by the change. The way I fell in love with you almost from the first moment – one might think I was out of my mind or that I was a girl with no shame –'

He kissed her.

'Don't worry about that,' he said, 'or you will make me terribly sad and anxious. Our souls recognised each other –'

'I have no question about that now,' she said. 'I believe that we have lived in Ireland often before now and we – our souls – were together and lived together. Therefore it was no wonder that we recognised each other so suddenly. But now, the work that is ahead of us in the new life, the new age ...'

'Yes,' said Ruairí, 'that is the great question –'

'It seems to me that it is very simple. In any lifetime, philosophy is of little benefit unless it can be given a practical application and put to use.'

He put his arm around her and they walked on slowly.

'You understand me well,' she said. 'I have been thinking hard about your situation and mine of late. I am happy to see you where you belong. Yes, Ruairí dear. Therefore I ask you not to get involved with this work

Father Dónall and his friends are doing, and another thing even more important than that –'

'More important than that! "That" is bad enough – asking me not to take part in a fight for intellectual freedom and opportunity! What is this terrible other thing?'

'It will surprise you at first. But I say, and say strongly, that you should give up being a travelling teacher, go home to the patch of land and –'

'To tell the truth, you are a real tyrant, Créide. For me to go home, to be a small farmer and to leave the Boyne, the cause, literature and, worst of all, yourself! You're not serious!'

'You wouldn't have to leave the cause or give up literature and, as for me, perhaps I'd be with you, living with you there – in a little while.'

'But Créide dear, you don't understand how hard life in the country is. You are poetic, educated and –'

'Ruairí, I am sick of those words "education" and "educated". It is in the country that Gaels with a little education are needed. In the "towns" we are usually like prisoners, far from civilisation, from the eternal tides, from the soul of the universe.'

'I admit that I love the country – that my heart delights in the "patch of land." But you, Créidc! In the Boyne valley, on the Dublin mountains, you are like a being from the otherworld or a spirit. But on bogland –'

'Dublin is far worse than bogland,' she said. 'It is a desert. There is beauty in bogland. I thought you were a poet! But you are afraid of having me live with you on bogland!'

Then she spoke about the dreams that she had been having every night of late about life on the patch of land. It was an otherworldly story.

At last he put his arms around her and kissed her. 'On

bogland or in a desert, in a cave, on a mountain ridge, on a wild island far out in the sea, or even in a prison, I would be happy if you were with me,' he said lovingly.

'Yes,' she said. 'We have made the bargain now. The life we will have on the patch of land will, with God's help, be wonderful.'

They had to go back to Navan then, for special trains don't wait a single minute for lovers any more than for other people. As they were going back, Créide spoke lightheartedly about the life poets had in the country from the days when Theocritus and Virgil lived to the time of Mistral himself.

XIV

Lying in his bed long after midnight, Ruairí had no desire to sleep. He was thinking about the *feis,* about Créide, about their conversation by the Boyne, and about the patch of land. Life there with her would be delightful. And the joy his father and mother and the neighbours would feel! He thought for a long time about what he would have to do with the old house. Without a doubt he would have to add other little rooms to it. One of them would become a nice, cheerful library. He thought about the books he would want in it. First of all, every book and pamphlet available in Irish. Perhaps with Créide's help he would be able to write a superb book, a really serious *épopée,* in Irish. He used often to think that it would be a great thing to base an *épopée* on the adventures, the wonder, the marvel relating to the islands and the sea in the west. There one found the noblest thoughts of the Celts, the high point achieved by the magic of the Gaelic spirit.

And the life they would have in the country day after day, summer after summer! And Dublin – the Boyne – literature – the Society of the Guiding Star – still – he would miss them badly – life was strange – did he agree with Créide about taking his leave of – of – of – he fell asleep.

Early in the morning he sat up suddenly, fully awake. He was amazed that he had not strongly opposed Créide about life in the country. The truth was not half as simple as she thought. The cities were not all they were made out to be either. They had plenty to do where they already were. And what would Father Dónall have to say if he ran home? To abandon the great intellectual cause! And to go to the middle of nowhere! What in the world had come over him by the Boyne? He was amazed and troubled.

He admitted that he had a great love for life in the country – in a way. But it was slight in comparison with the love he had for literary life, for currents of thought. And to live on the remote patch of land – it would be like exile from intellectual life. And his own family would not be happy if he returned to farm work.

But Créide would be with him! There would be magic in the country because of that. There would be, without a doubt. But wouldn't life on the patch of land be too hard on her? At any rate, would it be right to let her go there?

And marriage! He began to have doubts about it. Créide was like a being from the otherworld, like a spirit. And a being from the otherworld as a wife in an old house in the middle of bogland! 'The Brightness of Brightness on a lonely path.'

That is what was on his mind throughout the day: anxious at times, doubtful at times and, now and again, experiencing a joy he did not understand. That night in Navan he wrote and sent to Créide a long letter baring his heart and all of his thoughts. He said in conclusion that it was clear they had only been dreaming the night before. They would not be content with life on the patch of land. There was another life and other work in store for them.

But when the letter was gone he again experienced doubts and constant loneliness!

On the following morning he met Father Micheál Ó Gadhra and they walked by the Boyne for an hour. The young priest was very worried. He said the old clergy were enraged about Father Dónall Ó Dálaigh and especially about the speech he gave at the public meeting the day of the *feis*. It was being said in the Diocesan College that Father Dónall would very soon be silenced.

A week later, Ruairí got a letter from Father Dónall himself. He was about to go to America! To collect money for some schools the bishop wanted them to have in the diocese. He would be abroad for a couple of years.

'They are afraid of the journal,' he said. 'Now it has been postponed – for more than two years. Alas! But perhaps it is for the best. Perhaps the young people are not ready yet. Carry on, my friend! Spread the ideas. Sow the seed in good ground. We will have our *Renaissance* in due course.'

Father Dónall going abroad! Being exiled from Ireland! *Les rigoristes* had won the day.

Ruairí had only a bit more teaching to do at that time. The term was almost over and there would be no other classes until the autumn. Friends let him know that the Regional Committee was not agreed about re-appointing him as a travelling teacher. Certain people did not like him; his ideas and his opinions were 'too dangerous.' But there were other people on the committee strongly in his favour and it was likely there would be a fight come autumn.

He thought about the problem. It could not be solved. Apart from the teaching (in Meath or elsewhere), what did he have apart from the patch of land? If he were French or German or English, he would have a literary life ahead of him. Alas, literary life was just beginning in Ireland.

He met the man from the *Herald* in Navan that evening. He said he knew how things stood with the Regional Committee. 'Certain people are at work in the old way,' he said. 'But here in Meath we are not as timid as they think.

They should remember what happened when we stood up for Parnell. Don't worry, my boy! If the Regional Committee does not appoint you in the autumn there will be a job for you at the *Herald* and I promise you that we will have some fun. I am not a literary man and I like the quiet life, but if someone threatens me or one of my friends there will be a fight on the spot. That's the long and the short of it.'

Ruairí was very grateful to him, and he was pleased that the old man was so bold. But he thought that it would be a poor thing to be a reporter on a country newspaper – or, indeed, on a city newspaper. Reporters were drudges – as were sub-editors and editors as well. What he wanted was an intellectual, independent literary life – he sometimes felt that he had the material for a hundred books in his mind. But he told the editor he would think about the whole subject and they could discuss it in due course.

He explained the situation to close friends like Cathal Ó Cinnéide. Cathal wrote to him kindly, but he said that he was not surprised. The enemies of thought were too strong and the majority of the Gaels too timid and ignorant.

'I am sick of the Gaels,' he said. 'They have no courage or intellectual activity or understanding. I'm thinking that it would be as well for me to give up being a travelling teacher and become an organiser among the labourers – the foundation-stone of the nation. It would be best for you to do the same. We have all been dreaming for a long time. There will be no Gaelic culture in Ireland until we put an end to serfdom and poverty.'

Ruairí settled his affairs in Meath and was expecting to go to Dublin when he got a letter from Créide – he had been lonely because she had not written before this.

The letter surprised him.

'You're right, Ruairí. We were dreaming by the Boyne that night. I did not understand the situation. I don't understand the world. I don't understand myself. I was heartsick after getting your letter. But the strange thing is that the dreams come every night and they are more beautiful than they were before. I dream that we are happy on the patch of land. You are content farming and I am with you, as happy as a spirit from the otherworld. But at the same time the sea is out before us – and of course the actual patch of land is far from the sea – and the ancient heroes and the souls of all our friends are near us. You might say it's like a golden age. It's impossible to describe. I haven't been well lately. I'm very busy now. I'm about to go to the Gaelic college in Maoileann na Mara. From all I've heard, it's a peaceful, otherworldly place. I have always loved the sea. We often talked about a little otherworldly boat! Can you come? I thought that you would be in Dublin long before now. I will write to you often and unless you write to me every single day …'

I have to hurry, Ruairí said to himself. I'll be in Dublin by evening …

That is not what happened. He got a telegram. His father was again in danger of death. He had to return immediately to the patch of land.

XV

There were anxious days ahead of Ruairí on the patch of land, but everything turned out well within a month. His father recovered. One of his brothers came home from America with money. He wanted to live on the patch of land and help the old people. All was well and everyone was satisfied.

Ruairí then decided to go to Maoileann na Mara where Créide and many of his Gaelic friends were. The Gaelic college, its surroundings and the little islands in the sea west of it were famous. He knew the old otherworldly stories concerning all of them. He had never been in the area, but the surroundings and the sea and the famous little islands delighted him. And because Créide was there he thought he was now in *Tír na nÓg*.

The letters he had gotten from her during his visit to the patch of land initially delighted him and then surprised him. She spoke first of the beauty of the area near Maoileann na Mara, of her love of being out in a boat, of the enchantment of the islands. She wanted to live there forever.

'I was mistaken before,' she said. '"Myself" has not

made sense to me until now. The change of mind I have experienced is wonderful. It cannot be described. I think that the sea is extraordinarily magical and holy. I am near *Tír na nÓg* when I am out in a boat. And those dreams are more beautiful than ever. Indeed it's not right to call them dreams now. Ruairí, I feel that we are living together day and night.'

In another letter she said that the life of Dublin was like a dream to her now. She did not even feel an attachment to the Gaelic college. The sea and its magic were constantly luring her. 'Ruairí, now I understand that we – you and I – are not in tune with today's Ireland. It is too worldly. If we were working in the city or even in the country we would not be content and happy. There is another state of being and other work in store for us. You will realise that soon, my love.'

He could not really understand that however. He quickly put his affairs in order and went off to Maoileann na Mara.

He was tired as he boarded the train. In the evening he fell into a peaceful sleep and dreamt that he awoke immediately on a little island far out in the sea. Créide was waiting for him, looking loving and happy. They walked around the little island. There were hundreds of Gaels there, Gaels of the ancient times working diligently with modern Gaels. That was not at all surprising to either Créide or himself ... He woke up at last. The train was approaching Maoileann na Mara.

A strange story awaited him. Everyone at the Gaelic college was amazed and anxious.

Créide could not be found. There had been no sign of her at all for three days and three nights.

As she often did, she had taken a little boat out into the harbour in the afternoon. Cathal Ó Cinnéide, Eibhlín Ní Anracháin and other boys and girls were out in boats at the same time, the odd one in a little boat by herself like

Créide, most of them in twos or fours in other boats. The weather was calm, the water still and the young people were enjoying the *céilí* in the harbour. Some of them went out towards the nearest island, but they were all back by nightfall – except for Créide. They thought that she would soon be back, but a couple of hours passed and she hadn't come. They were surprised, but no one was worried since it was a fine moonlit night and they knew she was a skilful rower. Some of them had seen her when they were coming back. She was in her little boat not far from the mouth of the harbour, rowing easily and singing to herself.

Another hour went by, but still she had not returned. Around midnight every available boat was out in the harbour or further at sea in every direction. The night was bright and glorious, but no one laid eyes on Créide or her little boat anywhere.

Cathal Ó Cinnéide, Eibhlín Ní Anracháin and another boy and girl were in a boat by themselves. Around midnight they were sure they heard Créide's voice singing cheerfully and proudly. Their hearts rose. They looked around in every direction. There was no one at all to be seen. The other boats were far behind. The singing went on for a while and then, suddenly, it stopped. A deep silence fell over the sea. They felt an overwhelming loneliness.

The search was not given up until morning. But there was no sign of Créide anywhere. Some then said that perhaps she had gone to the nearest island. The college was cancelled for the day. The boaters went out to the islands. They went from one island where people were living to another. It was a wasted journey. Nobody on any of the islands knew anything about Créide.

Then it was discovered that there were no boats missing! And no boatman remembered Créide borrowing a boat from him the day she was last seen.

The old people shook their heads. They remembered the old stories about the magic of the sea and about an island far to the west, an eerie island on which no one had lived for ages.

That was how things stood when Ruairí reached Maoileann na Mara.

XVI

Ruairí was rarely to be seen in Maoileann na Mara in the days after that and when he occasionally met his friends they were surprised by how quiet, pensive, and preoccupied he was. He showed no sign of sorrow or loneliness; instead he seemed happy, but not even Cathal Ó Cinnéide could get him to talk.

He often went out alone in a boat on the sea far from the harbour. Even more often that that, after a couple of weeks he would walk all over the islands. By that time, the islanders knew about his situation and about what happened to Créide as well and they were very kind to him. But after a while he went away and it was said that he had gone off to a remote little western island, an eerie, ghostly place on which not even the boldest islander would want to set foot. The old people shook their heads when they heard that that was where Ruairí was.

'He will go farther,' they said.

When the end of the college term was approaching, Cathal Ó Cinnéide and other friends went looking for him. He was digging the soil industriously on the back of a ridge near the strand when they came ashore. He came down to the strand and welcomed them warmly. He spoke enthusiastically and amiably about how good the soil was; he hoped to have much of the little island a fine productive garden some day. They then went to a nice, airy hut that he had on the far side of the island facing the open sea. There were large caves under the cliffs. He said that he would spend a night in one of them now and again, but he still did not know how deep they were or where they ended; there were ancient symbols and ancient writings in some of them. His conversation was pensive but cheerful, and his mind appeared to be calm and happy.

Before they took their leave of him, Ruairí and Cathal had a private conversation while the other friends were walking here and there on the beautiful cliffs, by the strand, or in the caves. Ruairí spoke freely and forcefully about the work he had to do on the island and about how calm and active his mind was.

'A while ago,' he said, 'I would not have believed it would be possible that something like this could be in store for me. I was thinking about an intellectual fight in Ireland. That sort of thing isn't at all worthwhile; it's just a waste of soul. We must advance *la vie créatrice* quietly and faithfully and we will have the land of wonders and the Kingdom of Heaven as a result. The ancient stories had a great deal to say about the World of the Waters. There is a special magic in waters and our souls respond to the magic. The ordinary world, the World of the Waters, *Tír na nÓg*: that is the progression. I myself left the patch of land and then left Dublin – the ordinary world – for the Boyne and then came here to the sea. At the same time my soul was stirring and awakening. *Tír na nÓg* is the next state of existence, and I am preparing myself for that marvellous state. And as for Créide –'

'Oh,' said Cathal. 'I was afraid to mention her although I have been thinking of her the whole time. The story is, is, is –'

'Delightful, glorious,' said Ruairí. 'It was not difficult for her to go to *Tír na nÓg*. I understood some of what was going on from the letters she sent me when I was on the patch of land. How wonderful is her state in the islands and by this sea or should I say in the mystical islands, by the spiritual sea of which these are the body and shell. I am already near her – closer to her than if we were in the Boyne valley or in Killiney – and as I work the land and perfect my mind and my soul I will be with her in a more wonderful and spiritual way. Even now the meaning of life and the progress of the human race are much clearer to me than when I came here to Créide's Island – that is what I call it. But it's time for me to stop, Cathal my friend, or you will be certain that I am out of my mind altogether.'

'Everything that has happened amazes me,' said Cathal. 'But I do feel some magic in the little island, in the sea and in myself, and I am open to believing much that I did not believe before. But you will be lonely here, and another thing, you are needed in Ireland.'

'"Lonely?" you say, Cathal! I am in company the like of which does not exist under the sun. "Needed in Ireland?" Yes, without a doubt. We are all needed in Ireland. And where is Ireland, or what is it? That place where people are afraid of intellect and ideas; that place where there is constant wrangling over points of grammar; the place of greed, the place of poverty, the place of misery – that is just an insignificant part of Ireland. The great Ireland, the true Ireland, is an intellectual, thoughtful, spiritual entity. It is revealing itself to me at last in its majesty, in its beauty, in its loveableness. I hope that together with Créide I will do magnificent work for it. Until now I didn't really know what I could do.'

Cathal and his friends were pensive coming back to Maoileann na Mara. They did not understand Ruairí's state of mind. He was like someone from another world. But it was clear to them that he thought his situation was natural and happy.

'We Gaels talk a great deal about wonders,' Cathal said as they approached the harbour at Maoileann na Mara in the moonlit night. 'We acknowledge that there were extraordinary wonders in the distant past. But what about in our own time? What will people in Dublin say about the story of Ruairí and Créide?'

There was one person in Dublin who thought that the story was fitting and glorious. That person was Créide's father Fiontán Ó Conghaile. He was lonely and heartbroken after losing her, but his soul rejoiced that she had escaped peacefully and magically to a mystical, truly alive state of being.

Around this time he at long last got a letter from Eibhlín Ní Dhónaill. At first his heart leapt. The letter came from America and was very long. Eibhlín said that a few days earlier she had gone to a big *feis* the Gaels had organised. She was delighted by the report of representatives from Ireland concerning the vitality in modern Ireland. She was rich and she would be happy to assist the work. She explained how that wealth had come to her. Years ago, when she was poor and sad, she had married an elderly millionaire. She had regretted doing so ever since, for her heart had always belonged to Fiontán. Her husband had died a couple of years after the wedding. However rich she was, her life lacked happiness and peace as the years went by. She grew hopeful when she heard the story of the new Ireland. She wanted to serve Cathleen Ní Houlihan. She would go to Ireland if that is what Fiontán wanted.

Fiontán read the letter in his study. Then he thought for a long time. At last he got up slowly. He put the letter on the fire. He opened the window. He looked at the sky and the sea. He looked at the stars ... He came back to the table. There seemed to be tears in his eyes, but there was a hint of joy on his face. He took up a large manuscript. He went on writing in it quietly ...

Fearghas Ó Ruanaí met Cathal Ó Cinnéide one autumn night as Fearghas was going home after a meeting of the Society of the Guiding Star. They talked about Ruairí and Créide.

'It's strange that the story surprises people so much, particularly Gaels,' said Fearghas. '"People" go off in a strange way every year and there is no discussion of their leaving. For example, there is a young man who is poetic and pensive, his heart overflowing with love for his country and its cause. But for some reason, or for no reason at all, he loses his feeling for poetry, his great joy, his love and his loyalty and there is nothing left to be seen but a complainer, someone of no use. Yes, the great poetic person goes away although the same body remains among us. It is a terrible departure, but it does not surprise most of us. Ireland is losing intellectual and spiritual people every year because it is not itself intellectual and spiritual – it cannot keep them here, or if it does keep their bodies and their ordinary minds, their souls are no longer alive or engaged.'

Cathal acknowledged that he was right about that.

'As for Ruairí and Créide,' Fearghas said, 'it's a different story. They are both in an elevated state, especially Créide. That is something most of our friends do not understand. Many Gaels think that people cannot work for Ireland unless they can be seen amongst us on Irish soil. *Le matérialisme* has afflicted them without their realising it.'

He paused for a moment and then he said, 'I would love to be like Ruairí, far away on a delightful island in the sea of wonder – in a way I sometimes am – but I still have a great deal to do here in Dublin. I have great things to accomplish with the co-operative movement, great things no one else is willing to do at present. The co-operative movement is the hope of Ireland – the hope of the world. But there exists a mystical, mental and spiritual co-operation as well as a worldly co-operation; and Ruairí and Créide, especially Créide, help with that mystical co-operation, for she is in the most wonderful state of being. They are working in the great Ireland – a country holier and more profound than we perceive here in the ordinary Ireland.'

'That is beyond my understanding,' said Cathal. 'It's a pity that a poor person cannot discover the meaning of life without hard work, without difficulty –'

'Everyone has to work hard, as hard as he can – with his hands and with his mind every day of his life,' said Fearghas. 'Work and thought, thought and work – they are the best teachers; they are the servants of the soul.'

Cathal looked at the sky and the thousands of stars made him feel lonely and frightened.

'It is a vast and complex universe,' he said. 'It has no limit at all – corporeal, intellectual or spiritual. There is no explanation to be found for it – even the most profound is just a guess.'

'And isn't it a joy for us to be at work and on a pilgrimage in a universe that is so wonderful?' Fearghas said. 'There is no limit to our wealth. We walk through magic and through divinity. "The cities are full of Zeus, the harbours are full of Zeus, the myriad ways of people are full of Zeus".'

The End

Faoin Eagarthóir/About the Editor

In Worcester, Massachusetts a rugadh Philip O'Leary. Céim Ph.D sa Léann Ceilteach bainte amach aige – ó Ollscoil Harvard. Is é *An Underground Theatre: Major Playwrights in Irish: 1940–1980* (UCD Press, 2017) an leabhar is déanaí uaidh.

Philip O'Leary was born in Worcester, Massachusetts. He holds a Ph.D in Celtic Languages and Literatures from Harvard University. His most recent book is *An Underground Theatre: Major Playwrights in Irish 1940–1980* (UCD Press, 2017).